We Wasn't Pals

Canadian Poetry and Prose
of the First World War

T0164428

We Wasn't Pals

CANADIAN POETRY AND PROSE
OF THE FIRST WORLD WAR

NEW EDITION

Edited by

Bruce Meyer and Barry Callaghan

Preface and Introduction by
Bruce Meyer

Foreword by
Barry Callaghan

Afterword by
Margaret Atwood

The Exile Classics Series
Number Twenty-Seven

Fiction, Poetry, Translation, Drama and Nonfiction

Library and Archives Canada Cataloguing in Publication

We wasn't pals : Canadian poetry and prose of the First World War / edited by
Bruce Meyer and Barry Callaghan ; preface and introduction by Bruce Meyer ;
foreword by Barry Callaghan ; afterword by Margaret Atwood. -- New edition.

(Exile classics series ; no. 27)
Includes bibliographical references. Issued in print and electronic formats.
ISBN 978-1-55096-315-1 (pbk.).--ISBN 978-1-55096-408-0 (pdf).
ISBN 978-1-55096-446-2 (mobi).--ISBN 978-1-55096-447-9 (epub)

1. World War, 1914-1918--Literary collections. 2. Canadian literature (English)
--20th century. I. Atwood, Margaret, 1939-, writer of afterword II. Callaghan, Barry,
1937-, editor, writer of supplementary textual content III. Meyer, Bruce, 1957-,
editor, writer of supplementary textual content IV. Title: Canadian poetry and
prose of the First World War. V. Series: Exile classics ; no. 27

PS8237.W3W39 2014   C810.8'0358   C2013-902878-1
                                        C2014-901377-9

Design and Composition by Mishi Uroboros
Typeset in Palatino font at Moons of Jupiter Studios

Published by Exile Editions Ltd ~ www.ExileEditions.com
144483 Southgate Road 14 – GD, Holstein, Ontario, N0G 2A0
Printed and Bound in Canada in 2014, by Imprimerie Gauvin

Every effort has been made to trace the estates, ownership, and copyright holders
of the works presented in this anthology. Owing to the length of time that has passed
between the writing of these works and the publication of this volume, some works
have been impossible to trace. The publisher wishes to acknowledge the contribution
these writers have made and continue to make to Canadian culture.
This publication extends that contribution.

We gratefully acknowledge the Canada Council for the Arts
and the Ontario Arts Council for their support toward our publishing activities.

Canadian Sales: The Canadian Manda Group, 165 Dufferin Street,
Toronto ON M6K 3H6   www.mandagroup.com   416 516 0911

North American and International Distribution, and U.S. Sales:
Independent Publishers Group, 814 North Franklin Street,
Chicago IL 60610   www.ipgbook.com   toll free: 1 800 888 4741

INQUISITIVE PARTY: Exactly what difference do you find between fighting in the Ypres Salient and the Somme?
PEACE RIVER JIM: (*after judicial consideration*) Mud's browner.

—ANONYMOUS

Dull grey paint of war
Covering the shining brass and gleaming decks
That once re-echoed to the steps of youth...

Impromptu dances, coloured lights and laughter,
Lovers watching the phosphorescent waves;
Now gaping guns, a whistling shell; and after
So many wandering graves.

—H. SMALLEY SARSON

CONTENTS

Preface to this New Edition

Bruce Meyer

This new edition of *We Wasn't Pals* serves two key purposes: it continues the work of spreading awareness of Canadian poetry and prose of the First World War that was initiated by the original edition in 2000, and now, as it joins other culturally important works in the growing Exile Classics Series — for this we have included a lexicography, glossary, bibliography, and questions for discussion and essays — the texts reach out to a whole new generation of readers, whose perceptions of the conflict have not yet been awakened, or ingrained, in their own consciousness.

The original edition of this book in 2000 introduced Canadian readers to a lost decade of their literature — the trench writers of the First World War. These voices had been ignored for almost eighty years. They were missing from Canada's literature because they expressed a profound honesty to truths that were almost impossible to comprehend. The writers whose works are presented here were simply being honest, and honesty is as bitter to express as it is to receive. Honesty injures as much as it heals. Honesty leads a reader to the truth, no matter how dreadful that truth may be, but in doing so shares the wounds and the horrors it expresses with others. In 1918, Canadian readers were not ready to hear the truth.

What readers had to face with the initial offering of *We Wasn't Pals* was the battle to wrap their minds around an experience that was still beyond words after eight decades — as beyond words as the authors found it in 1918 when they struggled to share what they had witnessed and endured for four years of war. But readers did recognize the truth and the dark beauty in the truth of what is found in this book. That, in itself, is a testament to both the courage of the writers and to the dedication of readers.

Despite the additional apparatus and pedagogical addenda, this anthology still is what it is: a record of a war that was ignored for almost a century because it was so remote, so absurd, and so antithetical to what literature usually says and does. Nonetheless, Canadian readers paid a tremendous tribute to these authors by simply listening to what they had to say.

That this new edition is now not only possible, but called for by educators and young readers, suggests that the original edition did what it had to do: break the silence surrounding a missing era in Canadian literature and the authors who asked that we share the pain of a wounded generation. As a nation, we have learned that authors say what they say not to remind us of our own complacency and imaginative inertia but to point us beyond such shadows.

FOREWORD

Barry Callaghan

This is the place
you would rather not know about...
where the word why *shrivels and empties*
itself...

As a child growing up during the Second Great War I heard my mother and father singing songs from the First Great War. My mother said it was strange but there were no songs that anyone eagerly sang about the war against the Nazis — no song except "Lili Marlene" — and that was funny, my father said, because our soldiers were singing an enemy song that everyone said was beautiful because it made everyone feel sad. I didn't think it was funny because the only enemy soldier I had ever seen was on the back cover of my piano Conservatory practice book and he had cruel eyes like the eyes of the dog our neighbour kept chained to a steel fence post next door.

Mother had dark eyes full of light. She sang gay war songs when we went to my grandparents where she played His Master's Voice 78's on the Victrola that had a crank handle on the side: "My Buddy," "Over There," "Mademoiselle from Armentières," "They Can't Beat Us," and the bugle boy song, "Oh How I Hate to Get Up in the Morning." Even my father would sing along with my favourite:

> *Rosie Green was a village queen*
> *Who enlisted as a nurse,*
> *She waited for a chance*
> *And left for France with an ambul-lance.*
> *Rosie Green met a chap named Jean,*
> *A soldier from Paree,*

When he said, Parlez-vous *my pet,*
She said, I will but not just yet,
When he'd speak in French to her
She'd answer lovingly...

And then we'd all let go in a nasal cry,

Oh Frenchy, Oh Frenchy Frenchy...

I thought this was hilarious because an older boy had shown me a package of *Sheiks*, condoms, French safes, Frenchys, and I thought my mother and father didn't know what they were singing about.

Mother showed me, in an album of photographs that she had cut and pasted as a fourteen-year-old girl, a snapshot of herself, stylishly playful, wearing an army captain's hat, and another snap of Uncle Ambrose in uniform in 1918, astride his army motorcycle. She is sitting up to her neck in the sidecar, which looked to me like one of the tiny boats I had floated in my bath as a baby. I thought this was almost as funny as Ambrose's leggings that were wound like brown bandages from his ankles to his knees.

Years later, after going through that album again with Mother, surprised to see with what verve and swish her sisters were dressed, and surprised, too, at all their young women friends who were outfitted in nurses' uniforms, she gave me a little diary she had kept through the 1916-1918 years.

I knew she had been precocious as an art student at fourteen, but one paragraph took me aback. Amidst girlish entries about tea dances in Muskoka and outings on the sand beach by Scarborough Bluffs, and hugging a pillow at night in the way she wanted to hug a boy and kiss him, she wrote about the war with the angry conviction of innocence:

Thursday Afternoon, Sept. 12, 1917

Toots [her older sister] *has a fellow, Fred Ryan, a returned soldier coming to see her… There's a young aviator, nearly 20 yrs, coming to see Toots too. He's up at Camp Borden just now… Oh dear there's nothing but "conscription" around here. It's terrible. I just can't stand the thought of it. To think that after all the men Canada has sent that now they should spring this on us. It sure is coming I guess. I hope Ambrose doesn't have to go. It will be awful if he does. Poor Ronnie Lynn was killed on the 9th. Mrs. Lynn got a letter from him that was written on the 6th. This is terrible. Russia into civil war now. What on earth is this world coming to? Japan is going to join Russia. Dear, what will come of it? I hope the States will help some. We won't have any men left here at all. We know there's few enough as it is, but there soon won't be any. To hear some people talk….in their estimation every last boy should have been sent there long ago. They make me sick.*

As it turned out, an armistice was declared less than a year later, only a week or two before Ambrose was to take a train east to board a troop ship and go over there. Mother's three sisters never married. They stayed at home in the family house for forty years. Perhaps, once the death count at the Somme and Vimy Ridge and Ypres was completed, there really weren't enough men to go around:

> *the long, the short, the fat and the tall,*
> *over there…*

Of an afternoon during the next Great War, my aunt Vera ('Toots' — because she was so gaily tempered) would bring me gifts, often a box containing balsa wood and clear glue. I would spend hours making model planes — fighters, like the Spitfire and Mustang — spreading out plans on the dining-room table, learning to squeeze a perfect pin-head drop of glue into a balsa-wood joint, and one day my father got up from the long table where he wrote, typing on his portable Remington, and in a few minutes when he came back into the dining room he was carrying a silver trophy that he had won as a boy during the First War. Engraved on the cup was: *Special Prize — Model Aeroplanes — Donated By Long Branch Aviation School — 1916*. He said he had built a fighter with one set of wings above the other, a bi-plane, and he'd painted it cherry red. I asked him if any of his older schoolboy friends had gone to the war as pilots and he said, "No, but some went into the trenches. Some got gassed."

One Saturday night, when some of my parents' friends were visiting, I was excited because I had been to the afternoon cartoons. I had seen "Donald Duck In Nutzi Land." I determinedly sang, as if I were Spike Jones making farting noises on his Birdaphone,

> *When der Fuehrer says*
> *We is the master race,*
> *We Heil, Heil,*
> *Right in der Fuehrer's face.*
> *Not to love der Fuehrer*
> *Is a great disgrace,*
> *So we Heil, Heil,*
> *Right in der Fuehrer's face...*

That's it.

That's why these are notes to a preface that cannot be written.

That's all I knew about the First Great War, until years and years later, long after I had put aside the prankish laughter of childhood so that I could play like a man. I was in Majorca, at the home of the elder poet, Robert Graves. We were just outside the door. He was a big man, big bones, big hands, and he'd said Hello and put up his fists. We began to shadow-box, bobbing, feinting, laughing, and then he pursed his lips and said, "Poof, poof," as if he were blowing soap bubbles as a child. He put down his fists and asked, "Do you know Frank Prewett?"

I didn't know who he was talking about.

"Canadian poet. One of yours. Wartime. I published him."

I shook my head.

"Never mind. Come in, come in, sing for me."

He liked me to sing the "Agnus Dei" in falsetto, like a choir child.

Once home, I asked Bruce Meyer to find out who Frank Prewett was, and what he had written because he wasn't in any of the anthologies.

A few years later, I published his *Selected Poems*, among them, several "modern" war poems. Here was a poet who had first been edited by Robert Graves and praised by Virginia Woolf. Why had I never heard of him?

Was I living in a place where the word *why* empties and shrivels itself?

Then one day, Joe Rosenblatt — who has written in the voices of bumblebees, gorillas, serpents and fish — asked me if I had ever read *Generals Die in Bed*.

"No."

"Oh, it's the great war novel. The real thing."

I wanted to sing "Oh Frenchy, Oh Frenchy Frenchy," as if I knew something about that war. Instead I said to Bruce Meyer, "Let's find out if there were writers who really wrote about what they saw and did in those trenches…"

Years later we are publishing *We Wasn't Pals*. It is a kind a narrative selection of what we found, and some of it is astonishing.

Still, there is the question Why? Why did the men who shaped our taste, who told us what to read like E.K. Brown and A.J.M. Smith, consign this work to a great gap of unknowing? Why did Northrop Frye, who seemed to know everything, say nothing about these writers? Why did he ignore Prewett and Charles Yale Harrison?

Perhaps the answer lies in a little story about Frye himself.

One day during the First Great War he was playing the piano in his family house. His mother was listening, full of admiration. The postman came to the door with a letter that said Frye's older brother had been killed on the Western Front. His mother went into shock, she went deaf. She never heard Frye play the piano again. He never wrote about his brother, or the war, or the writers who came out of the war.

Silence. A wide-gaping silent laughter in the place we would rather not know about where

> *The razor across the eyeball*
> *is a detail from an old film.*
> *It is also a truth.*
> *Witness is what you must bear.*

INTRODUCTION
Bruce Meyer

This book is not an academic record of the literature of Canadians who fought in the First World War. Such a book would be like a listing of the names of the dead and the wounded, something that those at home during the war were greeted with, column after column, in the daily papers. Nor is it a memorial book. There have been countless memorial books with pictures, tributes, afterthoughts from a grateful nation. What this book does is allow the dead to tell their story in the authentic voice of their own experience. After all, that is one of the things that literature should do: it should serve as a record of our experience. But there is something more than chronicle here.

What emerges from the poetry, fiction, vignettes, letters and memoirs of that period (a period that until now has been almost completely ignored by scholars and readers) is a story that follows the psychological transformation of a nation from naïveté to horror to grim knowledge.

The voices included, such as the poet Bernard Freeman Trotter or polemicist L. Moore Cosgrave, suggest that Canada was not only unprepared for war militarily, but also psychologically. Their individual stories tell of a horrific transformation from Edwardian gentility to Modernist shock, an experience that went far beyond any known boundaries of art or sanity. During that process, the soldier poets and writers had to reinvent their means of telling. They were failed not only by the Virgilian attributes of loyalty, honour, justice, devotion to principle, nation and cause, and the assurance that somehow God and justice would see them through, but failed by a literature that had been their lens on the world.

In *The Waste Land* (1922), T. S. Eliot wrote: "These fragments I have shored against my ruins." Many of those writing at the time, even if they were not in the trenches, knew that the way literature had shaped the world was changing, or as Yeats said following the carnage of the Irish 1916 uprising, "Changed, changed utterly / A terrible beauty is born." Canadian humorist Stephen Leacock pointed to the change in his facetious essay, "Some Startling Side Effects of the War." He quoted former U.S. President William Howard Taft:

"There is no doubt," said Mr. Taft recently, "that the war is destined to effect the most profound uplift and changes, not only in our political outlook, but upon our culture, our thought, and, most of all, upon our literature"…Yes, the war is not only destined to affect our literature, but has already done so. The change in outlook, in literary style, in mode of expression, even the words themselves is already there.

Leacock, however poked fun at the trench writing, at the new language of brutality and frankness. Like most readers in Canada, the trenches were foreign correspondence to him. Home-front poets, such as Norah Holland, wrote of flowers blooming in the mud where the precious blood of youth had been spilt. Actually, men sat for weeks up to their thighs in that mud and slime, fighting off rats, only to die choking on poison gas. The gaping mouths of the young dead were the trench flowers.

A compromise between the poetic and the actual was struck in John McCrae's, "In Flanders Fields," a poem that became a mantra for the Allied troops of the Western Front after its publication in *Punch* in 1916. If "In Flanders Fields" accomplishes anything, it gives us images. Images are far easier to remember than the names of battles. Just about every Canadian school child has read, recited or memorized it. "…poppies blow, between the crosses row on row." A paraphrase of it even ended up on the wall of the Montreal Canadiens' dressing room. If the reading public of the war and post-war years shied away from the horrors, they at least accommodated the images. Everyone knows what poppies look like. Poppies had always been symbolic of martyrdom, sacrifice and eternal sleep. Pharmaceutically, they can be made into an opiate that can take one out of reality, distancing fear, pain, and even memory.

When November 11 rolls around each year, just about everyone in Canada has their own set of images, stories or ideas of what those four war years were about, and what those red poppies mean. Some dismiss the firing of guns and the whiff of cordite as a bellicose celebration of war: the truth is far from that. The day is set aside as a time not for military celebration, but for remembrance. The eleventh hour of the eleventh day of the eleventh month of each year marks the moment that the armistice was signed, ending the First World War. It marks a moment of victory, but a victory won at an enormous, inconceivable cost.

When I was four, my grandmother pinned one of those red poppies on me and took me down to City Hall on a raw November morning because, "there is something you need to see." I remember standing there as she clutched her black Persian-lamb coat at the throat. I spotted my Aunt Hazel in the crowd on the other side of the 48th Highland band — the same band that always opened each hockey season at Maple Leaf Gardens.

Aunt Hazel was a spinster. In her youth she had been a beautiful, brilliant woman. Even in age, as the tears rolled down her cheeks and the guns fired in salute to the playing of *The Last Post*, and the massive bells of the City Hall clock broke in upon the silence, she was still beautiful. Years later I learned the story of Hazel's beau. His name was Tom Kelly (maybe he is the Kelly that Stanley A. Rutledge mentions in "Like a Thief in the Night"). In any case, they'd been engaged. He'd gone off to France and disappeared without a trace at a place called Vimy Ridge. Listed as missing in action, his body was never found. Perhaps he was one of the countless soldiers "known but to God." Perhaps it is his body that was laid to rest in the House of Commons several years ago as a national memorial to the war dead. Each year I buy a poppy from a veteran or a child-cadet, and as I pin it on I say Tom Kelly's name.

When Parliament decided to honour those Canadians who have fallen in active service by selecting an anonymous body — now nothing more than a few shards of bones, if that — for interment in the tomb of the Unknown Soldier, they chose someone who had fallen at Vimy Ridge in 1917. Vimy is always cited as the apotheosis of Canadian participation in the First World War. It was the battle where Canadian troops accomplished in a matter of days what the British, the French and the Australians had failed to do in the previous two years of the war. It was at a terrible cost. Three thousand, five hundred and ninety-eight Canadians died there in the course of two days. But when the numbers at Vimy are placed alongside those from other battles — from First Ypres to Mons — the figures, as military historians put it in their cold language, represent "relative economy of loss."

During the dedication ceremonies for the Grave of the Unknown Soldier, the names of other battles were mentioned: Ypres in 1915 that wiped out a huge proportion of the First Contingent. There was the Somme on that hot July day in 1917 when inept British commanders sent tens of thousands to their deaths. There was Passchendaele, a muddy place that swallowed most of the Newfoundland Regiment, about which Edmund Blunden commented that he knew some sort of mortal passion would take place there when he first saw the name on a field map. And there were other battles that are rarely mentioned except on monuments — Courcelette, Arras, and Zillebeke. In John McCrae's letters to his mother, the sense of interminable slaughter, day after day, week after week, is closer to the truth of the First World War than the place names that appear neatly carved on war memorials in the cities and small towns of Canada. The reality of the First World War, not only for Canadians but for all those who fought in the trenches, was that the "fighting" consisted not of great events but of constant misery and fear punctuated by massive moments of slaughter. And what is more, as the literature of the period suggests, the experience of the war was a personal one for each individual voice. The war was not a series of abstract experiences tallied on a map, but real things that happened to people just like us.

In the decade following the Armistice, as the monuments went up in the cities, towns, crossroads, church halls and college doorways, and the war's grim reality became clear (Trinity College at the University of Toronto, for example, lost three-fifths of the graduating class of 1916), the books of war-writing began to appear. In the back stacks of a few research and public libraries, row on row, are the regimental histories, some fat volumes with fold-out maps, thick with technical language and details of what the generals did. For the most part, however, those regimental histories are unreadable. They are scientific in their precision and their accounts of which officer ordered which action, and which platoon seized which trench on such and such a day. They read with the passion of an engineering textbook. By 1920, U.S. President Warren G. Harding's cry for "a return to normalcy" was the readily received opinion in Canada. Within a decade, no one wanted to read about the war. Within two decades no one knew what to read.

By 1943, the noted critic E.K. Brown wrote in his influential work *On Canadian Poetry*:

The poetry of Drummond, Service and MacInnes was swept aside after the First Great War. It has not counted as an influence since 1918. The war brought a brief stimulus to poetry in Canada as in England; elder poets such as C.G.D. Roberts and Duncan Campbell Scott were stirred to exquisite laments; a few younger writers wrote lyrics with some quiet and lofty beauties; nothing good was achieved in the harsher manners; the one masterpiece was Colonel McCrae's "In Flanders Fields," where careful art, studied moderation in tone, and intense as well as perfectly represented emotion fused to produce a moment's perfection. The poetry of the war was also swept aside...

With that dismissal of "harsher manners" (while vastly overestimating "In Flanders Fields"), an entire era in Canadian literature went missing. He never examined the work of W.W.E. Ross, Frank Prewett, H. Smalley Sarson or any of the other writers from the war. He taught both the critics and the poet/editors who would shape the way our literature was read well into the late twentieth century — Northrop Frye and A.J.M. Smith. Neither mention the war writing in their works. Even though *The New York Post* had declared Charles Yale Harrison's *Generals Die in Bed* to be one of the best novels of 1928 (edging out Hemingway's *The Sun Also Rises*), or Ford Madox Ford had considered Peregrine Acland's *All Else is Folly* a major novel of the twentieth century, or that Virginia Woolf had written to Lytton Stratchey and declared that Frank Prewett was an important poet, the war writing of an era in Canadian literature went "missing in action."

Not only did Canadian trench writers meet with critical rejection: they met with public forgetfulness. The simple reality underlying works such as Harrison's *Generals Die in Bed* or James Hanley's *The German Prisoner* is that nothing in the literature of the Romantic, Victorian or Edwardian eras had prepared either the readers or the writers for what they would encounter in the war. There was a brutal honesty in this writing. It was the same stark violence, death and destruction that one encounters in Homer's *Iliad* or Virgil's *Aeneid*; yet frankness, absurdity and black humour did not register on the average reader. Literature was supposed to be about nature, not the unnatural. It wasn't supposed to do what Charles Yale Harrison was attempting when he wrote:

A shell lands with a monster shriek in the next bay.

The concussion rolls me on my back. I see stars shining serenely above us. Another lands in the same place. Suddenly the stars revolve...

I begin to pray.

"God — God — please..."

I remember I do not believe in God. Insane thoughts race through my brain. I want to catch hold of something, something that will explain this fury, this maniacal congealed hatred that pours down on our heads. I can find nothing to console me, nothing to appease my terror. I know that hundreds of men are standing a mile or two from me pulling gun-lanyards, blowing us to smithereens. I know that and nothing else..."

Obviously, Canadian writers were capable of what Ezra Pound in *Hugh Selwyn Mauberley* called for:

> *frankness as never before,*
> *disillusions as never told in the old days,*
> *hysterias, trench confessions,*
> *laughter out of dead bellies.*

I remember visiting the home of a friend of my grandparents when I was about four. In the midst of tea, Walter began to choke. His face turned purple and he choked and choked. I thought he was going to die. He left the room with his wife. She returned about ten minutes later. "Walter has to rest now," she said, and we got up and left. Walter had been gassed at Ypres. He had choked three times a day for almost fifty years.

About twelve years later, one New Year's Eve I was out with my parents at someone else's home. I grew bored from the conversation and made my way downstairs in search of a television (I am of that generation). Instead, in the half-darkness of the rec room, I found the host's father, an old man who had survived the war. When I shook his hand, the bones in his wrist rattled. He explained that he had taken shrapnel there, then retreated to his basement bedroom and came back with a piece of the German bomb, a bombardment map, and a photograph. "These are things you should see," he said. "You will probably be the last to see them." He spread the map on the floor. "Read the names," he ordered. Each trench was labelled: "Devil's

Way," "Hell Valley," "Bloody Bloor," and "Splattered Spadina." Hometown street names. This was how soldiers found their way through the thousand miles of trenches that ran north from Switzerland to the English Channel.

As he tossed the piece of shrapnel back and forth between his hands, he pointed out the names of men in the photograph — an artillery battery from Cobourg he had joined straight out of Queen's University. Placing a finger on each one, he told me how each had met his end. One was shot while crossing a bridge on November 12, 1918. Another simply "disappeared, we never knew what happened to him." "This one died of gas, and this one got too close to the recoil of the gun and it flipped over on him."

What has stayed with me since that New Year's Eve in the late Seventies was that this war was a personal war. It was not about numbers, or statistics, or even about the names of battles carved on war memorials and cenotaphs across the country. The reality of the war is closer to a memorial in Saskatoon that stands beside the Saskatchewan River. There is a statue of a boy holding a soccer ball. He is in short pants, and he looks as if he is about to run off and join his teammates on the playing field. Beneath him are the names of the fallen from that city. The statue had been intended, so I have been told, to commemorate a successful football team that had won an important championship in 1914. Over the next four years, the entire team fell in combat, and the statue — cast for the celebration of a victory — was rededicated as a war memorial.

Herein lies the paradox, as I see it. The voices in this anthology are who we remember and how we remember them. But they are also the celebration of the struggle to maintain a semblance of living in a place and a time that was dedicated to death. Their story, in their words, one selection after another, is relentless — how could it be otherwise? — but it is relentless in its authenticity, and relentless, therefore, in its humanness. For all the killing, for all the mindless military strategy that seemed to render life — and lives by the thousands per day — as worthless, ordinary men and women continued to manage moments of courtliness, moments of generosity, moments of laughter, muffled as it might be. I can see Berta Carveth, a young and innocent girl, helping to hold down a badly wounded soldier as his leg is eaten away by infection below the knee. I see Frank Prewett and his men coming across a shell-pocked field on the way back to their lines, their arms filled with the lilies they gathered in an abandoned French village. I see that anonymous "Battalion Bard" rhyming away in the muck and filth of the trenches, making poetry where no one thought doggerel was possible. And I see Stanley A. Rutledge, barely out of school, reading the diary of a fallen German soldier his own age, a schoolboy soldier who would have been happier discussing Hegel than fighting.

Our experience as a nation resides not only in ideas but in those voices that have expressed their experiences. These voices are waiting to be heard, not only in terms of their role in Canada's literature but in the experiences and warnings they share with us as contemporary readers.

We Wasn't Pals

Canadian Poetry and Prose
of the First World War

Major J. M. Langstaff

WAR-SHAPED DESTINY

I never thought that strange romantic War
Would shape my life and plan my destiny;
Though in my childhood's dreams I've seen his car
And grisly steeds flash grimly thwart the sky.
Yet now behold a vaster, mightier strife
Than echoed on the plains of sounding Troy,
Defeats and triumphs, death, wounds, laughter, life,
All mingled in a strange complex alloy.
I view the panorama in a trance
Of awe, yet coloured with a secret joy,
For I have breathed in epic and romance,
Have lived the dreams that thrilled me as a boy.
How sound the ancient saying is, forsooth,
How weak is Fancy's gloss of Fact's stern truth!

John Daniel Logan

WAR'S NEW APOCALYPSE

When I, full-armed, marched forth through Picardy
    (Not pleasant Picardy of yore),
The spectacles I saw in Picardy
    (In Picardy despoiled by war)
Were not alone the wastes I thought would be,
    Nor only deeds I should abhor,
But I beheld in town, in trench, on plain
    What may not be on earth again:
The forms of Faith and Hope and Charity
    Walk close with Death in Picardy.

The little village homes in Picardy,
    Shell-wracked and tenantless and bare,
Gaped lornly at the brown-clad soldiery
    That trooped by blithe and debonair;
But near the ruined Château Brevigny
    I saw three wan-faced women fare
'Mongst wayside graves, smile sweet as holy nuns,
    And bless the tombs of martyred sons.
Then I knew Faith had found safe sanctuary
    In widowed hearts in Picardy.

The once fair fields of fertile Picardy
    (Oh, ruthless was the conqueror!)
Stretched grey and fallow, far as I could see,
    Unploughed save by the shards of war;
But when I passed beyond Sainte Emelie
    I glimpsed an old man, bent and hoar,
At work afield while shells burst with their dread,
    Fell deviltries above his head.
Thus Hope held fast, and wove earth's livery
    Of green and gold in Picardy.

L. Moore Cosgrave

1915 – THE DEVELOPMENT OF HATE

War! What thoughts of romance — of chivalry — of splendid crusades of all ages, were inspired on that fateful 5th of August, 1914! Then followed the breathless excitement of preparation and the joyous rigour of training, mingling with that ever-present and proud realization that we were the standard-bearers of Canada's honour. We who formed part of that first Canadian Contingent pledged to help the Mother Country in her splendid and unselfish protection of the helpless smaller nations — the brave adventure o'er the great oceans in our modern argosies to that land of historic battlefields — Europe! That great Armada, in its three lines of ships, twelve deep and three abreast, bringing back vivid memories of Nelson's day.

No deep, intense hate pervaded our beings; merely an implicit belief that we were in the right and must help to punish some impersonal transgressor of the world's human laws; which deepened, as we neared the scene of the Homeric contest, into a sportsman's indignation against one-time fellow-players whose minds had become clouded, temporarily, with greed and self!

Then, like a flash of blinding lightning, came the awakening! The change from light-hearted, unthinking young adventurers to men! — men with a corroding hatred in their souls — a shame of their modernity as exemplified by "Teuton Kultur" in their hearts. And this hate came to us on that fateful day, April 22, 1915.

Who amongst us on that smiling Spring day, as we held the line in front of ancient Ypres, can e'er forget that silent, menacing, all-devouring, grey-green cloud of poison gas — let loose by, as the Algerians gaspingly cried, "The Father of All Evil." Men in their splendid strength sinking to the ground in dreadful contortions — dying after hours of agony — their dying words crying curses upon the fiends in human form who could be such damnable cowards, and could violate in such a manner all the tenets and creeds of a humane world! And what of the thoughts of us who survived, power-less to ease, by one iota, their terrible suffering and agony! Truly — an awakening! Changing clean, kindly disposed gentlemen into primitive beings with no thoughts beyond the lust to kill in any manner, those men — lower than the filthiest beasts, who had done or countenanced this vile thing! And as our hearts were indeed filled with the blackest, most hellish hate of fellowmen that this world has ever known.

Thus ended our first great trial, bringing us, after the shorter hells of Festubert and Givenchy, to the sodden trenches of the Bois de Ploegsteert; and thus began the long, dreary, soul-deadening trench warfare — that strange, unnatural life which made of some men angels and others devils!

Charles Yale Harrison

BOMBARDMENT
from GENERALS DIE IN BED

I run down the trench looking for prisoners. Each man is for himself.

I am alone.

I turn the corner of a bay. My bayonet points forward — on guard.

I proceed cautiously.

Something moves in the corner of the bay. It is a German. I recognize the pot-shaped helmet. In that second he twists and reaches for his revolver.

I lunge forward, aiming at his stomach. It is a lightning, instinctive movement.

The thrust jerks my body. Something heavy collides with the point of my weapon.

I become insane.

I want to strike again and again. But I cannot. My bayonet does not come clear. I pull, tug, jerk. It does not come out.

I have caught him between his ribs. The bones grip my blade. I cannot withdraw.

Of a sudden I hear him shriek. It sounds far-off as though heard in the moment of waking from a dream.

I have a man at the end of my bayonet, I say to myself.

His shrieks become louder and louder.

We are facing each other — four feet of space separates us.

His eyes are distended; they seem all whites, and look as though they will leap out of their sockets.

There is froth in the corners of his mouth which opens and shuts like that of a fish out of water.

His hands grasp the barrel of my rifle and he joins me in the effort to withdraw. I do not know what to do.

He looks at me piteously.

I put my foot up against his body and try to kick him off. He shrieks into my face.

He will not come off.

I kick him again and again. No use.

His howling unnerves me. I feel I will go insane if I stay in this hole much longer...

It is too much for me. Suddenly I drop the butt of my rifle. He collapses into the corner of the bay. His hands still grip the barrel. I start to run down the bay.

A few steps and I turn the corner.

I am in the next bay. I am glad I cannot see him. I am bewildered.

Out of the roar of the bombardment I think I hear voices. In a flash I remember that I am unarmed. My rifle — it stands between me and death — and it is in the body of him who lies there trying to pull it out.

I am terrified.

If they come here and find me they will stab me just as I stabbed him — and maybe in the ribs, too.

I run back a few paces but I cannot bring myself to turn the corner of the bay in which he lies. I hear his calls for help. The other voices sound nearer.

I am back in the bay.

He is propped up against his parados. The rifle is in such a position that he cannot move. His neck is limp and he rolls his head over his chest until he sees me.

Behind our lines the guns light the sky with monster dull red flashes. In this flickering light this German and I enact our tragedy.

I move to seize the butt of my rifle. Once more we are face to face. He grabs the barrel with a childish movement which seems to say: You may not take it, it is mine. I push his hands away. I pull again.

My tugging and pulling works the blade in his insides.

Again those horrible shrieks!

I place the butt of the rifle under my arm and turn away, trying to drag the blade out. It will not come.

I think: I can get it out if I unfasten the bayonet from the rifle. But I cannot go through with the plan, for the blade is in up to the hilt and the wound which I have been clumsily mauling is now a gaping hole. I cannot put my hand there.

Suddenly I remember what I must do.

I turn around and pull my breech-lock back. The click sounds sharp and clear.

He stops his screaming. He looks at me, silently now.

He knows what I am going to do.

A very white light soars over our heads. His helmet has fallen from his head. I see his boyish face. He looks like a Saxon; he is fair and under the light I see white down against green cheeks.

I pull my trigger. There is a loud report. The blade at the end of my rifle snaps in two. He falls into the corner of the bay and rolls over. He lies still.

I am free.

But I am only free to continue the raid. It seems as though I have been in this trench for hours. Where are the red flares? I look towards our lines and see only the flickering orange gun-flashes leaping into the black sky.

The air is full of the smoke of high explosives. Through the murk I see two heads coming out of the ground. It is an entrance to a dugout. The heads are covered with familiar pot-shaped helmets — we use a more vulgar term to describe them. Apparently this was a dugout our men had overlooked.

I cock my breech-lock and raise the rifle to my shoulder. The first one sees me and throws his hands high into the air.

"Kamarad — Kamarad," he shouts.

His mate does likewise.

Suddenly the sky over in the direction of our lines becomes smudged with a red glow.

The flares! The signal to return!

"Come with me," I shout into their ears. I start to drag them with me. They resist and hold back.

They stand with their backs glued to the side of the trench and look at me with big frightened eyes. They are boys of about seventeen. Their uniforms are too big for them and their thin necks poke up out of enormous collars.

"*Nicht schiessen!* — *bitte* — *nicht schiessen!*" the nearest one shouts, stupidly shaking his head.

I reassure him. I search them for weapons and then sling my rifle over my shoulder as an evidence of good faith. We start off down the trench towards a sap which leads out into No Man's Land.

We are back in the bay where he, with my bayonet in his ribs, lies in the corner. I pass him quickly as though I do not know him.

The one nearest to me throws himself on the dead soldier.

I spring upon him.

The red flares colour the sky. It is the signal to return, and here this maniac tries to keep me in this trench forever. I grab him by the slack of his collar and start to tear him away.

He looks up at me with the eyes of a dog and says:

"*Mein Bruder* — *eine minute* — *mein Bruder.*"

The red flares grow brighter in the sky over my shoulder.

The other prisoner looks at me with sad eyes and repeats:

"*Ja, ja, das ist sein Bruder.*"

"*Schnell,*" I shout into the kneeling one's ears. He nods and takes a few letters and papers from his brother's pockets and follows me into the sap.

The earth leaps into the air on all sides of us. I point towards our lines and we begin to run. The field is being swept by machine-gun fire.

I do not see any of our men. We are alone.

We run and stumble over stray bits of embedded barbed wire. We pick ourselves up and run again. It is miraculous how we can live, even for a moment, in this fire. A shell explodes about twenty yards from us. The brother falls. We pick him up and carry him into a discarded communication trench that runs from the German lines to ours.

The fire grows fiercer. We can distinguish shells of every calibre. The air begins to snarl and bark over our heads. They are using overhead shrapnel.

We stop and feel in the darkness for a funk-hole or a dugout. We find a hole in the side of the trench and wait there while the storm of living steel rages about us.

It is black inside. The unhurt prisoner pulls a stub of a candle out of his tunic pocket. I light it; it flickers with the force of the nearby detonations.

The brother hugs his wounded leg and rocks to and fro with pain. We examine him. He has been hit in the calf of his right leg. We take the emergency dressings from our tunics and pour iodine into the open hole of his flesh. He winces and then shrieks as the stuff eats into his tissue. I apply a gauze and his mate starts to bind the wound with bandages.

By signs and with my meager German I make them understand that we will wait here until the force of the barrage abates. I pull out a package of cigarettes and offer them one each. We light up from the candle and sit smoking.

I point to the wounded one's leg and ask him how he feels. He shakes his head and moans: *"Ach, ach, mein Bruder."* He points back towards the German lines.

He begins to weep and talk rapidly at the same time. I cannot understand. I can distinguish only two words — *"Bruder"* and *"Mutter."* The other prisoner nods his head solemnly, affirming what his comrade says:

"Ja, ja, das ist wahr — das ist sein Bruder, Karl."

I sit looking at them silently.

There is nothing to say.

How can I say to this boy that something took us both, his brother and me, and dumped us into a lonely, shrieking hole at night

— it armed us with deadly weapons and threw us against each other.

I imagined that I see the happy face of the mother when she heard that her two boys were to be together. She must have written to the older one, the one that died at the end of my bayonet, to look after his young brother. Take care of each other and comfort one another, she wrote, I am sure.

Who can comfort whom in war? Who can care for us, we who are set loose at each other and tear at each other's entrails with silent gleaming bayonets?

I want to tell these boys what I think, but the gulf of language separates us.

We sit silently, waiting for the storm of steel to die down.

The wounded one's cigarette goes out. I move the candle towards his mouth. He puts his thin hand to mine to steady it. The cigarette is lit. He looks into my eyes with that same doggish look and pats my hand in gratitude.

"Du bist ein guter Soldat," he says, his eyes filling with tears. I pat his shoulder.

With his hand he describes a circle. The motion takes in his trenches and ours, the thundering artillery, the funk-hole, everything. In a little-boy voice he says:

"Ach, es ist schrecklich — schrecklich..."

H. Smalley Sarson

THE SHELL

Shrieking its message the flying death
    Cursed the resisting air,
Then buried its nose by a battered church
    A skeleton gaunt and bare.

The brains of science, the money of fools
    Had fashioned an iron slave
Destined to kill, yet the futile end
    Was a child's uprooted grave.

Elverdinghe

H. Smalley Sarson

LAVENTIE CHURCH

Fragments left by a bursting shell
    Show where the altar stood;
A pile of bricks where the steeple fell,
    A Virgin carved in wood.
The crucifix, its burden gone,
    Stands awry in the nave,
The Christ lies under the scattered stone;
    Lost, like a felon's grave.

Stanley A. Rutledge

OVER BOYS AND AT THEM

It is here on the rolling Somme that France and Britain are gathering their men. Troops are herded on every plain. One climbs a hill and the whole landscape stretches below, indescribably full of black dots and streaks — men and transports scurrying here and there. As this scene is presented one gets an impression of energy, pulsing, chaotic it may be, but it is the secret of the new drive. We are "going at them." The staff work is better, more clean cut, more incisive, and tenacious of its aim. Veterans and "newly arrives" are carrying out. No more huts, no more Dugouts, but "active service with a vengeance," as one old-timer said. Attacks are called for on a moment's notice. Men go from their areas — "up and over," all in an hour's time. One has to be ready, always.

We are now past the German third line, and the fighting has taken on many characteristics of open warfare. The Huns, after each setback, work with frantic zeal at their new trenches. Our artillery rushes up at each new advance and begins another hammering. Right out into the fields, galloping horses plunge desperately in and out of shell holes. Men crawl into these indents and commence linking up the new line.

Crowded in the trenches the boys exchange a word or two, and then it is "over and at them," and the best of luck. Advancing in extended order they rush for fifty yards, it may be, and then dive for Mother Earth. The German machine guns are rattling away, the Fritzes, very brave with their rifles, open up rapid fire. Men stumble up and on — the whole scene one wild demoniacal dance — the dance of death.

Frank Prewett

CARD GAME

Hearing the whine and crash
We hastened out
And found a few poor men
Lying about.

I put my hand in the breast
Of the first met.
His heart thumped, stopped, and I drew
My hand out wet.

Another, he seemed a boy,
Rolled in the mud
Screaming, "my legs, my legs,"
And he poured out his blood.

We bandaged the rest
And went in,
And started again at our cards
Where we had been.

Stanley A. Rutledge

A LETTER HOME

Belgium, July 10, 1916

We came out of trenches last night. Our tour was very satisfactory, and Wilf and I came out unscathed. Today, there is the usual washing up. We are billeted in what was once the country residence of a person of some distinction. The grounds are spacious, with massive trees and well-arranged driveways. The house is of white stone, partially demolished now; and architecturally well conceived, of the chateau style, and surrounded by a moat. In the brave days of old this has been the home of a wealthy *citoyen* of Ypres. It is situated on one of the main roads to that "dead city."

Guerin, my sniping mate, and I occupy a unique dugout. A large tree has fallen, and with this protecting wall, a typical shelter has been made. My partner and I had very good results last time in. That sounds rather cold-blooded, doesn't it? But over here, one loses any compunction as regards to taking human life. Of course, if we "get" a man and see he is wounded, there is a further shot fired, even though opportunity offers. With our high-powered telescopes and telescopic rifle sights it is possible to see a fly on the enemy parapet, even five hundred yards away. Suppose an incautious German puts his head up for a second, and we happen to be "trained" on that spot, it means a crack of the rifle, and the observer, accustomed to this work, can actually follow the course of the bullet and ascertain the hit. Of course, one can give a quick peep and get down, but never show up in the same place. The German has patience, and is waiting for you.

Such is the work of a sniper — invaluable it is — we protect our men, let the enemy know we are on the job, observe new work on his parapet, locate loop-holes and machine-gun emplacements, smash periscopes and generally annoy and keep him "down." I think we have it on the German and his work. At least, my last two trips have shown this result. Our hours are very long, snipers being on the job in two shifts, from daybreak until the flares begin at dark. It is a great game...

Robert W. Service

MY MATE

I've been sittin' starin', starin' at 'is muddy pair of boots,
And tryin' to convince meself it's 'im.
(Look out there, lad! That sniper—'e's a dysey when 'e shoots;
'E'll be layin' of you out the same as Jim.)
Jim as lies there in the Dugout wiv 'is blanket round 'is 'ead,
To keep 'is brains from mixin' wiv the mud;
And 'is face as white as putty, and 'is over-coat all red,
Like 'e's spilt a bloomin' paint-pot—but it's blood.

And I'm tryin' to remember of a time we wasn't pals.
'Ow often we've played 'ookey, 'im and me;
And sometimes it was music-'alls, and sometimes it was gals,
And even there we 'ad no disagree.
For when 'e copped Mariar Jones, the one I liked the best,
I shook 'is 'and and loaned 'im 'arf a quid;
I saw 'im through the parson's job, I 'elped 'im make 'is nest,
I even stood god-father to the kid.

So when the war broke out, sez 'e: "Well, wot abaht it, Joe?"
"Well, wot abaht it, lad?" sez I to 'im.
's missis made a awful fuss, but 'e was mad to go,
('E always was 'igh-sperrited was Jim).
Well, none of it's been 'eaven, and the most of it's been 'ell,
But we've shared our baccy, and we've 'alved our bread.
We'd all the luck at Wipers, and we shaved through Noove Chapelle,
And...that snipin' barstard gits 'im on the 'ead.

Now wot I want to know is, why it wasn't me was took?
I've only got meself, 'e stands for three.
I'm plainer than a louse, while 'e was 'andsome as a dook;
'E always *was* a better man than me.
'E was goin' 'ome next Toosday; 'e was 'appy as a lark,
And 'e'd just received a letter from 'is kid;
And 'e struck a match to show me, as we stood there in the dark,
When…that bleedin' bullet got 'im on the lid.

'E was killed so awful sudden that 'e 'adn't time to die.
'E sorto jumped, and came down wiv a thud.
Them corpsy-lookin' star-shells kept a-streamin' in the sky,
And there 'e lay like nothin' in the mud.
And there 'e lay so quiet wiv no mansard to 'is 'ead,
And I'm sick, and blamed if I can understand:
The pots of 'alf and 'alf we've 'ad, and *zip!* like that 'e's dead,
Wiv the letter of 'is nipper in 'is 'and.

There's some as fights for freedom and there's some as fights for fun,
But me, my lad, I fights for bleedin' 'ate.
You can blame the war and blast it, but I 'opes it won't be done
Till I gets the bloomin' blood-price for me mate.
It'll take a bit o' bayonet to level up for Jim;
Then if I'm spared I think I'll 'ave a bid,
Wiv 'er that was Mariar Jones to take the place of 'im,
To sorter be a farther to 'is kid.

W. Redvers Dent
(Raymond Knister)

from SHOW ME DEATH

I awoke to find myself in the hole still, but it was evening now and dusk settling. I felt pains in my stomach, my jaw, and worst of all in my leg. I looked down at my leg, which was very stiff, and the puttee was soaked with blood. If I took it off the bleeding would start again, and if I left it on I would get gangrene. What the devil should I do? No. Hadn't I a shot of that dope? I'd leave it.

My jaw was bruised, only a slight cut, and my stomach had a very bad welt shaped like a gun butt. So that was it. My hand was bleeding again. What a mess! Good Heavens! Who was coming? Germans! I was behind the lines!

Two figures in grey with red crosses on their arms had stopped at the hole. I tried to look brave and snarl, but I'm afraid it was a very weak attempt.

They were stepping over the bodies at the bottom of the hole and around the edge. There were two or three other khaki figures lying there beside my own. I heard the moaning and groaning of wounded, but couldn't place them exactly. There seemed to be a lot.

The Germans gave me a look, and then one had compassion and gave me a drink. I wasn't worth worrying over. They went right through the officer's pockets, taking everything, even his boots, nice, soft, shiny ones. "The ----!" There was a Fritz wounded there in the hole, his jaw nearly off. My gun barrel did that, I said to myself.

At last they passed on, taking the Fritz with them. My head began to throb. Well, thank God the Fritzies weren't as bad as they said. They left me alone to die in peace.

In war you look after your own side first, naturally. When there were no German wounded to look after, they would come back for us. I couldn't help it — I thought I was alone among the dead, and I groaned, and groaned again. I would have given anything to cry.

Then a miracle happened. I thought I was dreaming, but the officer moved, slowly rolled over, oh, so slowly, and said, "Can you see any Fritzies?"

I said, "No."

"Thank God! Well, we sure are in one hell of a mess. Where did you get it?"

"All over," I replied between gasps. "The devils didn't leave a whole bone in my body."

He spoke again: "I got a beauty — a bayonet in the shoulder. The blighter was aiming at my belly, but I knocked his arm up. Are your hands free? Do you think you could bandage it?"

He groaned in spite of himself, and added, "It is pretty darn painful."

"Can you roll over?" I asked, and as he rolled toward me I rolled a little in his direction and stuck his field dressing on the wound. It surely was a mess — a long gash with cords sticking out. I couldn't tie it, though, with one hand, and said, "I can't make the bloody thing stick."

So we both thought it over for a minute; then he suggested changing his Sam Browne belt to the other shoulder to hold it.

I had a difficult time rolling him over and fixing his belt, as we daren't raise ourselves upward or we would get it. It was finally done, but, darn it all! I had broken open my leg wound, and, unwinding the puttee, found it was a bad hole through the calf. I could feel the shrapnel, a jagged piece, under the flesh. Oh, hell! What should I do now? I groaned again, my mouth dry, my head throbbing and throbbing.

I slid down and groped among the bodies until I caught a khaki tunic, groped, found the field dressing, tore it open with my teeth, and wrapped it round, but couldn't tie it unless I used my other hand, which was very stiff and burned and seared. Sweat poured off me, to the accompaniment of groans and grunts, as I tied the dressing. The officer was talking quietly to himself and groaning. He was delirious.

What should I do? I pulled him down to the bottom of the hole among the bodies, and finding a German pack with a great-coat, put it over him.

I hunted through my friendly Canadian's body for cigarettes and found some. Throb, throb. Would that damned engine in my head never stop? O God! Do something about this. I can't do much more. I hunted for my cigarette-lighter, crouched down in the hole putting my head between two bodies, cigarette in my mouth, lighter in my hand. Thank God, it lit quickly for once and my cigarette was going. What a relief.

I hunted among the water-bottles till I found one that gurgled, pulled the cork and, putting it to my mouth, found RUM. I said a prayer of thanks, drank long, and it immediately put fire into me. I had to put out my cigarette or lie down. Which should I do? I placed it carefully on the belt buckle of a Fritz and crawled over to the officer.

His mouth was open and I poured some rum into it. He spluttered, sending it all over his face, but he began to lick it with his tongue, mutely asking for more.

I gave him a little, and reserved the rest to see what would happen later. Throb, throb. Would that never stop? I hunted for my cigarette, and found it still going, so, holding my hand over the spark and blowing the smoke down to the ground, I smoked, smoked, smoked. It was dark now and felt cooler. Not a shell was dropping over us. They would have to be our guns, if there were any, I thought to myself. The German barrage was on ahead.

Evidently their wounded went by another route than through the wood, for we saw no one. Flares thrown up by the Germans convinced us they must be up on Observatory Ridge.

Rats! My God! I had forgotten about the rats. I could see their eyes gleaming, hear them rustle. Oh, I can't stand any more. And now rats! Haven't I stood enough, suffered enough? Oh, please, please send the rats away! Oh, please do, please! I am at the end of the rope. Haven't you done enough? Why do you allow it? You aren't a God, you are a joke! Damn you — damn you to hell!

I shuffled down beside the officer, hunted for his revolver, found it, and struck at them and cursed, lying across him to get at them. Scurry, scurry. I could see their eyes. Damn them! Curse them!

I forgot about my wounds, troubles, pains, aches, everything, and, like a snarling beast, struck and beat at them. I lay there in a world gone mad and dared God to do his worst, defied Him, preached to Him, and told Him I could run the world better than that.

A storm of rifle and machine-gun fire broke out, red and green flares floated in the sky, and the German artillery burst like a flood of bass drums, pounding in my ear.

The rats disappeared and figures rushed past, and I heard groans, and curses in German, then came men running, stumbling and someone fell into our shell hole.

I struck and struck and struck, and was still pounding him with the butt of the revolver when I heard voices, English, and good old Canadian curses.

They passed, following the Germans.

I still struck the figure, though he had given his last groan long before.

I was in a daze. I believe my mind was going. The officer still mumbled and groaned, another wave of men passed over, not even glancing at us.

Then came the third wave, and these were slower, hunting, hunting, listening for groans. I could see them by the flares, and I shouted and shouted.

A figure came toward us. "Hey, Joe, here are a couple!"

A welcome voice said, "You can stop hitting that poor blighter now, Bud."

My hand moved up and down, then somebody felt my body, and my mouth was opened and a pill of some kind thrust in.

"God, Joe, these are the C.M.R.'s, not our mob at all!"

"Well, what the hell do you think of that? C.M.R.'s. An officer, too, without any boots. Those ----s pinched his boots. How is your guy? Mine's off his bean but O.K., I think."

Then another voice broke in, "This beggar hasn't even a shirt. He's as crazy as a loon. Been pounding some poor ----'s face to pulp, and was still doing it till I told him to let up."

"Can yours walk? I think I can handle this one."

Joe's voice again: "By the looks of things these C.M.R.'s sure put up some fight. Say, we better get out of here before the barrage starts."

I felt myself being lifted, my arm put around somebody's shoulder, while my other arm still flopped up and down, up and down. I couldn't seem to stop it. Am I crazy? I must be. That chap said I was.

I felt all right, no pain, nothing, only that arm. I couldn't stop it. My mind seemed perfectly clear.

We stumbled on, and I heard my man trying encourage me.

Suddenly his nerve gave. "For God's sake stop flopping that arm! It gives me the creeps!"

I tried to cut it out, but couldn't. I didn't seem to have an arm. It wasn't there; I couldn't make a connection. Am I dead? Must be. Stumble, stumble. At last a road.

We moved along it and I heard the sound of an automobile idling. A heave, a push, and I lay on something hard, then rumble, rumble, rumble, and we were moving.

Somebody else is there now, too.

The sound of gasps, groans. Bump, rumble, rumble, bump.

Screams from somewhere, sounding like my own voice. Rumble, rumble. At last a stop, lights, doctors, stretchers, a funny smell, then sleep, blessed sleep, glorious sleep.

CORYDON'S TRENCH SONG

Original Music by R.G.D.

Fetch me a hunk of bul - ly beef,

And a pot of mar - ma - lade,.................................... And

H. Smalley Sarson

After Reading Herrick At Neuve Eglise, 1915

I

Within my heart I built a shrine
    Engarlanded with roses,
Where love's pure flame can ever shine
    Brightly and discloses
An altar my fond lips enlaid
    With ardent kisses tender—
All dedicated to the maid
    Whose homage thus I render.

II

My heart is sad since I have made
    You mistress of my thought;
Yet am I glad my soul has stayed
    To worship where it ought.

Could you but grant some small redress,
    My supplication ease,
No further want would I express
    To bruise Love's ecstasies.

III

Red is the curving petal of a rose
Yet redder are thy lips than any flower that grows
And sweeter too, their only food should be
Kisses, which I would gladly give to thee.

IV

Wealth I count a hindrance,
    Power and glory naught,
Wisdom seems but folly
    And is too dearly bought.
Ambition is a vast morass
    Wherein the unwary moan,
But love the pressure of your lips,
    Their warmth upon my own.

V

Within the rubbish heap of our
False loves, lost hopes and shattered dreams
We yet may find a gem that gleams
A bud that still may flow'r.

CUPID IN FLANDERS

"As long as this war lasts, dear boy, I can only be a sister to you!"

Berta Carveth

Diary of a Canadian Nurse
Unit Four

Thursday, June 29, 1916

Nothing new. Terrible burn dressing. Retter burned by explosion of smoke bomb. Miss Stroose's half-day. To town in evening. Front seat in ambulance going in. Fed on strawberries on way back.

Saturday, July 1, 1916

Heard heavy bombardment most of a.m. The sound of the guns could be heard all the way across the Channel here in England. Canadian games on cricket grounds. Unable to go. Colonel Osler on job. Two operations for Unit Four. Spent rest hours, three to five, snoozing in garden. Phone from Uncle Bert. In garden in evening. First letter from Sheldon. Report of sixteen miles of German first-line trenches taken by Canadians. Expecting more casualties soon. Beds clearing all too quickly.

Monday, July 3, 1916

Telegram at one p.m. from Lieutenant Robinson inviting me spend p.m. in Dover. Nothing planned for half-day so got pass from Captain and sent return telegram which never got there, so spent afternoon in Dover alone, mostly looking. Returned to Folkestone in time for tea, and home in ambulance. Convoy came in at seven p.m.. Twenty-four for our ward. All were Imperials.

Wednesday, July 5, 1916

Polishing and arranging flowers, etc. most of a.m. Princess Louise and party arrived at 3:15 a.m. and spent about two hours visiting units. Talked to and shook hands with each patient, leaving cigarettes with each. Just sister in charge presented. Photo taken in Unit Four.

Strawberries and cake, etc. served in library. Wrote letters in garden in evening. Letter from Mother.

Sunday, July 9, 1916
Doug phoned in a.m. Three-thirty off. Culley, Doug and I walked to Cheriton. Took taxi to town. Supper at Geronemo's. Took Culley to Ross Barracks in taxi, then on to QCMH (Queen's Canadian Military Hospital). Doug leaves in a.m. for Birmingham. Had telegram to report on Wednesday, a.m. Billy Givens and Captain Dixon called in evening. Air raid in a.m. No damage.

Saturday, July 22, 1916.
Beastly slow.

Monday, July 24, 1916
Half day for Miss Ross and I, spent in town, movies, shopping and Geronemo's. Planned to go to Hythe in ambulance in evening. Convoy arrived about one p.m. About fifty, almost all Australian, and some bad cases.

Thursday, July 27, 1916
Two band concerts today. One at four and one at evening. In hammock on rest hours and in evening.

Friday, July 28, 1916
Colonel on scene. Four ops in p.m. Last case (shoulder) returned at 6:55 in very bad shock. Condition improved by heat: interstitial rectal saline and whiskey, and strych. But suddenly worse at 8:30, died quite suddenly. Sister T3 on till after ten. Getting straightened. I was to special till ten. Someday alright. Good concert in garden.

Saturday, July 29, 1916
Beastly day. No morning luncheon. No tea. No time off and on duty till almost eight. Two leg amputations in a.m., one in bad shock. Old

case developed signs of tetanus. Doing dressings till almost seven p.m. Slept in hammock in evening. No letters today.

Sunday, July 30, 1916
Another bad day. Old case had very unexpected hemorrhage at 7:30 a.m. I was lucky enough to discover it immediately. Second hemorrhage at 9, to OR, intravenous while in surgery. Rest hours 1 to 3:30 spent in garden writing letters. Miss T3 last hours. Alone with V.A.D. on duty till almost eight. Went for long walk all alone. Too late for service in the garden.

Monday July 31, 1916
Troubles never cease. Amputation case had internal hemorrhage from absorption of poison. Gave interstitial, tried intravenous twice with no success. Then gave saline abdominally. No improvement — died at 12:20. Unit like Hades all a.m. Four dressings left for p.m. One hour rest. Slept in hammock. Letter from Doug. Spent evening in hammock. Unit Three tomorrow. Farewell to Unit Four.

Bernard Freeman Trotter

SMOKE

All the windy ways of man
Are a smoke that rises up.
                    — TENNYSON

Breath of the mine,
Wraith of the oak—
Who shall divine
The riddle of smoke?

        ℰℰℰ

Weave me a cloud,
Cover the sky;
Weave me a shroud:
Life is a lie!

Weave it not thin,
Weave it not fine;
Vivid as sin,
This, the design:

Beings of might
Toiling with death;
Frail things affright,
Gasping for breath;

Cities of doom,
Blackened and grim;
Battle-cloud's gloom;
Charred forests dim;

Crater and pit,
Furnace and pyre;—
Boldly in-knit
With garlands of fire.

Weave it! The dust
lies in the urn:
So at last must
All the world burn.

Take then your toll,
Weaver of cloud.
Follows the whole:
Weave me a shroud.

Weave me it true,
Weave me it well—
Weave me it, weave me it,
Vapour of hell.

Walter McLaren Imrie

REMEMBRANCE

Through the unshuttered windows of the ward, the shadows of the late afternoon steal quietly in. The Sergeant stirs restlessly in his bed. Above him hangs the Military Medal, and a last, lingering sunbeam, quivering obliquely on the bare white wall, touches the deep colours of the ribbon with wayward hands, and suddenly departs. Slowly the shadows lengthen.

The Sergeant's eyes are closed, and his dark lashes lie like twilight on his still face. He is a glorious lad — as splendid in his young manhood as an Athenian marble. In the gathering dusk, he assumes an almost luminous pallor. It is as though his departing spirit were already casting about him a halo of transplendent light. Softened by the approaching death, his features have assumed the deep impress of the final sleep, and folded above his heart, his hands lie nerveless and attenuated, like withered lilies.

For seven days I have watched his chart, but the hieroglyphic lines of temperature and pulse give no encouragement. Apparently there has been no resistance voluntarily offered, no heroic effort made; it is as though he knew the futility of hope, and, in his heart, was very glad — and waited. Some men fight their battles inch by inch; some men, not at all.

In the morning, and in the afternoon, and then at night, I do his dressing. He seldom speaks, so it is difficult to say just what degree of suffering he endures. Only once or twice have I found his dark eyes upon me, as I worked, and then, his gaze was so remote, so utterly removed, that to have challenged him, and brought him back to the grey horror of reality, would have seemed a desecration, almost, of some dim, spiritual aloofness of his own. So we have gone on, patiently, and in silence.

The surgeons have done what they could for him — probed and drained, and given blood transfusions; but from the very start, his chance was wretched. In his left lung there lies a great, torn fragment of shrapnel, and when he coughs, it turns and writhes within him, lacerating its way through muscle and tissue, and severing the vessels that obstruct its course. Then, stains of crimson steal across his lips, and presently, great basins brim with his own blood...

After supper, the trays are cleared away, the men quiet down, and the Medical Officer comes on his nightly round. Captain Bartholomew studies the Sergeant's chart, takes his pulse and temperature, and then calls me aside.

"I think we'd better have screens to-night, Corporal — he can't last very much longer, at this rate."

So I bring the screens and put them about the Sergeant's bed. The other men look on, unmoved, and whisper between themselves in a low monotone.

At nine o'clock, I fetch my dressing-tray from the instrument cupboard. The ward is very quiet now, and many of the men are asleep. With a soft, kindly radiance, the lamp-light floods the screen-enclosed area. The Sergeant's eyes are open, and he is moving his hands about, over the coverlet.

"Here we are again, old man! — You look pretty fit, tonight. Feeling better?"

"Oh, — I don't know — thanks." He turns his head wearily towards me, and tries to take an interest in what I am doing. His black hair looms like a shadow on the pillow.

I unbutton the coat of his pyjamas, and carefully remove the surgical pads that cover his wound. His body is burning to the touch — like the beating of the sun on a mid-summer's afternoon. Apparently his fever is up again on one of its periodic flights. Surely the end — the beginning of the end — is near.

The dressing takes some twenty minutes. When I have finished, and am gathering up my basins and tubes and instruments, and am about to depart, a waxen hand strays out from the bed, and detains me. I put down my tray on the floor.

"Yes, old man; what can I do for you? A drink?"

The Sergeant negatively closes his eyes, and then slowly opens them.

"No, I'm not thirsty, thanks, Corporal. I only wanted to know — if you'd — come back — and sit with me awhile — for, you see — I'm dying — tonight — and it's lonely here — behind these screens."

I take both his hands in mine, and hold them fast.

"We're not afraid, old pal. Try to sleep. I shall not leave you."

Thus draws his mortal day to its close.

Towards eleven o'clock he passes into a light delirium. His dreams are broken, disjointed — dim memories of dead days, lived long ago, and ever at their heels, urging them on, blood-stained remembrances of the more immediate past — the far prairies of his native Canada, gloriously golden under their Autumn harvest of wheat; his mother, patiently waiting; his brother; the battlefields of the Somme. A little strangled sob floats upwards for an instant, and dies in fluttering accents.

At midnight he rouses, and I give him water to drink. Thereafter, he seems easier, and does not care to sleep; so I talk to him quietly of Canada — of the prairies and the mountains and the sea — of the beauty and the gladness — that is *home*. Patiently he holds my hand, and listens. Backward I lead him, step by step, in memory.

When I believe him to be at the very verge of sleep; his fingers suddenly close hard on mine, and he stirs uneasily beside me.

"It's Eric, though, Corporal," his voice is very faint and I must stoop to hear, "Eric, my brother, that I'm longing for. Can't you see — he's dead, and I've been waiting for him — all this time.

What can I say? The cold hand trembles in my own.

"He was only a kid — was Eric — seventeen. Mother should never have let him go: but God, how he loved me — better than life itself — and he *would* come along. All his life before him, — and *happy*, — why, he never knew a care! — It seems years ago to me, now. — Only seventeen when he died! God, — the pity of it all!

"I was with him the morning he was killed; we'd never been apart, he and I, — just pals, — and he was a proper soldier, too, even though he was a kid.

"Yes, I've lived it all over a good many times, since I've been lying here, — that day he died. — I've only got to close my eyes, and Gad! — I'm back on that old road again, with Eric bedside me on the gun-carriage. We were drivers, you see, — he and I, — in the Somme. Been through some pretty heavy fighting, too.

"I'll never forget that day — the heat and the dust. There wasn't a breath of air. The old girl lumbered along, rattling and clanking like all-possessed. First, we were up on one wheel, and then we were down on the other — And what a road! — pools of water, green with slime, and Shell holes a horse could break his leg in. — The dust rose and fell like smoke, around us: we were grey with it, — we breathed it in with every breath. It drifted in shuddering clouds, — hung motionless in the still air. At times, we could not see the man ahead of us, — our own horses, even."

Faint, the Sergeant pauses for an instant, and his eyes slowly open. They mirror a horror, — a remembrance, that is beyond human words.

"The kid was half-asleep, you see, hanging on beside me, and jolting about. The sun was in his eyes, and he'd been up all night, besides. I tried to watch him, — God knows, — had my arm around him, most of the time so that he could put his head down on my shoulder, and sleep more easily. — It was all play to him; like a boy, he was tired out, and wanted to forget.

"Then — we struck a crater! — God, I thought we'd never stop; down and down, slipping and sliding. The horses were wild with fear. Struggling to hold them back, I wrenched my arm from the kid. It only lasted a moment, — then slowly, the great gun righted itself, — the wheels groaned, the chains pulled taut. — Out of the dust beneath me, — suddenly there came a cry! I looked for Eric; — he was gone!"

The Sergeant's eyes fill slowly with tears. They course unheeded down his wan face. He makes a supreme effort to regain his self-control. Out of his increasing weakness, and the mists of delirium, which are slowly gathering again, he wrests a final moment of lucidity.

"I left the horses standing, and went back. — At the bottom of the crater, I found him, face-downward in the dust, his arms spread out before him. There was blood on the sand, — great pools of it, that quickly sank and disappeared. — The wheels had gone over his chest, — poor kid, but his hands were still twitching when I reached him, — clawing the sand, and digging themselves in. — I tried to lift him up in my arms, but he was bent, and broken, and twisted. His blood poured over me, — my hands, my tunic. It was on my lips, and my eyes were blinded with it.

"Then, they shelled us there on the road, as I was burying him, and — and —"

Exhausted, he falls back. The watch, hanging above his head, ticks away the moments, listlessly. An oppressive silence weighs upon me. In the dim light, I conjure the terrible scene, — the devastated road, the shimmering veils of dust and heat, the crater, the plunging gun-carriage, the body, the sand, the blood.

I cannot breathe, and rise to go. The lifeless hand slips from my own. On the pale cheeks, the tears are slowly drying, leaving faint, brackish stains.

From the wall I take down the Military Medal, and place it between the relaxed fingers of the waxen hands. His eyes are glazing rapidly. The broken dreams rush headlong through his brain; — the Somme; the far prairies of his native Canada, gloriously golden under their Autumn harvest of wheat; — his mother, patiently waiting; — his brother.

Calmly, serenely, the lamp-light throws a dim radiance about him.

Berta Carveth

from
THE QUEEN'S MILITARY HOSPITAL ALBUM

Sir William Osler (seated center), Berta Carveth (second nurse from right, third row), and members of the Canadian War Contingent Association, Beachborough Park, 1916

Patients at Beachborough Park. Berta Carveth (standing, back row, second from right). c. 1916

Unknown unit at Beachborough Park

Christmas 1916 at Beachborough Park

Cartoon of Berta Carveth drawn by one of the patients in the
Queen's Military Hospital, Beachborough Park, 1918

Cartoon drawn by one of the patients, Beachborough Park, 1918

Hartley Munro Thomas

THE SONG OF THE CONTACT PATROL

There is war in the air! We go
Where bullets are swift and low,
(But we have bullets and bombs as well)
Into the path of the storm and shell.
Bullet for bullet, and bomb for bomb,
From Nieuport Bains to beyond the Somme,
We hurl from our dizzy machines—
That is what warfare means
    For them who make war in the air.

There is war in the air! We fly,
And sooner or later, die;
For we are trustful of flimsy wings,
Trustful of engine and "prop" that sings—
Bullet for bullet, and bomb for bomb,
From Nieuport Bains to beyond the Somme.
And, Oh! that the people be true,
Who make us our planes anew,
    Yea, they must be true to the air.

There is war in the air! We go
Though clouds and the rain are low.
For we have duty beyond the guns,
Bringing the curse of the air on the Huns—
Bullet for bullet, and bomb for bomb,
From Nieuport Bains to beyond the Somme.
And, Oh! that the people be wise
Who plan for the war in the skies,
    For we must wage war in the air.

John Barnard Brophy

DIARY OF AN AIRMAN

Monday, May 29, 1916

In the morning I went up to test a new engine, which ran all right. Aero engines are always run full out for a few seconds before going up, to see that they are giving their power, but they can't really be tested until actually flying and climbing in the air. I did some *camera obscura* work about noon, and registered some good shots at it. In the evening I started for the lines to do a patrol, with Knight as observer. Another of our pilots, Smith, who had since gone home with nerves, was also doing it in a Martinsyde...

Thursday, June 8, 1916

Started out at 5:35 [a.m.] to do a reconnaissance of several towns, including Bapaume...

The others, after turning behind Bapaume, stood away south-west at high speed. There was a regular hail of archies between me and them after I turned, so I couldn't follow but had to push off northwest towards Arras, along a much longer course. I got archied all the way until I crossed our lines, which latter thing was more or less of a relief because the zing of shrapnel on all sides is not calculated to instill joy in the heart of the average human.

Monday, June 26, 1916

We set out at 12 [noon] to do a three-hour test. I flew towards the coast and attempted to climb through the clouds. I got into very thick ones, after passing over Crécy Forest, and didn't see sky or ground for fifteen minutes. I didn't know whether I was upside down or flying in circles, so when I got to 9,000 and no sign of a let up, I came down a few thousand... I passed over Aire and went south...

The oil gave out before we got to Hesdin, and espying a huge chateau, I descended. We approached the chateau. We found two Tommies in charge... We immediately entered and phoned the aerodrome for oil and petrol, and settled down to wait for them... The chateau was a huge, beautiful, old thing with a long, broad driveway leading up to it. It belonged to the Allied Press people, and the sitting room was supplied with innumerable papers and books in all languages, so we read a good many copies of *Punch* and had tea. The tender arrived after three hours...

We got off in a rain storm, just skimming over a team of horses and terrifying them. The rain got worse but we managed to find the aerodrome. By then it was blowing a gale, and we could hardly see twenty feet. We came over the aerodrome at a hundred feet, and turned and came upwind. I had no goggles and was hardly able to see with the rain in my eyes. I never saw a machine get thrown about so much. We landed, missing all the holes in the aerodrome by pure luck, and to the great relief of the *garçons* who were assembled in the shed to watch us. We got home at 7:30, good and wet, and had a good dinner.

Saturday, July 1, 1916
Went to Lille again this morning, and bombed the station again. The big push started today, and we gained a couple of thousand yards between the Somme and Sommecourt.

In the afternoon I went on a bomb raid to Bapaume. We crossed our lines at Albert and went up to Bapaume, about twelve miles. We got archied as soon as we got to Bapaume. We dropped our bombs, trying for the railway and some stores. Then we lit out to Arras, being heavily shelled. I dodged all over the place, and managed to avoid any direct clouts, although they managed to sift a few odds and ends of shells through my machine. I found one shrapnel bullet stuck in the wood. They were going off on all sides, and above and underneath, near Arras, and I was quite pleased to cross our lines and get out of reach. They must have put up one hundred shells at me in fifteen minutes.

I followed the road to Doullens and landed OK and got the souvenir bullet.

Sunday, July 2, 1916

We didn't take part in any military activity but our troops advanced, and are fighting for Contalmaison. In the afternoon we had another bomb raid to Bapaume. Six of us went to bomb three targets. Mine was a chateau. We crossed the lines near Albert, at 8,000 feet, and got nearly to Bapaume before the archies got our range, and then they opened out on us rather warmly. I sighted on the chateau and let go. I hit right beside the chateau, which is a Hun headquarters, but I couldn't see what damage was done. It was probably a good deal, as these bombs each weigh 336 lbs and have iron bars in them, that are alleged to go through forty feet of masonry. I came back over Sommecourt, and found the archies less abusive than at Arras. In the evening, fires were reported at Bapaume.

Saturday, July 8, 1916

The General [Trenchard] appeared on the scene today, and said that Sir Douglas Haig wanted him to congratulate us on our work in the big push, and that the Flying Corps was a big factor in the success, as the Huns never came over our lines and our troops are free to move without being watched. The Huns have had their trains and supplies blown up, and our machines watch their movement. The RFC bombed eleven Hun observation balloons, and now the Huns don't put them up, and can't observe what their artillery is doing. Our machines range battery after battery on to Hun targets. One ammunition train was bombed, and the cars blew up one after another.

Sunday, July 9, 1916

Got up at 3:30 and went out on a bomb-raid. Hewson and I were flying last...

We turned south just beside Cambrai, and found our mark, Marcoing [railway] station. I let my bomb go and had to turn off quickly to dodge a bomb from another youth who was above me. I saw his bomb go down. Several lit on the tracks in the station yards, and probably ruined them. As soon as our bombs were dropped we turned and lit out for home, devil take the hindmost. He did. As poor old Hewson was picked off by a bunch of Huns, who attacked us from behind, and fired at us and went away. We haven't heard what happened to him, and hope he landed safely.

We flew over Crécy Forest, and went to the coast, and could just see England in the distance.

We went for a walk in the village in the evening.

Tuesday, July 11,1916

The chief kicks about our bomb-raids have been the poor formation, leaving us in danger of being separated, and "done in" by Huns. The Colonel decided he'd lead us to show us how. He was to lead and Capt. Carr and I were next, and four others in pairs behind, and nine scouts [from 60 Squadron]...

I got into place and Colonel went over to the lines, and kept circling to get higher for half an hour, right over the lines.

I thought this was a foolish stunt, as I know the Huns could see us, and would be waiting for us. I was very surprised that they didn't shell us, but there was a battle on, and they were probably too busy. We were right over Albert, as I recognized two huge mine craters that had been shelled July 1st.

When we did cross over with only two scouts, we hadn't been over more than a couple of minutes, before I saw three Fokkers coming towards us, and a couple of LVG's climbing up to us. Another Fokker was up above me, and behind, between our two scouts. I know he was going to dive at one of us, but expected the scouts to see him and attack him, so I didn't bother about him, but began to get the stop-watch time of my bomb sight to set it for dropping.

While I was doing this I suddenly heard the pop-pop-pop's of machine guns, and knew the Huns had arrived. I looked and saw them diving in amongst us, and firing. There were seven LVG's and three Fokkers as far as I could make out, but they went so fast I could hardly watch them. Our scouts went for them, and I saw the Colonel turn about.

My gun being behind me I couldn't get in a shot, and turned around after Carr and the Colonel. They fired some more as we went back but didn't hit me. The Colonel was hit and so the show was over. He had about a dozen bullets in his machine, and was hit in the hand. His gun was shot through, and his observer hit in the face. He probably won't try to lead us again.

Friday July 21, 1916

Was blasted out of my downy bed at 5 a.m. muttering imprecations. Devoured a couple of contraband eggs, that had come out with the First Contingent [CEF, in 1915], smacked lips, and seized the control handles of my old bus. Ascended into the blue vault of heaven, followed by six other *garçons* in similar buses, formed up at a given hour, fired a series of signals, and set out for Epehy station in Hunland, with the avowed intention of blowing the whole neighborhood of said station off the map of Europe...

Cooper was flying just ahead of me. The Huns dived past us, firing as they went. Cooper turned sharply and dived under me, and went down. His machine broke to pieces at about 4,000 feet. Oliver — Jones was his observer. Our escort dived at the Huns and let them have it. A Hun in front of me, turned up on his nose, and went down in a dive.

I was first to reach Le Trasloy, and registered two hits in the village. Going back we also got archied, but our scouts had beaten off the Huns. I've been on six consecutive bomb-raids, as we are short of pilots. We went for a walk in the evening, and retired early.

Sunday, July 23, 1916

Kenney went back home today, making the fifth to go with nerves since I came out. I am guard pilot tonight, and have to sleep in the Orderly Room.

Wednesday, July 26, 1916

Duggan came back today after two months in hospital. We also got news that we are to move in a day or two, back presumably near St. Omer, for a month's rest. It certainly is due to us, too, before the whole squadron develops nerves. The sixth pilot went back to England today, as the result of the nervous strain.

The Huns are getting too good with their archies. They now have a fire shell which explodes and sends up dozens of long shoots of liquid fire of some sort, which covers a great area, and one of which would cook us in a second if it touched the machines. Personally I have a peculiar antipathy to being cooked. They are the most fearsome things I've ever seen. I don't object to ordinary shrapnel whistling through my bus, but I draw the line at liquid fire.

Saturday, July 29, 1916

We flew straight to Cape Gris Nez. It was misty and cloudy over the Channel, so we couldn't see the water, and we couldn't see England at all. We steered a compass course north-west, and the wind blew us further west. I didn't see water once, crossing. When we got to England it was a bit clearer as the mist was over the Channel...

We reported and handed in the machines, and got a taxi and drove into London. It took us about an hour and a half. We went to the Cecil and it was crowded, so Watkins and I got a room at the Savoy. We had dinner at the Piccadilly Hotel, and everything seemed so funny, especially to hear the orchestra.

Frank Prewett

THE SOLDIER

My years I counted twenty-one
Mostly at tail of plough:
The furrow that I drove is done,
To sleep in furrow now.

I leapt from living to the dead
A bullet was my bane.
It split this nutshell rind of head,
This kernel of a brain.

A lad to life has paid his debts
Who bests and kills his foe,
And man upon his sweetheart gets,
To reap as well as sow.

But I shall take no son by hand,
No greybeard bravo be:
My ghost is tethered in the sand
Afar from my degree.

Frederick George Scott

MY SEARCH IS REWARDED
from THE GREAT WAR AS I SAW IT

We had now reached the middle of November, and the 4th Division was expected to come north very soon. My only chance of finding my son's body lay in my making a journey to Albert before his battalion moved away. I woke up one morning and determined that I would start that day. I told Ross to get my trench clothes and long boots ready, for I was going to Albert. At luncheon my friends asked me how I proposed to travel, for Albert was nearly fifty miles away. I told them that the Lord would provide, and sallied off down the road with my knapsack, thoroughly confident that I should be able to achieve my purpose. An ambulance picked me up and took me to the Four Winds crossroads, and then a lorry carried me to Aubigny. I went to the field canteen to get some cigarettes, and while there I met a Canadian Engineer officer whom I knew. We talked about many things, and as we were leaving I told him that I was going forth in faith as I hoped to get to Albert that evening. I said, "You know my motto is 'The Lord will provide.'" As we walked along we came to a turn in the road, where we saw at a little distance a sidecar with a driver all ready. I said to my friend, "It is just the thing I want. I think I will go to the owner of that car and say to him that the Lord has provided it for me." He burst out laughing and said, "I am the owner of that car, and you may have it." I thanked him and started off. It was a long ride, and at the end a very wet and muddy one, but I got to Tara Hill that evening and had dinner at General Thacker's Headquarters. I told the officers there of the purpose of my visit, that I was going to the front line the next morning, and asked if they would telephone to one of the batteries and tell the O.C. that I should arrive some time in the middle of the night. The Brigade Major of course tried to dissuade me, but I told him that I was going in any case, that he was not responsible for my actions, but that if he liked to make things easier for me he could. He quite understood the point, and telephoned to the 11th Battery. I then went back to the reserve headquarters of the 4th Division in the town, and prepared myself for the journey. When I had to make an early start in the morning, I always shaved the night before, because I thought that, of all the officers, the chaplain should look the freshest and cleanest. I was in the middle of the process of shaving, and some staff officers were making chocolate for our supper, when a German plane came over and dropped a huge bomb in the garden. It was about one a.m., and we could not help laughing at the surprise the Germans would have felt if they could have seen our occupation going on quite undisturbed by their attempt to murder us.

About half-past one, I started up the street which led to the Bapaume road. The moon was shining, and I could see every object distinctly. Near our old Headquarters I got a lift in a lorry, which took me almost to Pozières. There I got out and proceeded on my way alone. I entered the Y.M.C.A. hut and had a good strong cup of coffee, and started off afresh. That lonely region in the moonlight with the ruined village to one side and the fields stretching far away on either hand gave me an eerie feeling. I came upon four dead horses which had been killed that evening. To add to the strangeness of the situation, there was a strong scent of tear-gas in the air, which made my eyes water. Not a living soul could I see in the long white road.

Suddenly I heard behind me the sound of a troop of horses. I turned and saw coming towards me one of the strangest sights I have ever seen, and one which fitted in well with the ghostly character of the surroundings. It was a troop of mounted men carrying ammunition. They wore their gas masks, and as they came nearer, and I could see them more distinctly in the moonlight, the long masks with their two big glass eye-pieces gave the men a horse-like appearance. They looked like horses upon horses, and did not seem to be like human beings at all. I was quite glad when they had passed. I walked on till I came to what was known as Centre Way. It was a path, sometimes with bathmats on it, which led across the fields down to the battery positions in the valley. Huge shell holes, half filled with water, pitted the fields in every direction, and on the slippery wood I had great difficulty to keep from sliding into those which were skirted by the path. Far off beyond Courcelette I saw the German flare-lights and the bursting of shells. It was a scene of vast desolation, weird beyond description. I had some difficulty when I got into the trench at the end of Centre Way, in finding the 11th Battery. The ground had been ploughed by shells and the trenches were heavy with soft and clinging mud. At last I met a sentry who told me where the O.C.'s dugout was. It was then about half-past three in the morning, but I went down the steps, and there, having been kindly welcomed, was given a blanket on the floor. I started at 6 a.m. with a young sergeant for Death Valley, where I was to get a runner to take me to Regina Trench. The sergeant was a splendid young fellow from Montreal who had won the D.C.M., and was most highly thought of in the battery. He was afterwards killed on Vimy Ridge, where I buried him in the cemetery near Thélus. I had been warned that we were going to make a bombardment of the enemy's lines that morning, and that I ought to be out of the way before that began. I left the sergeant near Courcelette and made my way over to the Brigade Headquarters, which were in a dugout in Death Valley. There with the permission of his O.C., a runner volunteered to come with me. He brought a spade, and we started down the trench to the front line. When I got into Regina Trench, I found that it was impossible to pass along it, as one sank down so deeply into the heavy mud. I had brought a little sketch with me of the trenches, which showed the shell hole where it was supposed that the body had been buried. The previous night a cross had been placed there by a corporal of the battalion before it left the front line. No one I spoke to, however, could tell me the exact map location of the place where it stood. I looked over the trenches, and on all sides spread a waste of brown mud, made more desolate by the

morning mist which clung over everything. I was determined, how-
ever, not to be baffled in my search, and told the runner who was
with me that, if I stayed there six months, I was not going to leave till
I had found that grave. We walked back along the communication
trench and turned into one on the right, peering over the top every
now and then to see if we could recognize anything corresponding
to the marks on our map. Suddenly the runner, who was looking
over the top, pointed far away to a lonely white cross that stood at
a point where the ground sloped down through the mist towards
Regina Trench. At once we climbed out of the trench and made our
way over the slippery ground and past the deep shell holes to where
the white cross stood out in the solitude. We passed many bodies
which were still unburied, and here and there were bits of accou-
trement which had been lost during the advance. When we came
up to the cross I read my son's name upon it, and knew that I had
reached the object I had in view. As the corporal who had placed the
cross there had not been quite sure that it was actually on the place
of burial, I got the runner to dig the ground in front of it. He did so,
but we discovered nothing but a large piece of shell. Then I got him
to try in another place, and still we could find nothing. I tried once
again, and after he had dug a little while he came upon something
white. It was my son's left hand, with his signet ring upon it. They
had removed his identification disc, revolver and pocket-book, so
the signet ring was the only thing which could have led to his iden-
tification. It was really quite miraculous that we should have made
the discovery. The mist was lifting now, and the sun to the East was
beginning to light up the ground. We heard the crack of bullets, for the
Germans were sniping us. I made the runner go down into a shell
hole, while I read the burial service, and then took off the ring. I
looked over the ground where the charge had been made. There lay
Regina Trench, and far beyond it, standing out against the morning
light, I saw the villages of Pys and Miraumont which were our objec-
tive. It was a strange scene of desolation, for the November rains had
made the battle fields a dreary, sodden waste. How many of our

brave men had laid down their lives as the purchase price of that con-secrated soil! Through the centuries to come it must always remain sacred to the hearts of Canadians. We made a small mound where the body lay, and then by quick dashes from shell hole to shell hole we got back at last to the communication trench, and I was indeed thankful to feel that my mission had been successful. I have received letters since I returned to Canada from the kind young fellow, who accompanied me on the journey, and I shall never cease to be grate-ful to him. I left him at his headquarters in Death Valley, and made my way past Courcelette towards the road. As the trench was very muddy, I got out of it, and was walking along the top when I came across something red on the ground. It was a piece of a man's lung with the windpipe attached. I suppose some poor lad had had a direct hit from a shell and his body had been blown to pieces. The Germans were shelling the road, so with some men I met we made a detour through the fields and joined it further on, and finally got to the chalk-pit where the 87th Battalion was waiting to go in again to the final attack. I was delighted to see my friends once more, and they were thankful that I had been able to find the grave. Not many days afterwards, some of those whom I then met were called themselves to make the supreme sacrifice. I spent that night at the Rear Head-quarters of the 4th Division, and they kindly sent me back the next day to Camblain l'Abbe in one of their cars.

On November 24th I received a telegram saying that a working party of one of the battalions of the 4th Division had brought my son's body back, and so on the following day I motored once again to Albert and laid my dear boy to rest in the little cemetery on Tara Hill, which he and I had seen when he was encamped near it, and in which now were the bodies of some of his friends whom I had met on my last visit. I was thankful to have been able to have him buried in a place which is known and can be visited, but I would say to the many parents whose sons lie now in unknown graves, that, after all, the grave seems to be a small and minor thing in view of the glorious victory and triumphant life which is all that really matters. If I had not been successful in my quest, I should not have vexed my soul with anxious thought as to what had become of that which is merely the earthly house of the immortal spirit which goes forth into the eternal. Let those whose dear ones lie in the unrecorded graves remember that the strong, glad spirits — like Valiant for Truth in *Pilgrim's Progress* — have passed through the turbulent waters of the river of death, and "all the trumpets have sounded for them on the other side."

In June of the following year, when the Germans had retired after our victory at Vimy Ridge, I paid one more visit to Regina Trench. The early summer had clothed the wasteland in fresh and living green. Larks were singing gaily in the sunny sky. No sound of shell or gun disturbed the whisper of the breeze as it passed over the sweet-smelling fields. Even the trenches were filling up and Mother Nature was trying to hide the cruel wounds which the war had made upon her loving breast. One could hardly recall the visions of gloom and darkness which had once shrouded that scene of battle. In the healing process of time all mortal agonies, thank God, will be finally obliterated.

Stanley A. Rutledge

LIKE A THIEF IN THE NIGHT

Quite the most tragic thing one can observe is to watch the subtle inroads made by fear into the heart of a brave man. And yet it is common out here. I know of many chaps who were as iron in the beginning and who have "lost their nerve." The quoted phrase is common in soldier parlance. The breaking-down process — how damnable it is.

In our last tour I had occasion to be up in a zone which was being heavily shelled. It seemed as if the German gunners had poured out all their wrath upon this spot. The coal boxes whined and crumpled, tearing up every inch of ground. Whizz-bangs — those small shells which carry death's message with incredible swiftness — were breaching our parapets. Now, he, concerning whom I write, was one of our most intrepid bombers. At Hooge, at St. Eloi, at Kemmel, he was wonderful. The lust of blood seemed to course in his veins. After all, those are the chaps who kill the Germans — men who see the Hun as a mad beast — men who have no sentiment (unless the foe is wounded) — men who regard the German as directly responsible for every physical discomfort which came with the war — men who go about from day to day uttering fierce imprecations, and Kelly was in that class.

A small bombing attack was to be pulled off. The Germans had a detached post from which position much damage could be done to our line. It was thought best to send over a select party of bombers and snipers and endeavour to clear the strong point. The officer asked for volunteers, hoping to get the very men he might have selected. Kelly knew of the move, and was dreading to be asked if "he wanted to go over." I met him squatting in a "funk" hole, seeking protection from shrapnel. He told me the story.

"It's got me," he said. "After twelve months of this hell it's got me and got me right.

"Some of the chaps will laugh; Kelly the bomber has lost his nerve. He is done for, they will say, and it will be the truth.

"I think it was that shell at Courcelette that snapped my nerve. You know that afternoon when the gang were in the deep Dugout, and a shell came over and blew in the mouth of the Dugout? Well, since then I have never felt the same. Every shell seems to me to have my name and number on it. The old spirit has gone out."

Then, dropping his voice: "I hope they don't ask me if I want to go over."

Beckles Willson

A VISIT TO FRANCE'S "COLONIALS"

To turn a corner of a quiet country road and find a troop of Moorish cavalry, fully armed and garnished, bearing down upon you is a memorable experience. A little farther away, where the civil population has not been evacuated, a regiment of red-fezzed Senegambians, blacker than any negroes I ever set eyes on in the New World, is quartered, a source of perennial joy to the little French children, who have long ceased to feel any awe for them and regard them only as rare and delectable folks whom the extraordinary and mysterious power called war has cast amongst them for their entertainment. With the children in these favoured villages life is a perpetual circus.

Nearer the front the exotic and picturesque natives have it all to themselves. In one neglected villa garden with its rank growth of phlox and balsam, poppies and hollyhocks, and the grass a foot high on the once trim lawn, sprawled in groups, silent or animated, a platoon of swarthy and turbaned Moors. I was the first Canadian they had ever seen, and they could only dimly grasp the extent of the mighty waste of waters which separated me from home or of the land itself of which the maple leaf was the national emblem. But, after all, was it much less wonderful that they should be there than I — in the scourged and perilled land of the Franks, for whom forty races and five hundred tribes were fighting?

A little farther on the road to Compiègne I came to the village of C___ , where an entire Moroccan regiment was quartered, overflowing the cottages, barns, shops and stables into the cobbled streets, and lounging in picturesque attitudes on a little stone bridge over the river. It was a perfect riot of colour everywhere, in which crimson and yellows were noisiest, but the dazzling white of burnous and turban still the most salient. I went to the regiment's headquarters, where the colonel of this amazing regiment received me with much grace and cordiality. He is a handsome Frenchman — still youthful, who looks as if he might have stepped out of the pages of *Ouida* — so romantic and gallant was his bearing. His name was De Tinan — it might have been D'Artagnan. He limped slightly — the result of a thrilling adventure in the Algerian deserts: and his men followed his coming and going with such passionate devotion writ on their dusky faces that one could understand the command he has over them. Yet they are proud and haughty enough in their bearing, these stalwart Moors, Arabs, and Bedouins, with their burnished rifles, pistols, and scimitars slung about their bodies and their robes and *chechias* waving in the breeze.

"They are famous fighters," said the colonel. "Come with me and I will show you them at play."

We entered a garden and approached a low stone building, the upper part of which had been demolished. In the cellar of this structure, lit in Oriental fashion from above, some two hundred warriors of every tribe had assembled. They were packed as closely as our men pack a canteen, all seated on the ground from which a dense cloud of smoke from cigarette, hookah, and chibouque ascended through the great gash in the cellar roof. A pathway was somehow made for us to the farther end, and as we passed thither it was seen that a Moorish *danse à ventre* was in progress. Two male dancers endeavoured to stimulate the not altogether pleasant sinuosities of the desert *danseuse*, to the accompaniment of a cacophanous drum and the weirdest pipes I have ever heard. Moreover, at intervals they emitted a strange chant with a monotonous refrain, in which the assembled occasionally joined with relish. The dance lasted so long that I thought the performers gyrating, leaping, bending, twisting their hips, rolling their eyes and showing their dazzling teeth, would have dropped in sheer fatigue, and I was glad when coffee — oh such coffee! — in tiny brass cups — was passed around and furnished on occasion for whispered chat. Then other dancers appeared, and finally a very black demon of a fellow emerged from the background of crouching humanity and the Colonial murmured to me:

"He is our chief vocalist and *lion comique*. He is going to give us a patriotic song in French."

In a moment my gaze was riveted on this warrior's face. He had flaming, protruding eyeballs, and the thick, terrifying lips of a fairy-tale ogre, and in guttural, blood-curdling tones this is the jolly little *chanson* he sang — at least I give its purport as far as I could gather it:

"O come, all ye Bedouins and Moors and Algerians and Tunisians, come to the glorious blood feast. Come, O men of France, Russia, England, Italy, and lay hands upon the accursed Emperor William and squeeze him by the throat and cut off his head and dabble in his red, red blood!"

At this trait of humour the whole assembly roared with laughter, and all of us clapping our hands loudly, made him repeat his effort not once, but thrice.

And as I cast a glance around that sea of faces, as strange and magical a scene as ever pictured by Fortuny, I could not help wishing that that restless figure in Potsdam could himself be a witness of this miracle he had evoked — the spectacle of the outraged barbarian coming from the silence of the African desert to the relief of Western civilization in its peril.

H. Smalley Sarson

LOVE SONG

Twilight, the shadows darken on the leas,
The noises of the day are hushed at rest;
Even the wind, soft rising in the west
Falters and dies beneath the whispering trees.
No jarring human voices cry or speak,
Twilight, ah, Sweetheart, may I kiss your cheek.

Night, a pale moon rises through the haze,
A nightingale trills in a thicket near
As suddenly night's voices sharp and clear
Echo and re-echo through the maze;
For twilight's hold of silence falters, slips;
Night. Oh beloved Mine, give me your lips.

Bailleul.

FIGMENTS FROM FLANDERS

McGINNIS— Say, you two boobs. What did you think you were goin' to get when you saw us coming down on you?

PRISONERS (*in chorus, cheerfully*) — Cigarettes.

Frank P. Dixon

CIGARETTES

When the cold is making ice cream
    Of the marrow in your bones;
When you're shaking like a jelly
    And your feet are dead as stones;
When your clothes and boots and blankets
    And your rifle and your kit
Are soaked from hell to breakfast;
    And the Dugout where you sit
Is leaking like a basket, and
    Upon the muddy floor
The water lies in filthy pools,
    Six inches deep or more;
Tho' life seems cold and mis'rable
    And all the world is wet,
You'll always get through somehow
    If you've got a cigarette.

When you're lying in a listening-post,
    Way out beyond the wire,
While a blasted Hun, behind a gun
    Is doing rapid fire;
When the bullets whine above your head
    And splutter on the ground;
When your eyes are strained for every move
    And your ears for every sound;
You'd bet your life a Hun Patrol
    Is prowling somewhere near;
A shiver runs along your spine
    That's very much like fear—

You'll stick it to the finish, but
    I'll make you a little bet:
You'd feel a whole lot better if
    You had a cigarette.

When Fritz is starting something,
    And his guns are on the bust;
When the parapet goes up in chunks
    And settles down in dust,
When the roly-poly "rum-jar" comes
    A wabbling thro' the air
Till it lands upon the dugout
    And the dugout isn't there;
When the air is full of dust and smoke
    And scraps of steel and noise,
And you think you're booked for golden
    Crowns and other heavenly joys;
When your nerves are all a-tremble
    And your brain is all a-fret,
It isn't half so hopeless
    If you've got a cigarette.

When you're waiting for the whistle,
    And your foot is on the step,
You bluff yourself it's lots of fun,
    And all the time you're hept
To the fact that you may stop one
    'Fore you've gone a dozen feet,
And you wonder what it feels like
    And your thoughts are far from sweet;
Then you think about a little grave
    With R.I.P. on top,
And you know you've got to go across
    Although you'd like to stop;

When your backbone's limp as water,
    And you're bathed in icy sweat.
Why, you'll feel a lot more cheerful
    If you puff your cigarette.

Then when you stop a good one,
    And the stretcher bearers come
And patch you up with strings and
    Splints, and bandages and gum,
When you think you've got a million wounds
    And fifty thousand breaks,
And your body's just a blasted sock
    Packed full of pains and aches;
Then you feel you've reached the finish,
    And you're sure your number's up
And you feel as weak as Belgian beer
    And helpless as a pup;
But you know that you're not down
    And out; that life's worth living yet
When some old war-wise Red Cross
    Guy, slips you a cigarette.

We can do without Maconachies,
    And bully and hard tack,
When Fritz's curtain fire keeps
    The ration parties back;
We can do without our great coats,
    And our socks and shirts and shoes;
We might almost—though I doubt it—
    Get along without our booze;
We can do without "K.R.S.O." and
    Military law;
We can beat the ancient Israelites
    At making bricks and straw;

We can do without a lot of things,
    And still win out, you bet.
But I'd hate to think of soldiering
    Without a cigarette.

Stanley A. Rutledge

WILLIE GIERKE

As one comes from the trenches at St. Eloi it is possible, indeed very desirable, that one passes through Scottish Wood. You will remember St. Eloi was the Belgian village which happened to be right on the firing line. And it was here that the huge mines were sprung. Pass-ing through the woods one has to traverse an open space before getting back into a sheltered forest, known mapically as Ridgewood. A very good trail is met with, and, if the powers of observation are keen, on the right will be seen a military cemetery. It is typical of a number of these last resting places of our boys. One may be prompted to step over the barbed wire and look for the name of some old pal. In one corner, not set aside, can be seen a cross bearing these words:

"In Memory of Willie Gierke,
214th German Regiment.
Died June 19, 1916."

Let me tell you something of Willie. He was, no doubt, a student in one of the Berlin universities; twenty-one years of age and a bright chap. This I learn from the intelligence report containing his answers to questions put on the night he died. You see, his stay inside British lines was very short. He had been to the "front" since September of last year. At first his regiment had been placed opposite the French, but two months ago they came up to Ypres. The Germans say the fel-lows out in the front do not come back from Ypres. Willie was not a very good soldier. His heart was not in the bloody business. He would rather read Kant. On a sunny afternoon, when everything was silent as at eventide, Willie could be found sitting on the firestep, reading mother's letter and idly philosophizing.

Then one night the sergeant came up: "Gierke, you are on 'listen-ing post' tonight with Nerlick." Not the dangerous duty that many imagine it to be, but still a crawl into "No Man's Land" is rather risky.

I remember the night well. Our battalion was waiting for a favourable night to "pull off" a raid. It had been dull all day, a scurrying of heavy clouds, and one had a sort of feeling that it would be a dirty night. That favoured our plans. But let me return to Willie. The sergeant came along at "stand to," and told him that the listening posts would go out in one hour's time. Half an hour went by and the British parapet was becoming very indistinct. A little later, if one had been watching, two figures, overcoated, with bombs in their pockets, could be seen getting over the parapet at bay 14, trench 36. They crawled past the cans and rubbish, through the near entanglements and took up their place in a shell hole, about thirty feet from their own wire. Lying flat they listened intently for a few moments, breathing rather heavily. The rifle bullets were cracking overhead. Willie nudged Nerlick and pointed to what he thought looked like a man in the tall grass. Nerlick peered into the dark. There was no movement. Then Gierke rolled over and Nerlick ran. You see the suspicious object was one of our scouts, and the bullet found Willie. Our patrol rushed up and Stevenson threw the wounded lad over his shoulder. The scurry was sufficient to send up flares from the Huns, who did not know but what an attack was on. Machine guns started to spit out viciously. Our patrol lay flat, not a move, sir, not a move. The tall grass gave good protection.

Soon the narrow strip of front quieted down. The flares became intermittent, and our boys made their way home, coming by way of an old trench. Willie was badly wounded. He told us so, and his face told us more. After alleviating the pain — the bullet was in the lung, and breathing difficult — he gave some valuable information. His letters and diary were found, and the officer had a kind smile for the boy. He knew Willie hated war. He knew Willie was a mother's pride. He was just like our own boys now. But the breathing was difficult. We knew. Willie knew that the tide was fast ebbing. He knew the war would soon be over, and in a little while his eyes turned in answer to the last call. Next day we buried him in our cemetery.

A. Audette

NO MAN'S LAND

The rain will help—I'm not so thirsty now;
How cool it falls upon my burning lips!
Thirst is a frightful thing—I realize how
It drives men mad, like scores of scourging whips.

The still cool dark is better than the light!
The sun beats down so fiercely through the day,
It seems to burn away my very sight—
And shrivel me to nothing where I lay.

This "No Man's Land" is strange—a neutral ground,
Where friend and foe together come to sleep,
Indifferent to the shaking hell of sound—
To shell still searching for more grain to reap.

Kincaid died very well! Before he went
He smiled a bit and said he hoped we'd won;
And then he said he saw his home in Kent,
And then lay staring at the staring sun.

That German over there was peaceful, too,
He looked a long, long time across their line,
And then he tried to sing some song he knew
And so passed on without another sign.

Well this won't do for me—I'd best get back,
I'm just a little sleepy, I confess,
But I must be in time, we may attack—
The lads would miss me too at evening mess.

A moment more, and then I'll make a start—
I can't be shirking at a time like this,
I'll just repeat—I know them all by heart—
Some words of hers that ended in a kiss.

Why do I seem to feel her tender hand?
To see her eyes with all their old time light?
Is she beside me? Ah, I understand—
I think perhaps I'll sleep here through the night.

A C.E.F. ALPHABET

A   is the Army which has sailed overseas.

B   stands for Byng, whom we're eager to please.

C   is for Canada, Connaught, and Currie

D   is for Sir Douglas, whom nothing can hurry.

E   is for Empire for which we would die.

F   stands for France, our most valiant ally.

G   is the German — we hope to outlive him,

H   is for Hell we are going to give him.

I   is the Insect we feed in the trench.

J   stands for Joffre, C.-in-C. of the French.

K   is the Kaiser who raises our dander.

L   stands for Lipsett, a gallant commander.

M   is for Mercer, whose loss we all rue.

N   is our Nurse — a trim angel blue.

O   is for Ours — and the O.C. we prize.

P   is the Pats who do NOT advertise.

Q   is the Question "When will this war end?"

R   's the Recruit whom we welcome as friend.

S   stands for Sam, who raised this great host.

T   is for Turner, who scorneth to boast.

U   's the Ultimatum which began the great fight.

V   is for Victory now clearly in sight.

W   is Watson whose front name is Dave.

X   is the cross on our dear comrade's grave.

Y   stands for Ypres, where we battled so long.

Z   Zillebeke is and the end of my song.

1916

Peregrine Acland

from *ALL ELSE IS FOLLY*

It was a day of blue sky and bright warm sunlight. There was a gayety in the weather — gayety such as graced the morning when Alec and Adair last rode together at Bendip. But the sky above these French fields had a deeper clearness than is often found over the grey downs of England. It was more like the skies in western Canada under which Falcon...it seemed so many years ago...had driven his herd of cow ponies...

"Steady!"

He could scarcely hear his voice as he shouted to his men. And they, trudging wearily across the field, their shoulders bowed by the heavy packs on their backs and the heavier fears in their hearts, heard him not at all.

They could hear nothing but the stupendous roaring of artillery as the barrage of bursting shells crept gradually forward...and the swishing overhead of millions of bullets from thousands of machine guns, concentrating indirect fire on the enemy's supports.

Yet it wasn't what he heard that perturbed Falcon. It was what he saw.

The barrage of bursting shells — the upspoutings of black earth — had advanced beyond the German trench. He could see that trench clearly now. Battered but far from demolished, it was crowded with Germans, armed, active, defiant.

Where was his own company? The five platoons which had gone over in the last few minutes? He looked around, ahead of him, to right and to left. He couldn't see anywhere a trace of the men who had preceded him, except here and there, bodies writhing, their cries inaudible beneath the roar of the artillery, and, on the forward slope of the German parapet, other bodies of khaki-kilted Highlanders lying prone on the earth, curiously still.

Falcon found his mind now, as if whipped up by a powerful drug, working in flashes.

For him, with his handful of men, to advance straight on that trench crowded with Germans would be not fighting but self-slaughter, a gesture that would accomplish nothing. Yet he couldn't go back. He would have to go forward.

Even now, the German machine-gunner, traversing, was moving down the men on Falcon's left, was swinging the gun slowly towards Falcon... That machine-gunner must have wiped out nearly the whole company.

Useless to go up directly against that machine gun.

Falcon looked to the right, remembered an old communication trench. The trench from which he had jumped off a minute ago was an old German trench, captured less than a fortnight ago by the British. From that trench, at one time, a communication trench had run into the German front line which Falcon's company had just now so vainly assaulted. That communication trench had long since been blocked in, of course, but Falcon could see a stub of it now, running forward like a sap a few yards out of the German line.

For that stub of trench he ran. He had cast aside all thought of orders to advance at a walk. With him he took a runner. He grabbed the runner by the arm, put his mouth to the runner's ear, shouted at the top of his voice, "Follow me."

He had tried to get the attention of his other men with whistle blasts, with signals, but in vain. In the midst of those eardrum-smashing concussions, they couldn't hear his whistle. And they were so intent on their own immediate danger that they didn't see his waving arm.

Followed by the runner, Falcon dashed to the communication trench through a crackle of bullets. Leaped down into the short stub of trench. Found himself confronting three heavily built Germans.

These, startled by the onslaught of the big, black-browed Canadian who had so suddenly thrown himself into their midst, drew back towards the main trench while they swung their rifles towards him.

Falcon pumped back with his automatic.

The Germans stumbled, fell back, disappeared.

"Can you," Falcon roared into the ear of his runner, "lob a bomb into the main trench?"

The runner had a bomb, but he wasn't a well-trained bomber. He was nervous, fumbled, forgot to pull the pin, lobbed a bomb which was no more dangerous than a baseball.

Falcon meanwhile had with speedy fingers re-loaded. If only he had a rifle in place of this automatic! He looked around. Then instinct made him look up.

So now it was coming. Inescapably.

Sailing through the air towards him, describing a neat arc of a circle, came a German bomb. A "potato masher."

It was well aimed. It would land beside him in that little stub of trench. There would be no way at all of avoiding its explosion.

No time to climb out of the trench. And if there had been, he would have been riddled with rifle bullets in doing it. No, there was no time. He would just have to take what was coming. If only it would be swift and certain death. But to lie there, after it, for minutes that would seem hours, a huddled mass of bleeding eyes, guts, testicles...

During the second that remained before that bomb dropped he would keep on killing. Even as the bomb fell at his feet he banged with his automatic at an incautious, helmeted head that peered around the corner.

By doing that, he lost the one slight chance to pick up the bomb and toss it out of the trench before it exploded... Unless it exploded in his hand at the very moment of tossing.

Nevertheless, he reached for the bomb. But another peering head just then demanded attention.

Another second had gone. The bomb had not exploded.

A dud! Falcon breathed deeply in relief. The enemy, too, must be nervous, must have forgotten to release the catch.

Falcon picked up the bomb casually, tossed it away.

The problem of capturing that main trench remained unaltered. If only he had more men...

"Hello, Alec!"

A great voice roared in his ears. A hand hit him on the shoulder. He looked into the flashing dark eyes, the handsome, strong-jawed face of his fastest friend, Alastair Irvine. Irvine, commanding the company on Falcon's right, had found the advance of his left flank held up, had gone to help, and so had come to Falcon's aid.

With Irvine was a big, black-bearded private — the only private in the whole battalion who had permission to wear a beard.

Alec, forgetting present ranks, shouted joyously: "Colonel Carson!"

Private Carson, as he released the pin of a bomb, shouted back, "Hello, Alec!"

With Carson's strong, sure arm lobbing bombs into the German main trench, Irvine and Falcon were free to go forward. Following Irvine, as he scrambled up on the right side of the communication trench, Falcon found himself suddenly somehow getting across the German trench, over a rubble of earth and sandbags, at a point where that trench had been blown in. Irvine and he were, by now, behind the German front line.

They were both lying flat. Shooting into the crowded German trench. Shooting the Germans in the back.

Falcon, in the process of that scramble, had picked up a rifle. A dead man's. Surer to shoot with than his hard-kicking automatic.

Irvine and Falcon picked out, deliberately, the leaders in the German trenches — those who were evidently, by their activity, the best men. Carefully, swiftly, they shot them down.

It was hard to tell, often, whether you hit or not. The Germans, startled by death that came from the rear, had turned on the two Canadians. Falcon would see a face shoved up over the back of the German trench, a rifle levelled at him. He would shoot. The face would disappear...

Men from Irvine's company and a few of the remainder from Falcon's had followed them. There were soon a dozen Canadians behind the German trench, shooting the Germans in the rear.

Falcon aimed at the grey back of the German machine-gunner. A courageous fellow that must be, to be still sticking to his gun even though he swayed in his seat with the pain of a wound. But the braver he was, the better man he was, the greater the need to kill him.

Falcon wasn't bothering to lie down now. He was in a state of such intense exhilaration — an exhilaration not of delight in killing, but of cold terror that if he did not kill he would be killed — that he had no thought of safety. The only thing that mattered was to see the job through.

He knelt. With left elbow resting on his left knee to steady the rifle, he looked through the sights, took careful aim, pulled the trigger.

"I guess we both got him," a private shouted in his ear.

Falcon looked. The private was right.

In the middle of the machine-gunner's back, right between his shoulder blades, was a big, dark, rapidly growing stain.

But the sight that held Alec, with the peculiar fascination of horror, was the machine-gunner's head.

As the grey-coated body drooped forward, with great convulsive shudders, over the machine gun, the top of the head opened up and vomited a scarlet torrent... Brains... The mind of a man!

"We've got the trench," shouted Irvine. "They're sticking up their hands."

As Irvine jumped down into the German trench, followed by a group of his men, Falcon, looking far down the trench, saw a troop of grey, shovel-hatted figures, a hundred or more of them, clambering out of the back of it, retreating towards the German second line.

They must not escape. If they did, they would have to be fought later. They must be captured now. Or killed. The thing to do was to close in on them with the bayonet, jab a few, make the rest put their hands up, drive the crowd back as prisoners to the Canadian front line.

Falcon turned to the men behind him, shouted at them to charge. But in all that din they could not hear. He ran in front, signalled them, started off to charge the Germans himself in the hope that the men would follow.

But those Canadian backwoodsmen liked rifles better than bayonets. They were kneeling and shooting at the retreating Germans. Falcon, in front of them, came near to being shot himself. A nice thing, that, if an officer attempting to lead a charge got shot in the backside by his own men. Falcon gave up the attempt to rouse his men to a charge, joined them in shooting.

Only a dozen or so of the Germans dropped to earth. The greater part of the hundred escaped in safety and made their way back towards their second line.

Falcon now looked down into the trench nearby, where Irvine had lately leaped. In spite of all the killing that had been done, Falcon saw more Germans in the trench now than he had seen there when the attack started. Unarmed Germans with their hands up were pouring out of dugouts. Excited Canadian soldiers were starting to bayonet them, hands up or not. But Irvine was stopping them...that warm-hearted, cool-headed giant.

A great crowd of Germans for those few Canadians to handle. For even though more of Irvine's company had joined them, there were only a score or so of Canadians to more than a hundred — it seemed like two hundred — Germans. And the Canadians couldn't stay to guard those Germans. They had to advance on the second line.

Irvine and Falcon shouted at the Germans. Pointed back to the Canadian trenches. By a violent waving of arms they indicated that the prisoners must run back to the Canadian lines. That was all that could be done, to chase them back to the Canadian trenches, where the holding battalion could handle them.

Soon all those grey-clad, coal-scuttle-helmeted Germans, lately objects of terror, now of derision, started scurrying back to the Canadian front line. Tall Germans, short Germans, fat Germans, thin Germans. All scurrying, scurrying, with hands held high.

Irvine and Falcon kept their revolvers trained on their prisoners until the whole crowd neared the Canadian line, the foremost dropping over the parapet.

Falcon turned to go on with the advance, on towards the German second line. But just as he was turning, he noted, out of the corner of his eye, an ugly, hard-faced Hun drawing out of the rear of the party of prisoners, falling into a Shell hole, picking up a rifle, looking towards him.

Swinging round with a shout — useful in that hubbub only as a release to pent-up feelings — Falcon aimed his revolver at the Hun and leaped towards him with long strides.

The German dropped the rifle, stood up, shaking. Knees knocking together. Hands again up in the air.

Falcon resisted the temptation to shoot him. A fat, disgusting object. But terror-stricken, pitiable, comic.

Gesticulating violently, Falcon made as if to kick the Hun in the backside. Threatened to boot him, to shoot him, until he saw him run towards the Canadian trench and drop into it.

Falcon, turning to rejoin his men, stumbled over the body of a Canadian private. The upper half of the face was blown away, but below that red mess stuck out a square black beard. And there was only one private in the MacIntyres who was allowed to wear a beard.

Poor old Carson! Without his courageous bombing the success of that whole desperate quarter of an hour of fighting could not have been achieved.

Falcon went on. Only to be sickened by another sight... Alastair Irvine sitting propped up by a private. Jacket and shirt open. A red hole in the middle of his broad white chest.

Falcon ran towards him.

Irvine held out his hand.

"They got me, Alec. Shrapnel."

Irvine's face was pale, but not the greyish-green that hints fast-coming death.

"You'll pull through, old man," reassured Falcon as he pressed Irvine's hand.

"Look after my company," Irvine begged him. "The subalterns are only kids. Good kids, but green."

Falcon gave his word, wished good luck, went hurriedly on.

How long before his own turn would come? But there was no use thinking about that.

There were not many Canadians left in that section of the advance. In place of six waves, one. And that, very thinly manned. Falcon would have to reorganize the line as they advanced.

But before he could go another yard forward there was one thing he *had* to do. Or burst. The agonies of Gulliver before he put out the flames in the royal castle at Lilliput were nothing to the agonies that Falcon felt now. After the nervous strain of the past quarter of an hour, his whole system shouted for relief.

So he stood there with the green-faced dead around him, with the sweet, evil scent of explosives in his nostrils, with shrapnel ping-pinging overhead — for the Germans, knowing that the Canadians had taken their trenches, were now shelling vigorously their own former front — and amidst all that ruin and all that danger, he poured out a steady stream. Satisfying...immensely...so to christen newly captured soil.

Then on he went. Ran about among the men. Broke up groups. Scattered them out into a wave, three yards between man and man. Kept them advancing.

So they went forward three hundred, four hundred yards. Always in front of them the advancing British barrage, that great cloud of greyish-green smoke which hid them from their enemies, and which kept them, too, from knowing what lay immediately ahead.

Looking to the left, Falcon saw that the line there was not advancing. The men were dropping into Shell holes.

With loping strides he crossed over. Bullets crackled around. He and his men must be very close here to the next line of German trenches.

But the men must keep advancing. If they didn't persistently press forward, they would lose all the protection of that barrage. Then, stranded here in the open, they would be easy prey for the Germans.

He must rouse them out of their Shell holes.

Not so easy, when neither his voice nor his whistle was audible. Nor did the pantomime of signals suffice to arrest their attention. He could, then, only run from Shell hole to Shell hole, digging out the men in each, urging them forward...

He dropped into the first shell hole, found a Lewis-gunner and a private there together.

"Whazzamatter?" Falcon roared in the Lewis-gunner's ear. "Why don't you go forward?"

The Lewis-gunner only half heard him. Laughing hysterically, he shook his fists towards the German trenches.

"The bastards!" the gunner shouted. "They shot the cigarette out of my mouth. And it was the last cigarette I had!"

"We must go forward," Falcon bellowed again into the ear of the Lewis-gunner. "I'm going on to rouse these other fellows to the left. Keep your eye on me. When I go forward, that's the signal to advance."

The Lewis-gunner nodded.

Falcon jumped up — started with long strides towards the next group that he could see in a shell hole, a dozen yards away.

He had taken one stride, he had taken two, when he became aware that the barrage had lifted, that he was facing, almost running head-on into, the second line German trench. It certainly wasn't a hundred yards away, not much over fifty. He saw, beneath coal-scuttle helmets, stubble beards on dirty, drawn faces...

He hadn't time to do anything. He could only, in a flash, see all: four Germans aiming their rifles at him. He could see their eyes. Two of the four wore steel-rimmed spectacles. One looked a little like an old cobbler who had done jobs for him at home...

A good target he, Falcon, must make for them. Six feet two in his boots. And so evidently an officer, trying to direct, to lead the attack.

Three steps, four. Would he make the next shell hole — any shell hole — with the bullets cracking through the air beside his ears?

Five steps. What rotten shots! But they, too, must be nervous.
Six steps.

"*Ah-h-h!*"

In the chest. On the left side. Like a steel spike driven in by a sledgehammer.

So this was it, at last.

Carried along by his rush, he reeled into the nearest shell hole. Fell there, on his back, gasping... Bullets still crackled very close to his ears. The Germans, then, didn't know whether or not they had hit him...were determined to make a sure job.

On his back, in the shell hole, a copy of the London *Times* seemed to spread open before his eyes. The page headed "Roll of Honour." In the middle of the column headed "F" he saw his name.

"Falcon, Major Alexander, D.S.O, Can. Inf. Battn. Killed in action."

So that was what it would look like, tomorrow or the day after. That little line of type.

The illusion vanished. Everything was growing confused.

This immense pain in taking breath. This feeling of being smashed in, as if the whole side had been caved in. This bitter gasping for breath. This twisting of the throat. This gasping for breath... breath.

A stretcher-bearer suddenly was stooping over him. The stretcher-bearer tore open Falcon's jacket, cut open his shirt, looked at a huge hole near the heart. Had that been an expanding bullet?

Or had it, perhaps, struck something in the pocket, turned, gone down so?

The stretcher-bearer bandaged the wound as well as he could. Gave Falcon a quarter-grain tablet of morphia.

"Water," gasped Falcon. His throat was so dry with this battle for breath.

The stretcher-bearer undid the water-bottle hanging from Falcon's belt. Put it to the wounded man's lips. Then, the thirst for the moment quenched, he put it in Falcon's hand.

He looked at Falcon, looked at the greenish-greyness of his face. "Have you any messages to send home?" he asked.

Falcon shook his head.

"I've...sent them," he with difficulty whispered.

He had attended to all that. He was too seasoned a soldier not to think of all that. Rough business this for his mother and his father. And Adair... *"The strain is beginning to tell,"* she had written. This wouldn't be good news for her. Now, when she was ill. Afterwards, perhaps, it might ease the strain...

Why hadn't he got a bullet right through the middle of his forehead — as he had dreamed so vividly?... Months ago he had dreamed that, back in the days when he used to go reconnoitering in No Man's Land at night. Up near Wytschaete-Messines road. One morning, sleeping in a dugout that reeked with the stomach-turning smell of dead men, he had dreamed that a German patrol had got behind him on a reconnaissance, that he had had to fight his way through, only, in the end, to receive a bullet right between the eyes. Through many months that dream had stayed in the background of his consciousness, had seemed sure presentiment...

"I'm afraid that's all I can do for you, sir." The stretcher-bearer looked at him regretfully.

"More morphia." murmured Falcon. If he was dying, why not lessen the intolerable agony of this struggle for breath?

The stretcher-bearer shook his head.

"It's against orders, sir, to give more than one tablet. We might think a man was through, yet he might, after all, have a chance. Besides, I haven't many tablets. And there are a lot of wounded."

"I have some," whispered Falcon. "Right-hand breast pocket."

A private had joined them in the shell hole, was bending over Falcon. Heard his words, opened the pocket, took out the little glass bottle with the morphia tablets.

The private looked at the stretcher-bearer. "Shall I...?"

The stretcher-bearer hesitated. "Well, in this case... I suppose you might as well."

Falcon took a tablet. Washed it down with a swallow of water poured in by the hand of the private. Another tablet. Another swallow. Another tablet...

He took five times the dose that regulations allowed. The strain of the breathing eased a little.

He was taking a sixth tablet when he realized that the pain was now, at least, endurable.

He spat out the tablet, grinned feebly at the private and the stretcher-bearer. "If there's any chance at all, I'll fight for it."

"Good!" The stretcher-bearer rose. "I'm sorry, sir, but I must go. There are others..."

Falcon himself, before the attack, had stressed the order to the stretcher-bearers in his company not to waste time on the severely wounded, but to give chief attention to the slightly wounded who could go on fighting... Before everything, the success of the attack.

"Take these tablets with you," he whispered to the stretcher-bearer.

The private, too, had to go. Before going, he propped Falcon up as well as he could. He put the waterbottle in Falcon's left hand, and the automatic, as Falcon requested, loaded, in his right... "For emergencies."

The private went to rejoin the advancing line. Falcon found it an agony to loosen his grip of that rough hand. He could understand Nelson's "Kiss me, Hardy." It wasn't just Hardy that the stricken Nelson had wished to embrace before he faded out into nothingness. It was the whole warm spirit of humanity.

Now — to die or not to die — Falcon lay alone, on his back, staring at the blue sky and the bright white clouds. The bullets no longer crackled close to his ears as when he had first fallen, but shells continued to swish overhead, to rock with their concussions the ground on which he lay.

A wounded man stumbled into his shell hole. A big man with a bleeding shoulder and a strained, grey face.

"Why, Alec!" Cud Browne bent over him.

"Can't talk much, Cud," whispered Falcon, pointing to his side.

Cud took Alec's hand. Gripping it, he said: "I'm going back with this wound. It's nasty, but I can walk. I'll tell them... Is there anything else I can do for you?"

"How's the line?" asked Alec.

"Pretty thin. We have hardly any men. It looks as if we'll have to fall back."

Falcon shook his head. If the line retreated, he would fall into the hands of the Germans. He didn't want that — in this condition. Still, he had, in his right hand, his automatic. Seven shots in the magazine...

Falcon pointed to the pocket holding his field message-book. He whispered:

"Take a message."

Helped by Cud, he wrote a message to the Commanding Officer of the McIntyres.

"Took first trench with lots of prisoners. Hard fighting. Lost most of company. At German second line now. Very few men left. We can hold on if you send up reinforcements, officers and men..."

He paused. This was the time when a man with any real grit would send a stirring message, but he didn't care now about that. All he cared about was to get back, if he could, alive, to Adair...

He added to the note: "I'm down. Shot through chest near heart. May pull through if you can send out stretcher-bearers."

He signed the message: "Alexander Falcon, Major, O.C. 'B' Company."

Cud Browne gripped his hand again, went on.

A rotten message, thought Falcon... None of your heroic do-or-die stuff...just a plea for help.

He had had his chance to write something memorable. And he had missed it. He hadn't had the grit to rise above his own intense pain.

But what else mattered if he got out of here alive? He might then accomplish something worth more...

His vision of blue sky was again blocked by a khaki figure bending over him.

A corporal, his face grey with fatigue, his eyes anxious, troubled, was talking...

"I'm the last N.C.O. left, sir. No officers, no sergeants, no corporals but me. And not more than forty men..."

A fast hour's work, thought Falcon. With that extra platoon his company had been nearly up to strength at the start. Two hundred men with five officers. Now, a corporal and fifty men. "One crowded hour of glorious strife..." Humph! "We can't go any farther forward," the corporal was saying. "We have formed a new line where we lie. But if the Germans counter-attack I don't see how we can hold it. We have so few men. Hadn't we better fall back?"

Falcon shook his head.

"No," he whispered.

He wasn't thinking only of the line. He was thinking of himself. It would be death to be taken, this way, a prisoner. He would fight for his life. The men must fight for the line.

"Then, sir, we'll have to have reinforcements. Officers and men." The corporal spoke imploringly. It was a terrific responsibility for him, so little used to command, to assume...responsibility for a company's frontage on a battle-field.

Falcon, drawing his slow, laboured breaths, looked at the corporal steadily. He whispered: "I have sent for reinforcements... Hold on until they come."

The corporal looked at this man from whom he had so long taken orders, heard him commanding even now...

"All right, sir!" He rose from his squatting position, vanished into the rim of the shell hole as he returned to his men.

Falcon again was left alone. On his back. Staring at the sky. Water-bottle in his left hand, automatic in his right.

If the Germans broke through, he, lying there by himself, would never know it until some big figure in field-grey loomed above him, thrust at him, perhaps, with a bayonet.

He could stop that, if he had to, with his automatic. Drop a man or two. Then finish himself with a shot through the head.

Drowsy as the morphia made him, he refused to lose consciousness. Suppose that, after all, stretcher-bearers came for him, saw him lying inert with eyes closed, mistook him for dead and passed on? He must keep his eyes open. He was fighting for life.

Not that it would be so much of a life. From the feeling of the left side he imagined that his entire left lung was destroyed. No further career of adventure for him. But he could, at any rate, turn to writing... Now, surely, if the stretcher-bearers came for him soon he would have his chance. It was only a lung that was damaged. His head, which was all that could matter in writing, was unhurt...

All the afternoon he lay there, on his back, staring at the sky.

Once, in mid-afternoon, there dropped into his shell hole a subaltern from Alastair Irvine's company. A bold, energetic youth with bright eyes and with cheeks usually fresh-coloured but now pale with weariness. Lucky enough to be still unhit.

"I heard you were here," he said to Falcon. "We'll get you in later, if we can."

"How's it going?" Falcon whispered.

"A bit quieter now, but we've certainly had a rough party. I seem to be the only officer with these two companies. But I had word to expect reinforcements. We're all right if the enemy don't counter-attack before the reinforcements come."

After this brief visit Falcon was again left to himself. Occasionally he would hear footsteps passing close by. A wounded man going back to the dressing-station, or a runner with a message on his way to headquarters. Falcon, not knowing what was happening during the long hours of the afternoon, tried to call to these men. But he couldn't raise his voice. They passed by, unheeding.

Hour followed hour, and no stretcher-bearers came. Falcon lay there, half awake, waiting. It wasn't so difficult to keep awake. The intense pain in his side made sleep impossible.

Sunlight faded into dusk, the blue sky into darkness. Falcon lay, looking at the stars, waiting.

Stretcher-bearers might, after all, on that big battlefield, be quite unable to find him until too late. That subaltern who had come to see him might have been himself killed. No one perhaps would remember in which one of those hundreds of shell holes he lay.

There was such a lot to be done after an attack, and there were always so few men to do it. So few stretcher-bearers, too, as the advance proceeded…

And if you lie out too long, even if they did in the end find you, you would in all likelihood be rotten with gangrene. And you would be rescued too late.

As the hours of the night passed, and no help came, despair began to settle upon Falcon. Two or three times, at long intervals, he attempted to rise, but movement doubled the violence of the aching in his side. He didn't know anything about chest wounds, but he had heard of people dying of hemorrhages. It would certainly do no good to move, if movement only brought on a hemorrhage. So he remained there on his back, looking at the stars…afraid to sleep…waiting…listening.

Hurried feet passed him, but he could not summon them to his aid. What if those feet were not the feet of wounded Canadians returning, but of Germans advancing, breaking through the newly formed line?

Lying there alone, so long, in the darkness, he couldn't know how the attack went. He pondered the possibility of disaster.

This attack might prove like so many others. You made an advance, but you lost nearly all your men. The enemy counter-attacked. You were too weak to hold your gains. You had to fall back, halfway or farther.

That was what might have happened here… How could he know — he, who had seen no one, had spoken to no one for hours?

He looked at the luminous dial on his wristwatch. The hands showed a few minutes past three o'clock. It couldn't have been much past one o'clock in the afternoon when he was hit. Now, past three o'clock in the morning. He had been lying out nearly fourteen hours.

After a while the shelling, which for some hours had been light, became again heavy. High explosives — rocking the earth nearer and nearer to where he lay. Not very pleasant. Once more he tried to move. But it hurt his side so. He lay back again. He was probably safer here than anywhere. It wasn't a very deep shell hole, but even a shallow depression gave some protection from shell fragments. His whole body was below the surface of the ground. Only his head projected a little above the edge of the hole.

The shells now thundered to earth so fast and so quick that they formed a curtain of fire.

Whose barrage? Was it the enemy trying to smash up reinforcements that struggled towards the new British front line? Or was it the British artillery, forestalling attempts at counter-attack by the Germans?

Falcon didn't know. He had no means of knowing where the present British front line was, on which side of it he lay.

He was aware only that the barrage of shells was falling ever closer to his shell hole. If he didn't get out of here, surely he would get blown up. Yet if he did get out, into the open, he would be naked amongst all those explosions. Better lie quiet until the shelling was over...

A roar and a burst of red-yellow light. A crash that struck him from forehead to chin.

He was dazed, but he was still conscious. The blow had been bad enough, but not nearly so painful as that in the chest. It was rather like a terrific wallop on the head in a boxing match, that knocked you groggy, but didn't knock you out. He had had punches like that when he had been able to keep on fighting afterwards, but had hardly known what he was doing...

This was something like that... Yet different.

His right eye, surely, must be out. He couldn't see with it at all. The blood was pouring down his cheek. He put his hand to his right cheek. A gob of warm bleeding flesh hung there. He wondered if that was his right eye?

The end of his nose, too, was cut. Almost cut off. The flesh hung loose.

And his mouth was split in two. Upper and lower lips, split through in the center.

"What a hell of a sight!" he thought to himself.

He had heard of men with no faces. He would be like that. If he lived, he would have to live all to himself. He would see no one, not even Adair. No, he certainly wouldn't see Adair. He would go to some distant city, where nobody knew him. He would live alone. And he would write. With one good eye and one good lung, he could at least write... Such pictures of the war...

It was a life worth making a try for.

The shelling was not quite so heavy now. The shells were not bursting quite so close.

He must get out of this shell hole, or he would bleed to death, rot to death. He had no way to bandage this wound that had split his face from forehead to chin. If dirt got into it...

He detached the straps on his shoulders, which he had already loosened, the straps which held the light haversack he had carried in place of a pack. He took a last swig of water from his water-bottle. He left the water-bottle in the shell hole with the rest of his equipment. He left everything except his automatic. He might need that.

With immense difficulty — and not without starting up again the racket in his side, but he would have to disregard that — he struggled to his feet. He stood up.

With his one eye he looked about, bewildered.

Just where was he? Looking around the horizon, he saw the interlacing arcs of multitudinous flarelights on all sides but one. In that direction he could see only spasmodic flashings of batteries that illumined the rim of the sky. The flashing, surely, from British batteries.

Towards that flashing he headed.

Even if he had been a whole man, it would not have been a simple journey. To wander back at night, over a shell-pitted battlefield, stumbling over corpses, through big shell holes, up and down trenches that led you knew not where, with shells bursting, very often uncomfortably close. But he would have to take his chances on that. After all, he still had, in his right hand, his automatic.

His left hand he kept pressed against his side. With each step that he took, at the beginning of his journey, the wind seemed to sough from that hole in his side. He supposed that the lung hadn't quite collapsed before...was still collapsing. Like the pin-pricked bladder of a football.

He was only vaguely conscious of his direction. He floundered along with his left eye fixed on the gun-flashes. He came at last to a trench. No one in it. Except, here and there, a dead man... Plenty of them... He stumbled over a corpse. Sat down beside it, on the firing-step, exhausted. Rested a little while. Then rose. Floundered along through that trench a long way. Then came to a place where it was blown in. Struggled out into the open again. Then, after a time, he struck another trench. Or was it the same trench, running at a different angle? There might be someone in it.

He got down into it. He struggled along for a couple of bays. Joy of joys! A living man, a private in the Canadian infantry, stood before him.

Falcon spoke — the only way he could speak — with twisted words out of the left corner of his mouth:

"I'm...a major...in the MacIntyres... Eye out...lung gone. Can you help me...to the dressing-station?"

The private answered in broken English. He was a French-Canadian. He didn't know just where the dressing-station was.

Falcon, almost delirious with the throbbing in his head and the aching in his side, thought perhaps if he could give the man a tip of some sort...

"Here's my revolver... Take it." He held out his automatic to the private. "It's worth a lot of money... You can keep it, if you'll take me back."

"Je ne sais." The private was not sure of the way. But he would find out. If zee Major would wait, he, the private, would go and inquire. He would be back very soon.

He took the revolver. He went.

Falcon leaned against the side of the trench, resting as best he could.

It was a long wait. Five minutes passed, ten minutes, a quarter of an hour.

The private didn't come back.

Perhaps he had lost his way. Perhaps he had been himself injured by a shell explosion. Perhaps, having taken that revolver, worth a month's pay, he was no longer interested. At any rate, he didn't come back.

Falcon would have to shift for himself.

He wandered along the trench in the direction the private had taken. He found bay after bay, empty, deserted. Except, of course, for the corpses. He came again to a place where the trench had been blown in by a shell. He clambered up over the débris to the open.

He struggled along in the open, still heading for the gun-flashes. He was near collapse, but he would not give in. Not now, when he must be so nearly home. He had been on his legs, by this time, for nearly an hour, trying to find the way back. His legs would keep on going. Legs which, before the war, had so often done twenty, thirty, forty miles in a day. Those legs, though staggering now, would take him back.

He heard, at last, voices in the darkness — voices that spoke with a strong Scotch burr.

He came on a party of Canadian Highlanders, digging — remaking a trench. Or burying the dead. What did he care which?

Falcon again spoke with his split lips. Told who he was, how wounded, asked for help.

They crowded round him, offering welcome, help. There were no stretchers handy, they explained. All the stretchers were out forward, for bringing in the wounded. But one of the party volunteered to help Falcon down to the dressing-station.

Falcon leaned on the arm of this sturdy Scotch-Canadian. Was piloted by him down through a maze of trenches. So far to walk …so far…

Dawn was just breaking when they reached the dressing-station, a square-mouthed hole in the chalk-white wall of a railway cutting.

As Falcon lurched through the door of the dressing-station, leaning still on the arm of the private, the first person he saw coming towards him with outstretched hand was the white-haired Divisional chaplain.

Canon Hargraves saw this officer swaying in, one half of his face unshaven, the other half covered with blood, his jacket open, the left side of it drenched… He looked at the undamaged left eye. He recognized his late penitent.

"By Jove! You fellows…" the old man exclaimed.

The lanky medical officer in charge of the dressing-station came forward. He had worked all night over the hundreds of wounded, but was none the less cheery as he helped Falcon onto a stretcher.

"How about a shot of morphia?"

Morphia…bandages on his head…fresh bandages on his chest.

"The eye is still in," said the M.O. "There's a fair chance of saving it."

Falcon napped a little. Woke to find he was being carried out of the dressing-station on a stretcher. Men in field-grey were carrying him — German prisoners. Beside his stretcher walked the Highlander who had helped him back.

It was a bright autumn morning. The sunlight fell very pleasantly on the unbandaged part of Falcon's face and on the white chalk walls of the cut. Less pleasantly, there fell on his ears the swish and crash of high-explosives, the "ping" of shrapnel. Shells were bursting very close, searching this road, so congested with traffic of incoming troops and outgoing wounded.

Had he come through so much only to be finally smashed up on the way to the clearing-station?... But his good luck, such as it was, held.

The stretcher-bearers brought him out to the high-road, placed him and his stretcher in an ambulance. He dozed and woke, dozed and woke, as the ambulance rumbled over the cobblestone roads. He found himself, at last, being carried into the clearing-station.

"You've *got* to rush this case," he heard someone say. "He's been lying out in the open for God knows how long."

He was placed on a table, beneath a glare of light.

A. Audette

COMPLIMENTARY DINNER
"SOMEWHERE IN FRANCE"

Zero 7.00 pip enma. Be ready when barrage opens.
EATS, ETC.
Lewis gun cocktail just for a starter:
Cheer oh m'lads!
Hors d'oeuvres, pip-squeaked on toast,
rum jar sauce.
Mill's Bomb Soup (passed by Censor).
Adjutant's Dressing.
ANTI GAS RELISHES.
Tomatoes, Cabbage (pickles to the ears).
Celery, Nuns Alley Cukes.
Shell Dressing Mowatt Pickles.
(He'd get-em anyhow)
Casualty Joints (marked for duty by the M.
Prime ribs de youthful oxen.
(Imported by Pringle & Co., Inc.)
Five Point Nine Spuds—au pip.
Beaucoup Legumes.
(Swedish for "Have another Bob")
Creamed and Boiled pomme de terre.
Barbed Wire Peas.
Harrison Sweets (Trocadero Flavour).
Ammonia Capsule Merangue.
(detonated with Lemons).
Fruits, Nuts, Smoke Bombs, Toothpicks.
Libations: Coffee Noir, Tea the same way.
Wines, Water, Porter, drawn from the wood.
More Water, Liquers, Etc.

Some European Disease Germs as Observed by
an officer of the C.A.M.C.

L. Moore Cosgrave

1916 – THE PERSONAL HATE CHANGES TO IMPERSONAL LOATHING

Thus came we, after twelve long months of daily struggle with our almost invisible but ever-present enemy — *"Les Execrables!"* Changed we were — grimmer, harder in mind and body — our souls revolted by the tales, which crept through the lines, of hideous secret atrocities, perpetrated on innocent women and children, on defenceless wounded, on unprotected seaside villages! And imperceptibly, that great personal hate changed to a greater, but impersonal loathing! — Not of those men a few hundred yards away who represented our tangible enemy which we were pledged to destroy for humanity's sake; but against that greater, unseen, Machiavellian Being who bent them to his will — who outraged all our instinctive feelings of right and honour and decency.

These thoughts were vague, unformed, but steadily growing and assuming definite form and cohesion — at times, even, we almost felt a fellow-feeling for those individual enemies we came into contact with, in our patrols, our raids, our minor and major battles. For were they not undergoing similar privations, hardships, and dangers to ours? Then, again, would recur, at lengthening intervals, that first primitive hate, and we would again take a strange savage pleasure in avenging our helpless comrades' death.

So ran our thoughts and feelings throughout that long-drawn, bloody year of warfare — 1916 — the desperate local struggles around the craters of St. Eloi — the shell-torn trenches at Hooge, when whole battalions were swept into eternity in the holocaust of Sanctuary Wood. The dreadful, futile months on the Somme, with its acres of sacrificial corpses — all testifying to the selfishness of Man in his support of the Christ-principle of right. Always numerically inferior to the German hordes — but infinitely superior in morale — our knowledge of the right and our God-given power of justice, as bearers of the Torch, handed to us to carry on, from those martyred comrades of 1914 and 1915.

And still our souls struggled to present to our frail mortality the true perspective of right and wrong, of that greater humanity which the Supreme Being was trying to convey to a strangely distorted world.

S.F.L.

The Battalion Bard

We have a poet in our battalion. His name is *not* Browning. We have an N.C.O. of that name, but of course it would never do for him to write poetry. At the first couplet the shadow of a mighty name would come to blot him right out of existence. The justly celebrated volumes of his namesake would fall on him like a parapet stimulated by a *minenwerfer* shell. No, our poet's name is Perkins. He used to say that away off in Saskatoon he never had a chance even if the divine afflatus *had* struck him. Poetry bubbled in his soul, but it couldn't come out except when he took a pinch of bicarbonate of soda, which made him think for years it was indigestion that troubled him. But it wasn't; it was poetry, and the way he discovered that was curious.

He was humming "Tipperary" to himself one morning about 2 a.m., when he made one of a wiring party. He was thinking of the various other places where he would like to be and the first place he thought was the prairie, which he was delighted to find rhymed with Tipperary. Whereupon he promptly amended the current version of the celebrated ballad and read it out to us in the evening. At least, he read out as much of it as we would let him read, for we had had a hard day and our feelings were raw and we were looking for blood anyway. But Perkins was not to be suppressed. He wiped the plum jam from his face and clothes (which took some time, because we had rubbed our reprobation in) and said we'd be sorry. Whether we would have been or not is difficult to say, if a certain incident hadn't occurred which converted Perkins into a chartered libertine of verse, so to speak, for we had a terrific strafe by the Boche next day and old Perkins behaved so infernally well under fire that he was commended by the O.C. and recommended for the Military Medal.

After that would could we do? He became battalion poet, and spent all his leisure composing verses which were passed along the line and occasionally enlivened the Officer's Mess. I am not going to quote any of these early effusions, although I remember one chaste effusion beginning:

> *Here I sit in my lonely trench*
> *Waiting for orders from General French.*

This was about the time we changed commanders, when Perkins brought forth the following:

> *There's nothing weak and nothing vague*
> *About our noble General Haig.*

Perkins took as his motto — *Nulla die sine linea.* I am glad I cannot remember any more. He wrote them all out in a book which he said he was going to publish after the war under the title *Tropes from the Trenches.* But I think his muse got steadily better, for at a concert in rest billets he produced what I am told was his masterpiece. It was set to music (we were told it was music) and chanted (this doesn't seem the right word) by Company B's baritone, assisted by a corporal with a concertina. It had rather a grandiloquent title, "The Canadian." Here it is in full and it shows poor old Perkins at his best:

THE CANADIAN
By Private D.J. Perkins, Saskatoon Lancers

To Jack Canuck, drink a toast for luck,
He's had many jobs in his day, sir;
The forest and the farm have yielded to his arm,
And many stiff things came his way, sir.
And now he stands with a rifle in his hands
Ready for the wily Hun,

He'll never tire of the trenches or the fire
Until his job is done.

Refrain

Oh, a thousand leagues across the sea
He has come to do or die, sir,
And here he will stay for ever and a day,
Till he's marched through the land of the Kaiser.

He came from the west where they treat him best,
But he's moving eastward still, sir,
And he'll never turn around till he's captured all the ground,
And given Fritz his pill, sir.
Through Flanders and France he'll make him dance,
Paying for the blood he's shed,
Which may not be till 1923
And most of us are dead.

Refrain

Then came the smash-up at St. Eloi, and Perkins lay out in No Man's Land for two days with a broken leg until the Germans — to their credit — brought him in, and he is now — or was — a prisoner of war. But for weeks he was reported dead, and (to show the influence of example) a name board was prepared and passed solemnly from hand to hand bearing this touching inscription:

R. I. P.
Ye who love the Poet's Muse,
Shed a tear to hear the news:
Grave of D. J. Perkins this —
Whizz-bang hoisted him to bliss.

It just shows that inoculation is the only way to deal with certain ailments, and that even when what our M.O. calls "germ carrier" is weeded out it is too late and the bacteria have been passed on to another victim.

Nellie L. McClung as told by Private Simmons

THE PRISON CAMP
from THREE TIMES AND OUT

The Guard took me to Camp 6, Barrack A, where I found some of the boys I knew. They were in good spirits, and had fared in the matter of food much the same as I had. We agreed exactly in our diagnosis of the soup.

I was shown my mattress and given two blankets; also a metal bowl, knife, and fork.

Outside the hut, on the shady side, I went and sat down with some of the boys who, like myself, were excused from labour. Dent, of Toronto, was one of the party, and he was engaged in the occupation known as "reading his shirt" — and on account of the number of shirts being limited to one for each man, while the "reading" was going on, he sat in a boxer's uniform, wrapped only in deep thought.

Now, it happened that I did not acquire any "cooties" while I was in the army, and of course in the lazaret we were kept clean, so this was my first close acquaintanceship with them. My time of exemption was over, though, for by night I had them a-plenty.

I soon found out that insect powder was no good. I think it just made them sneeze, and annoyed them a little. We washed our solitary shirts regularly, but as we had only cold water, it did not kill the eggs, and when we hung the shirt out in the sun, the eggs came out in full strength, young, hearty, and hungry. It was a new generation we had to deal with, and they had all the objectionable qualities of their ancestors, and a few of their own.

Before long, the Canadian Red Cross parcels began to come, and I got another shirt — a good one, too, only the sleeves were too long. I carefully put in a tuck, for they came well over my hands. But I soon found that these tucks became a regular rendezvous for the "cooties" and I had to let them out. The Red Cross parcels also contained towels, toothbrushes, socks, and soap, and all these were very useful.

After a few weeks, with the lice increasing every day, we raised such a row about them that the guards took us to the fumigator. This was a building of three rooms, which stood by itself in the compound. In the first room we undressed and hung all our clothes, and our blankets too, on huge hooks which were placed on a sliding framework. This framework was then pushed into the oven and the clothes were thoroughly baked. We did not let our boots, belt, or braces go, as the heat would spoil the leather. We then walked out into the next room and had a shower bath, and after that went into the third room at the other side of the oven, and waited until the framework was pushed through to us, when we took our clothes from the hooks and dressed.

This was a sure cure for the "cooties," and for a few days, at least, we enjoyed perfect freedom from them. Every week after this we had a bath, and it was compulsory, too.

As prison-camps go, Giessen is a good one. The place is well drained; the water is excellent; the sanitary conditions are good, too; the sleeping accommodations are ample, there being no upper berths such as exist in all the other camps I have seen. It is the "Show-Camp," to which visitors are brought, who then, not having had to eat the food, write newspaper articles telling how well Germany treats her prisoners. If these people could see some of the other camps that I have seen, the articles would have to be modified.

The routine of the camp was as follows: Reveille sounded at six. We got up and dressed and were given a bowl of coffee. Those who were wise saved their issue of bread from the night before, and ate it with the coffee. There was a roll-call right after the coffee, when every one was given a chance to volunteer for work. At noon there was soup, and another roll-call. We answered the roll-call, either with the French word *"Présent"* or the German word *"Hier,"* which was pronounced the same as our word. Then at five o'clock there was an issue of black bread made mostly from potato flour.

I was given a light job of keeping the space between A Barrack and B Barrack clean, and I made a fine pretense of being busy, for it let me out of "drill," which I detested, for they gave the commands in German, and it went hard with us to have to salute their officers.

On Sundays there was a special roll-call, when everyone had to give a full account of himself. The prisoners then had the privilege of asking for any work they wanted, and if the Germans could supply it, it was given.

None of us were keen on working; not but what we would much rather work than be idle, but for the uncomfortable thought that we were helping the enemy. There were iron-works near by, where Todd, Whittaker, Dent, little Joe, and some others were working, and it happened that one day Todd and one of the others, when going to have teeth pulled at the dentist's saw shells being shipped away, and upon inquiry found the steel came from the iron mines where they were working. When this became known, the boys refused to work! Every sort of bullying was tried on them for two days at the mines, but they still refused. They were then sent back to Giessen and sentenced to eighteen months' punishment at Butzbach — all but Dent, who managed some way to fool the doctor, pretending he was sick!

That they fared badly there, I found out afterwards, though I never saw any of them.

Some of the boys from our hut worked on the railroad, and some went to work in the chemical works at Griesheim, which have since been destroyed by bombs dropped by British airmen.

John Keith, who was working on the railroad — one of the best-natured and inoffensive boys in our hut — came in one night with his face badly swollen and bruised. He had laughed, it seemed, at something which struck him as being funny, and the guard had beaten him over the head with the butt of his rifle. One of our guards, a fine old, brown-eyed man called "Sank," told the guard who had done this what he thought of him. "Sank" was the "other" kind of German, and did all he could to make our lives pleasant. I knew that "Sank" was calling down the guard, by his expression and his gestures, and his frequent use of the word "*blödsinnig.*"

Another time one of the fellows from our hut, who was a member of a working party, was shot through the legs by the guard, who claimed he was trying to escape, and after that there were no more working parties allowed for a while.

Each company had its own interpreter, Russian, French, or English. Our interpreter was a man named Scott from British Columbia, an Englishman who had received part of his education at Heidelberg. From him I learned a good deal about the country through which I hoped to travel. Heidelberg is situated between Giessen and the Swiss boundary, and so was of special interest to me. I made a good-sized map, and marked in all the information I could dig out of Scott.

The matter of escaping was in my mind all the time. But I was careful to whom I spoke, for some fellows' plans had been frustrated by their unwise confidences.

The possession of a compass is an indication that the subject of "escaping" has been thought of, and the question, "Have you a compass?" is the prison-camp way of saying, "What do you think of making a try?"

One day, a fellow called Bromley who came from Toronto, and who was captured at the same time that I was, asked me if I had a compass. He was a fine big fellow, with a strong, attractive face, and I liked him, from the first. He was a fair-minded, reasonable chap, and we soon became friends. We began to lay plans, and when we could get together, talked over the prospects, keeping a sharp lookout for eavesdroppers.

There were difficulties!

The camp was surrounded by a high board fence, and above the boards, barbed wire was tightly drawn, to make it uncomfortable for reaching hands. Inside of this was an ordinary barbed-wire fence through which we were not allowed to go, with a few feet of No Man's Land in between.

There were sentry-boxes ever so often, so high that the sentry could easily look over the camp. Each company was divided from the others by two barbed-wire fences, and besides this there were the sentries who walked up and down, armed, of course.

There were also the guns commanding every bit of the camp, and occasionally, to drive from us all thought of insurrection, the Regular Infantry marched through with fixed bayonets. At these times we were always lined up so we should not miss the gentle little lesson!

One day, a Zeppelin passed over the camp, and we all hurried out to look at it. It was the first one I had seen, and as it rode majestically over us, I couldn't help but think of the terrible use that had been made of man's mastery of the air. We wondered if it carried bombs. Many a wish for its destruction was expressed — and unexpressed. Before it got out of sight, it began to show signs of distress, as if the wishes were taking effect, and after considerable wheeling and turning it came back.

Ropes were lowered and the men came down. It was secured to the ground, and floated serenely beside the wood adjoining the camp... The wishes were continued...

During the afternoon, a sudden storm swept across the camp — rain and wind with such violence that we were all driven indoors.

When we came out after a few minutes — probably half an hour — the Zeppelin had disappeared. We found out afterwards that it had broken away from its moorings, and, dashing against the high trees, had been smashed to kindling wood; and this news cheered us wonderfully!

A visitor came to the camp one day, and, accompanied by three or four officers, made the rounds. He spoke to a group of us who were outside of the hut, asking us how many Canadians there were in Giessen. He said he thought there were about 900 Canadians in Germany altogether. He had no opportunity for private conversation with us, for the German officers did not leave him for a second; and although he made it clear that he would like to speak to us alone this privilege was not granted. Later we found out it was Ambassador James W. Gerard.

It soon became evident that there were spies in the camp. Of course, we might have known that no German institution could get along without spies. Spies are the bulwark of the German nation; so in the Giessen camp there were German spies of all nationalities, including Canadian.

But we soon saw, too, that the spies were not working overtime on their job; they just brought in a little gossip once in a while — just enough to save their faces and secure a soft snap for themselves.

One of these, a Frenchman named George Clerque, a Sergeant Major in the French Army, was convinced that he could do better work if he had a suit of civilian clothes; and as he had the confidence of the prison authorities, the suit was given him. He wore it around for a few days, wormed a little harmless confidence out of some of his countrymen, and then one day quietly walked out of the front gate — and was gone!

Being in civilian dress, it seemed quite likely that he would reach his destination, and as days went on, and there was no word of him, we began to hope that he had arrived in France.

The following notice was put up regarding his escape:

NOTICE!

Owing to the evasions recently done, we beg to inform the prisoners of war of the following facts. Until present time, all the prisoners who were evased, have been catched. The French Sergt. Major George Clerque, speaking a good German and being in connection in Germany with some people being able to favorise his evasion, has been retaken. The Company says again, in the personal interest of the prisoners, that any evasion give place to serious punition (minima) fortnight of rigourous imprisonment after that they go in the "Strafbaracke" for an indeterminate time.

Giessen, den 19th July, 1915.

Although the notice said he had been captured we held to the hope that he had not, for we knew the German way of using the truth only when it suits better than anything they can frame themselves. They have no prejudice against the truth. It stands entirely on its own merits. If it suits them, they will use it, but the truth must not expect any favours.

The German guards told us quite often that no one ever got out of Germany alive, and we were anxious to convince them that they were wrong. One day when the mail came in, a friend of George Clerque told us he had written from France, and there was great, but, of necessity, quiet rejoicing.

That night Bromley and I decided that we would volunteer for farm service, if we could get taken to Rossbach, where some of the other boys had been working, for Rossbach was eighteen miles south of Giessen — on the way the Switzerland. We began to save food from our parcels, and figure out distances on the map which I had made.

The day came when we were going to volunteer — Sunday at roll-call. Of course, we did not wish to appear eager, and were careful not to be seen together too much. Suddenly we were called to attention, and a stalwart German soldier marched solemnly into the camp. Behind him came two more, with somebody between them, and another soldier brought up the rear. The soldiers carried their rifles and full equipment, and marched by in front of the huts.

We pressed forward, full of curiosity, and there beheld the tiredest, dustiest, most woe-begone figure of a man, whose clothes were in rags, and whose boots were so full of holes they seemed ready to drop off him. He was handcuffed and walked wearily, with downcast eyes —

It was George Clerque!

"I know that in 50 years we'll recall with terror this crossing through."

Theodore Goodridge Roberts

A BILLET IN FLANDERS (1915)

Within, the frowtsiness and gloom;
Without, the chill and sodden dark;
Within, pitiful, pale and small,
Christ crucified on the mildewed wall.

Without, the grind of wheels; the ring
Of hoofs and heels on greasy stone:
Within, the old bed, high and damp;
A candle and a smoky lamp.

There I was lonely for sane things:
There I was heartsick for glad days:
And there I knew, with dawning near,
That indecision men call fear.

Heated with wine or caked with mud—
(A revel spent or a day's work done)—
Slowly I turned to that dreary bed
And the pale regard of the imaged dead.

I thought of death; and it did not seem
So dull a thing, nor so sad a jest,
As the dismal nights and the weary round
Of keeping alive on the muddy ground.

Flat ruins now, that house and room
Where I was caged with my soul's gloom
And poor Christ languished, pale and small
In agony on the mildewed wall.

Hartley Munro Thomas

FESTUBERT

Were you there?
>> Mud and blood and evil smell,
>> And barking parapets of hell,
>>> And each redoubt
That sputtered out
>> Its snapping death, and every shell
> Are branded on your memory
>>> Since Festubert.

Oh, wind so fair,
>> Ghosts were scattered on your path,
>> Each flying blindly in his wrath
>>> To heaven or hell
>>> (They could not tell).
>> And every thought and prayer man hath
Were thrown upon your fleeting breath
>>> At Festubert.

And children there,
>> Story-seeking at the knee,
>> For tales of ghosts and chivalry,
>>> Must listen here
>>> With childish fear,
>> The tale that tells so bitterly
Why they have played at soldier games,
>>> Since Festubert.

Harold Peat

THE CANADIAN GOLGOTHA
from PRIVATE PEAT

The night of April twenty-second is one that I can never forget. It was frightful, yes. Yet there was a grandeur in the appalling intensity of living, in the appalling intensity of death as it surrounded us.

The German shells rose and burst behind us. They made the Yser Canal a stream of molten glory. Shells fell in the city, and split the darkness of the heavens in the early night hours. Later the moon rose in a splendour of springtime. Straight behind the tower of the great cathedral it rose and shone down on a bloody earth.

Suddenly the grand old Cloth Hall burst into flames. The spikes of fire rose and fell and rose again. Showers of sparks went upward. A pall of smoke would form and cloud the moon, waver, break and pass. There was the mutter and rumble and roar of great guns. There was the groan of wounded and the gasp of dying.

It was glorious. It was terrible. It was inspiring. Through an inferno of destruction and death, of murder and horror, we lived because we must.

Early in the night the Fighting Tenth and the Sixteenth charged the wood of St. Julien. Through the undergrowth they hacked and hewed and fought and bled and died. But, outnumbered as they were, they got the position and captured the batter of 4.7 guns that had been lost earlier in the day.

This night the Germans caught and crucified three of our Canadian sergeants. I did not see them crucify the men, although I saw one of the dead bodies after. I saw the marks of bayonets through the palms of the hands and the feet, where by bayonet points this man had been spitted to a barn door. I was told that one of the sergeants was still alive when taken down, and before he died he gasped out to his saviours that when the Germans were raising him to be crucified, they muttered savagely in perfect English, "If we did not frighten you before, this time we will."

I know a sergeant from Edmonton, Alberta, who has in his possession today the actual photographs of the crucified men taken before the dead bodies were removed from the barnside.

Again I maintain that war frightfulness of this kind does not frighten real men. The news of the crucified men soon reached all the ranks. It increased our hatred. It doubled our bitterness. It made us all the more eager to advance — to fight — to "get." We had to avenge our comardes. Vengeance is not yet complete.

In the winter of 1914-1915 the Germans knew war. They had studied the game and not a move was unfamiliar to them. We were worse than novices. Even our generals could not in their knowledge compare with the expertness of those who carried out the enemy action according to a schedule probably laid down years before.

We knew that on the day following the terrible night of April twenty-second we must continue the advance, that we dare not rest, that we must complete the junction with the right wing of the British troops. And the enemy knew it too.

Frank Prewett

A STRANGE WAR STORY

It was the summer of 1917. The Germans had retreated from the Somme, destroying buildings and roads, and even orchards and gardens, and leaving booby taps everywhere. We supposed that we had defeated them and that they were retiring into Germany. We speculated on the attractions of Berlin. But during the past week or two we had been ambushed several times on our jaunt to Germany. The day before, the divisional artillery had been severely mauled as they trotted in open order across the downs towards a supposedly undefended hamlet which was designated Y Ack.

I was serving in heavy trench mortars, which were useless in this new style of war which dispensed with trenches and dashed about in the open. So the heavy trench mortars were living in bliss in the ruins of a sugar refinery. Every morning at ten minutes past eight and every afternoon at ten minutes past four, for the space of ten minutes, the Germans shelled the refinery.

It was a bore to have to stir oneself at eight and four o'clock each day and leave the refinery. But the rest of the day and all the night were peace. We would not have believed there was so much peace left anywhere in the world. We wrote letters, and slept, and lazed in the sun which shone all day long. The abandoned corn and sugar beet fields were waist-high in poppies. The skylarks fluttered upwards, singing as they rose, and glided earthward with a thin long-drawn trill

My bliss of body and mind where I lay daydreaming in the shade of a poplar tree, was shattered by my batman.

"Guvner wants to see yer — immediate."

My batman was named Smith. He was an East Londoner, short and stout, with a pale broad face, swollen ears, and flattened nose. His peace-time trade was prize-fighting, at which he could sometimes make as much as thirty shillings in an evening.

I presented myself to the major commanding divisional heavy trench mortars. The major was known as the Gorilla. His skin was yellow from many years in Tropical Africa, and his arms were abnormally long. His face was large, ugly, and ape-like around the eyes. He had to be named Gorilla.

"Come in, you," he addressed me. "You've just come back from leave, haven't you? The other old hands haven't had their leave so they can't go on this job. Can't send any of the new boys — not enough experience. Lose their way, get killed, have to do the job over again. That means you're going to do it, see?"

"Yes sir," I said. "What's the job?"

"The general wants to know whether the Bosches are occupying Y Ack, or whether they just happened to drop in yesterday when they caught our guns. We're unemployed, so we've got the job of finding out, see?"

"Yes sir. Any detailed orders?"

"None, except get into Y Ack, and get out again, and tell me whether the Bosches are there. If they're there, how many are they and have they got any guns. Manage it your own way. Better take your sergeant along. You're always wanting him to have a medal. Now's his chance. But don't take that boozy, punch-drunk killer that you call your batman. No fighting, mind, unless you're cornered, so don't get cornered. It might turn out tricky, so use caution all the time. Remember, this is a serious reconnaissance. The general wants to know if Y Ack is occupied, and that's all he wants to know. He might lose interest in that little affair with the Australians in Amiens if you get the information back before three o'clock, see? The infantry post have been warned you'll be going through."

"Yes sir."

My sergeant was an Indian, lately a student at London University. He was small, strong, and girlishly pretty. He took it bitterly that he could not be commissioned in the British Army because he was an Indian.

We walked down to the infantry screen, taking cover perfunctorily. The infantry subaltern said that of course he knew we were going out and of course they wouldn't shoot at any movement in the grass, at least not until we got back.

There were occasions, sometimes bitter occasions, when it was useless to try to reach assurance, by explanation and amplification, that a Scottish subaltern and a platoon of Scottish riflemen would not fire at any time at anything that moved.

My sergeant and I hoisted ourselves out of the hollow in a grove of stunted oak trees where the infantry subaltern lived. We studied our position with care, as to how it would look from Y Ack. We had no wish to wander against some other platoon on our way home. Then we spaced ourselves ten feet apart and began to squirm on our bellies towards Y Ack.

The hamlet Y Ack was distant half a mile. The Germans would probably have some posts in front of the village. They would let us go through them, to find out what we were up to, before shooting us. An alert sentry would see our wake in the long grass and weeds. My heart was pounding and my whole inside was tight and dry as we wormed our way forward. I felt light-headed with fear. But for the larks and the insects, silence was complete. When either of us made a slight jangling noise with his weapons or grated a stone with the toe of his boot we halted in panic while noise resounded as of a London railway terminus. We expected the slow, deadly hammer strokes of the machine gun. We were suffering very badly from nerves.

Slowly the hamlet came nearer and loomed larger as we peered at it through the long grass. A hundred feet from the first cottage we halted and whispered together. I cautiously studied the village through my field glasses. There was neither sight nor sound of movement. I left my sergeant and crawled to the cottage. I crawled round it. I beckoned my sergeant forward. We wriggled along the street, seeking cover in doorways or in shell holes or behind walls. We were old hands and could have become invisible on an empty dance floor. We reached the far end of the hamlet and still all was silent. There had been no whip of sentry's rifle bullet.

By this time we were no longer squirming on our bellies, but dashing on foot from cover to cover. My heart had ceased pounding and there was moisture in my mouth when I swallowed. Our whispers became cautious speech. The grating of our boots did not resound as with doom. We walked boldly back through the village, side by side. I felt inclined to sing, for it was another day of perfect sunshine. We had looked into every passage and yard and we were alone. Then I froze in horror. From the ruins of a cottage came a hideous, loud, rattling noise. Trapped. My own bloody fault, too, sauntering about as if we were on the sea front. I tugged for a grenade. A tabby cat emerged delicately from the open doorway. She came forward, mewing us a welcome. We burst into hysterical laughter.

We could not cease from laughing. We were long in draining ourselves of the intolerable accumulated tension of the past two hours.

As we tramped down the street I saw a garden of many madonna lilies. We went into the garden and filled our arms with them. Then we saw, behind the lilies, a patch of strawberries. We ate them greedily, all danger forgotten. We were light-headed, but with happiness now, not fear. The tabby cat rubbed herself against our legs. She followed us to the end of the hamlet, and a little beyond. There she stopped, but we strode boldly towards our lines. We had not a care in the world. Somewhere in the back of our minds we must have known that we might be sniped from behind, and that we had the Scottish platoon in front of us. But we had no room for other thought than that we were returning from a happy picnic, and we soon leapt into the infantry post, beaming with well-being. We still carried our madonna lilies.

My batman met me at the sugar refinery.

"You ain't 'arf copped it with the Guvner. 'E wants yer inside — immediate."

I made my report to the Gorilla well before three o'clock. I assured him Y Ack was unoccupied.

"I know damn well it's unoccupied, because you walked back. You walked back, didn't you, and you let the Bosches know where our infantry line is. You were always the clever boy, weren't you? And you used caution, too — like hell you did."

The Gorilla's rage was mounting out of control.

"And what's this I hear about flowers — my God, coming in from a reconnaissance with your arms full of flowers. The infantry phoned you were back but out of your minds. Out of your minds, see? Who's got to live this down? Me, as usual. And now I suppose you expect me to smooth things down with the general the same as I did over the Australians."

The Gorilla had a nasty way of reviving the past delinquencies, or misfortunes, of his junior officers.

"That wasn't my fault sir. The Australians asked for a bout when they heard Smith was a boxer."

"And who told them he was a boxer? And who was laying the odds? A nice example of an officer, you are."

"Anyway, sir, Smith was told not to hurt the Australian. It was an accident that he got his jaw broken. Smith didn't mean to hit him hard. As to the concussion, the Aussie must have bumped his head on the floor, or something. You remember, sir, it was a stone floor—"

"Shut up, you."

"Well anyway, sir, Y Ack is unoccupied."

"Listen, you," he said, "I've had enough of you. Get out of my sight, and out of my reach, quick, see?"

"Cheer up," my batman said. "What's the Old Man been creatin' about?"

"He's been creating about you."

"Me. Just because you didn't take me with you, and it's a proper batman's right to go with 'is officer where 'is officer goes. That's the rules. Not good enough for your lordship, not eddicated enough. I suppose it was sarge 'ad the idea about the lilies! As 'e got a boudoir?"

"Listen, Smith, I've had just about enough of you. And since you're so well informed of batman's rights you might remember their duties. One of them is to show respect to commissioned officers."

"Now, sir, don't take on so. It slipped me mind. I give yer my word, sir, I'll never lay 'ands on another Aussie, no, not if a dozen Aussies pitches on me together. Money couldn't tempt me."

I looked into the bland battered face that showed so much innocence and concealed so much guile.

"It's getting on for four o'clock. I've reserved your usual seat for the Bosch concert. Tell you what, sir, I was 'avin' a look round the quartermaster's stores, saw the corporal was settled down to vanty in the cookhouse, thought yer boots might 'ave come in—"

"Smith, shut up and get out of my sight, see?"

"What 'ave I done now?"

"Nothing, nothing, but please go away."

"That's alright, guvner, sir. Reckon yor're wrought up and 'avin' a reaction. Same with the ring, but bless yer, it passes in no time an'yer boxes on."

Frank Prewett

THE VOID BETWEEN

Of shattered youth the reliquary
Is still to seek, still hope to find
Dawn grows insidiously strong.
The damned chiefly desire to be saved.
Man in woman seeks lost innocence;
Woman in man her lost child.
Though we cling together we are isolate
And reach vainly to close the void between.

John McCrae

LETTERS: WITH THE GUNS

[N.B. These letters, written by McCrae in the form of a diary to his mother, are woven into Andrew MacPhail's memoir of the author of "In Flanders Fields" that serves as the afterword to McCrae's volume of poetry. MacPhail presents the diary entries out of sequence in order to show how McCrae's experiences were evolving the poem.]

Sunday, May 2, 1915

Heavy gunfire again this morning. Lieutenant H___ was killed at the guns. His diary's last words were, "It has quieted a little and I shall try to get a good sleep." I said the Committal Service over him, as well as I could from memory. A soldier's death! Batteries again registering barrages or barriers of fire at set ranges. At 3 the Germans attacked, preceded by gas clouds. Fighting went on for an hour and a half, during which their guns hammered heavily with some loss to us.

Monday, May 3, 1915

A clear morning, and the accursed German aeroplanes over our positions again. They are usually fired at, but no luck. Today a shell on our hill dug out a cannon ball about six inches in diameter — probably of Napoleon's or earlier times — heavily rusted.

Sunday, May 9, 1915

Firing kept up all day. In thirty hours we had fired 3600 rounds, and at times with seven, eight, or nine guns, our wire cut and repaired eighteen times. Orders came to move, and we got ready. At dusk we got the guns out by hand, and all batteries assembled at a given spot in comparative safety. We were much afraid they would open on us, for at 10 o'clock they gave us 100 or 150 rounds, hitting the trench parapet again and again. However, we were up the road, the last wagon half a mile away before they opened. One burst near me, and splattered some pieces around, but we got clear, and by 12 were out of the usual fire zone. Marched all night, tired as could be, but happy to be clear.

Northern France, Monday, May 10, 1915
For seventeen days and seventeen nights none of us have had our clothes off, nor our boots even, except occasionally. In all that time while I was awake, gunfire and rifle fire never ceased for sixty seconds, and it was sticking to our utmost by a weak line all but ready to break, knowing nothing of what was going on, and depressed by reports of anxious infantry...

This, of course, is the second battle of Ypres, or the battle of the Yser, I do not know which. At one time we were down to seven guns, butthose guns were smoking at every joint, the gunners using cloth to handle the breech levers because of the heat...

And behind it all was the constant background of the sights of the dead, the wounded, the maimed, and a terrible anxiety lest the line should give way...

None of our men went off their heads but men in units nearby did — and no wonder.

France, May 17, 1915
Our guns — those behind us, from which we had to dodge occasional prematures — have a peculiar bang-sound added to the sharp crack of discharge. The French 75 has a sharp woodblock-chop sound, and the shell goes over with a peculiar whine — not unlike a cat, but beginning with *n* — thus, — *neouw*. The big fellows, 3000 yards or more behind, sounded exactly like our own, but the flash came three or four seconds before the sound. Of the German shells — the field guns come with a great velocity — no warning — just whizz-bang; white smoke, nearly always air bursts. The next size, probably 5 inch

howitzers, have a perceptible time of approach, an increasing whine, and a great burst on the percussion — dirt in all directions. And even if a shell hit on the front of the canal bank, and one back of the back, five, eight or ten seconds later one would hear a belated *whirr*, and curved pieces of shell would light — probably parabolic curves or boomerangs. These shells have a great back kick; from the field gun shrapnel we got nothing *behind* the shell — all the pieces go forward. From the howitzers, the danger is almost as great behind as in front if they burst on percussion. Then the large shrapnel — airburst — have a double explosion, as if a giant shook a wet sail for two flaps; first a dark green burst of smoke; then a lighter yellow burst goes out from the centre, forwards. I do not understand the why of it.

The 10-inch shells: a deliberate whirring course — a deafening explosion — black smoke, and earth 70 or 80 feet in the air. These always burst on percussion. The constant noise of our own guns is really worse on the nerves than the shell; there is the deafening noise, and the constant whirr of shells going overhead. The earth shakes with every nearby gun and every close shell. I think I may safely enclose a cross section of our position. The left is the front; a slopedown of 20 feet in 100 yards to the canal, a high row of trees on each bank, then a short 40 yards slope up to the summit of the trench.

Friday, May 28, 1915
Newspapers which arrive show that up to May 7th, the Canadian public has made no guess at the extent of the battle of Ypres. The Canadian papers seem to have lost interest in it after the first four days; this regardless of the fact that the artillery, numerically a quarter of the division, was in all the time. One correspondent writes from the Canadian rest camp, and never mentions Ypres. Others say they hear heavy bombarding which appears to come from Armentières.

Wednesday, April 29, 1915
This morning is the sixth day of this fight; it has been constant, except that we got good chance to sleep for the last two nights. Our men have fought beyond praise. Canadian soldiers have set a standard for themselves which will keep posterity busy to surpass. And the War Office published that the 4.1 guns captured were Canadian. They were not: the division has not lost a gun so far by capture. We will make a good job of it — if we can.

Saturday, May 1, 1915
This is the ninth day that we have stuck to the ridge, and the batteries have fought with a steadiness which is beyond all praise...

Flanders, March 30, 1915
The wounded and sick stay where they are till dark, when the field ambulances go over certain grounds and collect. A good deal of suffering is entailed by the delay till night, but it is useless for vehicles to go on the roads within 1500 yards of the trenches. They are willing enough to go. Most of the trench injuries are of the head, and therefore there is a high proportion of killed in the daily warfare as opposed to an attack. Our Canadian plots fill up rapidly.

Tuesday, June 1, 1915
100 miles northeast of Festubert, near La Bassee
Last night a 15 pr. and a 4-inch howitzer fired at intervals of five minutes from 8 till 4; most of them within 500 or 600 yards — a very tiresome procedure; much of it is on registered roads. In the morning I walked out to Le Touret to the wagon lines, got Bonfire, and rode to the headquarters at Vendin-Les-Bethune, a little village a mile past Bethune. Left the horse at the lines and walked back again. An unfortunate shell in the 1st killed a sergeant and wounded two men; thanks to the strong emplacements the rest of the crew escaped. In the evening went around the batteries and said goodbye. We stood while they laid away the sergeant who was killed.

Kind hands have made two pathetic little wreaths of roses; the grave under an apple tree, and the moon rising over the horizon; a siege-lamp held for the book. Of the last 41 days the guns have been in action for 33. Captain Lockhart, late with Fort Garry Horse, arrived to relieve me. I handed over, came up to the horse lines, and slept in a covered wagon in a courtyard. We were all sorry to part — the four of us have been very intimate and had agreed perfectly — and friendships under these circumstances are apt to be the real thing. I am sorry to leave them in such a hot corner, but cannot choose and must obey orders. It is a great relief from strain, I must admit, to be out, but I could I wish that they all were.

John McCrae

In Flanders Fields

In Flanders fields the poppies blow
    Between the crosses, row on row,
    That mark our place; and in the sky
    The larks, still bravely singing, fly
Scarce heard amid the guns below.

We are the Dead. Short days ago
We lived, felt dawn, saw sunset glow,
        Loved and were loved, and now we lie,
           In Flanders fields.

Take up our quarrel with the foe:
To you from failing hand we throw
    The torch; be yours to hold it high.
    If ye break faith with us who die
We shall not sleep, though poppies grow
        In Flanders fields.

Charles Yale Harrison

LONDON
from GENERALS DIE IN BED

It is three o'clock in the morning.

We are weary with the long hours of travel. I walk out of the soot-coloured ugly Waterloo Station and hail a cab. I give the driver the name of a little hotel.

I am taken up to a room. I ask where the bathroom is. In a few minutes I am scrubbing myself vigorously.

It is five o'clock when I turn in. I stretch myself royally between the cool white sheets. Outside I hear the rumble of early morning traffic. I listen hungrily.

The hollow, echoing sound of horses' hoof-beats. The roll of wheels on the macadam. The growl of an omnibus as it passes my window.

I snuggle contentedly under the sheets and fall asleep.

It is late afternoon when I awake.

I dress leisurely, soaking in each quiet moment. The room is peaceful. It is years since I have been alone like this. I polish my boots, shine my buttons and leave the hotel.

On the steps I light a cigarette and look around me. Nobody notices me. The traffic of the city flows on all sides of me.

It is dusk and the few lights permitted are shaded so as not to be visible from the air. I walk to the corner. A woman passes me and whispers:

"Hello, Canada."

Too early for that.

First I must get a drink and then a bellyful of food.

I walk into a restaurant on Shaftesbury Avenue. I order a meal and a bottle of wine. After the first few mouthfuls I notice that I am not very hungry. I drink a glass of wine and light a cigarette.

Well, I am happy, anyhow.

The waiter sees the insignia on my shoulders. He is a tall, pale cockney. He hovers over me.

"'Ow is it over there?"

I do not feel like talking.

"Lousy," I reply.

A pretty girl sits opposite me. She leans across the table and asks for a match.

I give her a light.

We walk out of the restaurant together.

Her name is Gladys. We walk along the streets talking and laughing. She is an excellent companion for a soldier on leave. She does not mention the war.

We are in the Strand near Fleet Street.

"Let's have a drink," she says.

"Sure."

"Don't say 'sure,'" she says, "it sounds American. Say 'of course.'"

"But I am an American."

"I don't like Americans."

"All right, then I'm a Canadian."

We walk into the family entrance to a pub and order two double-headers of Scotch. We sit and drink and talk.

"Where shall we go to-night?"

"Anywhere you say."

"Do you want to go to the Hippodrome?"

"Yes."

We order another drink. I feel flushed.

We walk out of the public-house and into the humming streets.

She puts her arm in mine and we walk up the street. Her body is close to mine. I feel its contours, its firmness. There is an odour of perfume.

"Love me?"

She looks at me with wide-open eyes.

"Yes. I love all the boys." She squeezes my arm. I do not like her answer.

I frown.

She hastens to explain: "I have enough for you all, poor lads."

My frown breaks a little.

"Now, then, let's not talk of things like that," she says.

The whisky is racing through my veins. I feel boisterous. I swagger. The thought of the trenches does not intrude itself now.

I buy the tickets for the theatre. Inside the performance has started.

On the stage a vulgar-faced comic is prancing up and down the apron of the stage singing. Behind him about fifty girls dressed in gauzy khaki stage uniforms, who look like lewd female Tommies, dance to the tune of the music. Their breasts bob up and down as they dance and sing:

> *Oh it's a lovely war.*
> *What do we care for eggs and ham*
> *When we have plum and apple jam?*
> *Quick march, right turn.*
> *What do we do with the money we earn?*
> *Oh, oh, oh, it's a lovely war.*

The tempo is quick the orchestra crashes, the trombones slide, the comic pulls impossible faces.

The audience shrieks with laughter. Gladys laughs until tears roll down her face.

The chorus marches into the wings. A Union Jack comes down at the back of the stage. The audience applauds and cheers.

I feel miserable.

The fat comic — the half-undressed actresses — somehow make me think of the line. I look about me. There are very few men on leave in the theatre. The place is full of smooth-faced civilians. I feel they have no right to laugh at jokes about the war.

I hear Gladys's voice.

"Don't you like it, boy?"

"No, these people have no right to laugh."

"But, silly, they are trying to forget."

"They have no business to forget. They should be made to remember."

The comic on the stage has cracked a joke. The audience goes into spasms of laughter. My voice is drowned out.

Gladys pats my arm.

A jolly-faced rotund civilian in evening dress sitting near me says:

"I say, he's funny, isn't he?"

I stare at him.

He turns to his female companion. I hear him whisper:

"Shell-shocked."

I cannot formulate my hatred of these people. My head is fuzzy but I feel that people should not be sitting laughing at jokes about plum and apple jam when boys are dying out in France. They sit here in stiff shirts, their faces and jowls are smooth with daily shaving and dainty cosmetics, their bellies are full, and out there we are being eaten by lice, we are sitting trembling in shivering dugouts.

Intermission.

I feel blue. The effect of the Scotch has worn off.

"Come on, let's have a drink," Gladys says.

We go to the back of the auditorium and order two drinks. It is a long wait and we have several drinks before the curtain goes up again.

Finally the show ends and we go out into the street.

Swarms of well-dressed men and women stand about in the lobby smoking and talking, waiting for their motor-cars. There are many uniforms but they are not uniforms of the line. I see the insignia of the non-combatant units — Ordnance Corps, Army Service Corps, Paymasters.

I feel out of place in all this glitter.

"Come on," I say to Gladys, "let's get out of here."

She is angry with me as we walk down the street.

"You're spoiling your leave. Can't you forget the front for the few days you have before you?"

We are back in the pub.

More drinks.

She tells me amusing little bits of her life and I listen.

"...so when he left me I decided I'd stay on in London. I didn't know what to do so I took rooms in Baker Street and make a living that way. But I'm not like other girls..."

So!

Inside of her room a fire burns in the grate.

It is warm and cheery.

She takes off her hat and gloves, and prepares to make tea. The room is furnished with the taste of a woman of her profession. Ah, but it is welcome after two years in the line! I sit on a dainty settee facing the fire.

She comes back with tea and a small bottle of rum.

"Shall I lace it for you?"

I nod. She pours a little rum into the hot tea. We sit back and drink. She nestles up against me and with her free hand she takes off her shoes, then she slips off a stocking. As we talk she slowly undresses. Finally she stands up in only a gauzy slip.

The rum is tingling in every nerve. The fire throws a red glow over her white skin. She sits on my lap and then jumps up.

"My, but your uniform is rough."

I take a roll of pound notes out of my pocket. I put them on the table close at hand.

"Listen," I say. "I like you. Let me stay here for my ten days."

"I was going to say that to you, but I was afraid you might misunderstand me. Most of my boys spend their whole leave with me. I don't like them running off in the morning. It's a little insulting —"

She ends with a little laugh.

The fire crackles in the hearth. The rum sings in my head. The heat of the fire beats on my face. Her slim white body entices me.

Bang! An explosion in the street.

I leap to my feet.

My heart thumps.

She laughs.

"Silly. That's only a motorcycle backfiring. You poor thing! Your face is white."

She puts her hands on my face and looks anxiously at me.

I try to laugh.

We lie in bed. From a neighbouring clock the hour strikes. It is three o'clock.

One day gone!

Gladys's head lies in the crook of my arm.

"Happy?"

Her body makes a friendly, conscious movement. It is one of the many ways that lovers speak without works.

"Yes," I say in a whisper.

A tear comes to life and rolls down my face. She puts her hands to my eyes and wipes them.

"Then what are you crying about?"

I do not answer.

"You won't be cross if I tell you something?"

I shake my head.

"Promise?"

"I promise."

"I always feel sad when the boys cry in my bed. It makes me feel that it is my fault in some way."

Silence. Then:

"You're not angry because I have mentioned the other ones?"

I shake my head.

Cool hands on my face.

Her silken hair brushes against my cheek.

"Now, now — go to sleep, boy."

The clock booms the quarter-hour. I close my eyes.

I wake with the odour of grilled bacon in my nostrils. The curtains in the room are drawn. I do not know what time it is but I am rested. Rested and famished. In another room I hear the sizzling sound of cooking.

Gladys comes into the room. She is dressed in a calico house-dress. She smiles at me and says:

"Tea?"

She brings a cup of tea to me and we talk of the plans for the day.

I dress and come into the other room which is a combination dining and sitting-room and parlour.

There is a glorious breakfast on the table; grilled bacon, crisp and brown, two fried eggs, a pot of marmalade, a mound of toast, golden yellow and brown, and tea. I fall to.

Gladys looks on approvingly. How well this woman understands what a lonely soldier on leave requires.

"Eat, boy," she says.

She does not call me by name but uses "boy" instead. I like it. In a dozen different ways she makes me happy: a pat on the arm, a run of her hand through my hair.

She is that delightful combination of wife, mother, and courtesan — and I, a common soldier on leave, have her!

I slip into my tunic which by some mystery is now cleaned and pressed and we go out into the street and walk towards the Park.

The days slip by.

It is a week since I have been here with Gladys.

We are at table. She is a capable cook, and delights in showing me that her domestic virtues are as great as her amourous ones. I do not gainsay either.

We are drinking tea and discussing the plans for the evening. I do not like a moment to slip by without doing something. I am restlessly happy.

"I should like to go to Whitechapel this evening," I say.

She looks at me with surprise.

"Why?"

"I've heard so much about it. I want to see it."

"It's not nice there."

"I know, but I want to see more of London than just its music-halls, Hyde Park and its very wonderful pubs."

"But very low people live there, criminals and such things — you will be robbed."

"Well, I don't mind. I am a criminal. Did I ever tell you that I committed murder?"

She looks up with a jerk. Her eyes look at me with suspicion.

"It was some time ago. I came into a place where an enemy of mine was and I stabbed him and ran off," I explain.

Her eyes are wide open. She is horrified. She does not speak.

I laugh and relate that the murder took place in a trench and that my enemy wore a pot-shaped helmet.

Her face glows with a smile.

"You silly boy. I thought you had really murdered someone."

Westminster Abbey

Brown — musty — royal sepulchre.

I am alone.

I walk past statues of dead kings.

I yawn.

As I walk out in the bright sun-lit street I heave a sigh of relief. Well, I have been to Westminster Abbey. It is a duty.

As I come out, an Anglican curate sees my listless face.

It is wartime and no introductions are necessary.

"Hello."

"Hello."

"You look tired."

"Yes."

"On leave?"

"Yes. Going back tomorrow."

"Itching to get back, I'll wager."

"I'll be itching after I get back."

He laughs. He is the type known as a fighting parson — very athletic and boisterous.

"Ha, ha, that *is* a good one — you'll be itching *after* you get back. I must remember that one."

He asks if I will have tea with him at a nearby tea-room. The mustiness of the Abbey has dulled my wits and I can think of no ready excuse, so I accept.

We are seated at the table. He asks me innumerable questions about the war.

Isn't the spirit of the men simply splendid? Sobered everyone up. West End nuts who never took a single thing seriously leading their men into machine-gun fire armed only with walking sticks.

I remark that this is bad military procedure and add that it sounds like a newspaper story.

"Absolutely authentic, dear boy; a friend of mine came back and told me he saw it with his own eyes. Here, have a cigarette." I take one. I sit and smoke and listen to his views on the war. I am ill at ease and want to get back to Gladys.

He talks on.

"...but the best thing about the war, to my way of thinking, is that it has brought out the most heroic qualities in the common people, positively noble qualities..." He goes on and on.

I feel that it would be useless to tell him of Brownie, of how Karl died, of the snarling fighting among our own men over a crust of bread.

I offer to pay for the tea. He protests.

"No, no, by Jove, nothing too good for a soldier on leave — this is mine."

We part at the corner of the street.

"Good-by."

"Good-by, good luck, and God bless you, old man."

I hurry back to Gladys. Tonight is our last night together.

Morning.

The last day.

I am to leave Waterloo Station at noon. I have slept late. Gladys and I eat breakfast in silence. She is sad that I must go, of that there is no doubt. As I pack my things she brings a parcel to me which contains food, a bottle of whisky and cigarettes. I kiss her lightly as a gesture of thanks; she clings to me and hides her face from me.

Well, these things come to an end sooner or later...

We are at the station. The waiting-room is crowded with soldiers coming to London on leave. I envy them.

I say good-by to Gladys. She puts her arms around me. I feel her body being jerked by sobs. I kiss her passionately. She is all the things I have longed for in the long months in the trenches — and now I must go.

Her eyes are red and wet with tears. Her nose is red.

She looks up to me pathetically with weepy eyes.

"Have you been happy, boy?"

I think of the beautiful hours we have spent together and I nod.

Crowds mill on both sides of us. We are jostled.

I do not know how to go. I decide to be abrupt.

"Well, I think I'll have to be going."

Once more we embrace. She holds me tightly. I feel tears springing to my eyes. I lift her face to mine and kiss her wet eyes.

I run through the gate.

I look back.

She waves a crumpled handkerchief at me.

I wave my hand.

I climb into the carriage

The train begins to move.

H. Smalley Sarson

Two Fine Ladies

I saw two ladies in their car
    With seven Pekingese.
I know where your sisters sob
  The dragging hours away,
Where ever-toiling factories rob
  Children of their play.
Where squalid hovels like a scar
Hide Christ's humanities.
Two fine ladies in their car
    With seven Pekingese.

I have heard a mother cry
    Her anguishing distress
That her first-born had to die
    To please the passionless.
And I have watched your children mar
    Their beauty by disease
Two fine ladies in their car
    With seven Pekingese.

I know where your youth has died
In suffering and pain,
    That you might keep your honoured pride
To glory in your gain;
And I have watched an evening star
    Weep for their agonies.
Two fine ladies in their car
    With seven Pekingese.

I have smiled to hear you talk
    Of statesmanship and art,
I've watched your self-important walk
    And analysed your heart.
I know you for the fools you are
    Your puny vanities.
Two fine ladies in their car
    With seven Pekingese.

Hyde Park 1916

R.L.

SEGREGATION

"What's all this talk about 'Segregation of Canadian wounded,' Bill?" asked the Ontario man, applying a bit of chalk to his bandage where his cigarette had burnt a hole in it.

The Manitoba casualty shifted his crutch and his quid, and considered the subject deliberately.

"It's like this, Edward. They want all our fellows to be together instead o' being mixed up in English hospitals."

"But why shouldn't we be together — us and the English Tommies? We can learn a lot from one another. I guess they're afraid we'll be overheard cussin' our politicians — that's what it is."

"No, Edward, you haven't got the drift o' the idea at all. Do you happen in your benighted constituency to have heard of a French motto called *Shershy la femme*?"

"I'm an Orangeman," retorted the other, "an' I ain't goin' to incriminate myself. But I get your drift. Go on."

"Well, it's this way. I'm for segregation and I'll tell you why. It gives our Canadian nurses a chance. An' it's heaps more fun for our bunch. Now you know what an English nurse is like. You know she's a good nurse, a hard-working, kind-hearted, respectable nurse. But she ain't very young, and she ain't very gay. Mind you I wouldn't speak a word against her for the price of a Fort Garry town-lot, but does she, can she, compare with our saucy Canadian sky-blue lieutenants, with their pretty tresses done up in aprons? And not one of 'em over twenty-five summers! Why, to look at 'em alone is a treat. To have 'em hold your hand is a darn sight more amusing than getting' a D.C.M. from King George at Buckminster Palace. To my mind, Edward, them Canadian nurses, with their smiles and trim figures and Confederate cavalry hats and admirals overcoats (that they ought to wear inside out), are amongst the chief glories of this blamed war.

There's nothin' to beat it. It makes a fellow want to be wounded again an' again to go back to 'em, bless 'em."

"But what's all this got to do with segregation, Bill?"

"He has a right to one o' them sweet critters, instead o' havin' to put up with the homely, quiet, middle-aged Sisters that take your pulse and hand you out your dope in the English hospitals. Do you get me?"

"Yep, I get you all right. But you've forgotten something. You're an Imperialist, ain't you Bill?"

"Sure."

"Well, then, listen to me. What's our poor British brother done that he's to be shut off from this female treat that you've been so eloquently expropriating upon? We've nearly busted ourselves showing him what the boys of Canada can do in this war, and I guess we've impressed him some. Well, what about the girls of Canada? Ain't they to be given a show? We know 'em, we've seen 'em, we've feasted our eyes on 'em and flirted with 'em, and our officers are goin' to marry 'em all after the war. But what are we so darn selfish about? What are you goin' to build a high fence for 'em for? What it all comes to is that we're goin' to segregate our nurses, as if we was a lot o' benighted Mohamedans, so as the English Tommy couldn't get a sight o' one o' the finest Canadian products that ever made an immigrant's mouth water. It's mean policy an' I'm agin' it. We've made our sacrifices on the battlefield — let's make it in the hospital ward. I'm all for giving to Lieutenant Gladys and Lieutenant Esmeralda a chance to show these Yorkshire and Essex fellows that we raise something to beat prize pumpkins and No. 1 Hard. Do you get me, Bill?"

The Manitoba warrior cogitated. "You're puttin' up a tough proposition, Edward," he said at length, "but I guess this war is plumb full o' sacrifices."

Frank Prewett

I Stared At the Dead

When I awoke I had slept brief,
I waked to strangling of heart,
And I stood attempting new belief
That I thought, yet, was life apart.

I stood and stared at me dead:
Well folded my hands on my breast,
My stretch easy as in my bed,
And I grew troubled at my quest.

This is death before death, desire
Is now, I may know how to die
Before dying and at last acquire
News for all doomed ignorantly.

But while I stood I was seized
And forced into the body on the bed
With hardly a glimpse appeased
Of my soul when I had been dead.

Nellie L. McClung as told by Private Simmons

THE BLACKEST CHAPTER OF ALL
from THREE TIMES AND OUT

When the days were at their longest, some of the Russians who had been working for the farmers came into camp, refusing to go back because the farmers made them work such long hours. There is daylight-saving in Germany, which made the rising one hour earlier, and the other end of the day was always the "dark." This made about a seventeen-hour day, and the Russians rebelled against it. The farmers paid so much a day (about twenty-five cents) and then got all the work out of the prisoners they could; and some of them were worked unmercifully hard, and badly treated.

Each night, a few Russians, footsore, weary, and heavy-eyed from lack of sleep, trailed into camp with sullen faces, and we were afraid there was going to be trouble.

On the night of July 3rd, three tired Russians came into camp from the farms they had been working on after we had had our supper. The N.C.O. was waiting for them. The trouble had evidently been reported to Headquarters, and the orders had come back. The Commandant was there, to see that the orders were carried out.

In a few minutes the N.C.O. started the Russians to run up and down the space in front of the huts. We watched the performance in amazement. The men ran, with dragging footsteps, tired with their long tramp and their long day's work, but when their speed slackened, the N.C.O. threatened them with his bayonet.

For an hour they ran with never a minute's breathing spell, sweating, puffing, lurching in their gait, and still the merciless order was *"Marsch!" "Marsch!"* and the three men went struggling on.

When the darkness came, they were allowed to stop, but they were so exhausted they had to be helped to bed by their friends.

We did not realize that we had been witnessing the first act in the most brutal punishment that a human mind could devise, and, thinking that the trouble was over, we went to sleep, indignant at what we had seen.

In the morning, before any of us were awake, and about a quarter of an hour before the time to get up, a commotion started in our hut. German soldiers, dozens of them, came in, shouting to everybody to get up, and dragging the Russians out of bed. I was sleeping in an upper berth, but the first shout awakened me, and when I looked down I could see the soldiers flourishing their bayonets and threatening everybody. The Russians were scurrying out like scared rabbits, but the British, not so easily intimidated, were asking, "What's the row?"

One of the British, Walter Hurcum, was struck by a bayonet in the face, cutting a deep gash across his cheek and the lower part of his ear. Tom Morgan dodged a bayonet thrust by jumping behind the stove, and escaped without injury.

When I looked down, I caught the eyes of one of our guards, a decent old chap, of much the same type as Sank, and his eyes were full of misery and humiliation, but he was powerless to prevent the outbreak of frightfulness.

I dressed myself in my berth — the space below was too full already, and I thought I could face it better with my clothes on. When I got down, the hut was nearly empty, but a Gordon Highlander who went out of the door a few feet ahead of me was slashed at by one of the N.C.O.'s and jumped out of the way just in time.

All this was preliminary to roll-call, when we were all lined up to answer to our names. That morning the soup had lost what small resemblance it had had to soup — it had no more nourishment in it than dishwater. We began then to see that they were going to starve everyone into a desire to work.

We had not been taking soup in the morning, for it was, even at its best, a horrible dish to begin the day with. We had made tea or coffee of our own, and eaten something from our parcels. But this morning we were lined up with the Russians and given soup — whether we wanted it or not.

After the soup, the working parties were despatched, and then the three unhappy Russians were started on their endless journey again, racing up and down, up and down, with an N.C.O. standing in the middle to keep them going. They looked pale and worn from their hard experience of the night before, but no Bengal tiger ever had less mercy than the N.C.O., who kept them running.

The distance across the end of the yard was about seventy-five feet, and up and down the Russians ran. Their pace was a fast trot, but before long they were showing signs of great fatigue. They looked pitifully at us as they passed us, wondering what it was all about, and so did we. We expected every minute it would be over; surely they had been punished enough. But the cruel race went on.

In an hour they were begging for mercy, whimpering pitifully, as they gasped out the only German word they know — "*Kamerad — Kamerad*" — to the N.C.O., who drove them on. They begged and prayed in their own language; a thrust of the bayonet was all the answer they got.

Their heads rolled, their tongues protruded, their lips frothed, their eyes were red and scalded — and one fell prostrate at the feet of the N.C.O., who, stooping over, rolled back his eyelid to see if he were really unconscious or was feigning it. His examination proved the latter to be the case, and I saw the Commandant motion to him to kick the Russian to his feet. This he did with right goodwill and the weary race went on.

But the Russian race was nearly ended, for in another half-dozen rounds he fell, shuddering and moaning, to the ground — and no kick or bayonet thrust could rouse him.

Another one rolled over and over in a fit, purple in the face, and twitching horribly. He rolled over and over until he fell into the drain, and lay there, unattended.

The last one, a very wiry fellow, kept going long after the other two, his strength a curse to him now, for it prolonged his agony, but he fell out at last, and escaped their cruelty, at least for the time, through the black door of unconsciousness.

Then they were gathered up by some of the prisoners, and carried into the *Revier*.

Just as the three unconscious ones were carried away, three other Russians, not knowing what was in store for them, came in. We did not see them until they walked in at the gate. They also had been on farms, and were now refusing to work longer. They came into the hut, where their frightened countrymen were huddled together, some praying and some in tears. The newcomers did not know what had happened. But they were not left long in doubt. An N.C.O. called to them to *"heraus,"* and when they came into the yard, he started them to run. The men were tired and hungry. They had already spent months on the farms, working long hours: that did not save them. They had dared to rebel, so their spirits must be broken.

Our hearts were torn with rage and pity. We stormed in and out of the huts like crazy men, but there was nothing we could do. There were so few of us, and of course we were unarmed. There was no protest or entreaty we could make that would have made any appeal. Orders were orders! It was for the good of Germany — to make her a greater nation — that these men should work — the longer hours the better — to help to reclaim the bad land, to cultivate the fields, to raise more crops to feed more soldiers to take more prisoners to cultivate more land to raise more crops.

It was perfectly clear to the Teutonic mind. No link in the chain must be broken. *Deutschland über Alles!*

At noon the Russians were still running — it is astonishing what the human machine can stand! The N.C.O. impatiently snapped his watch and slashed at the one who was passing him, to speed them up, and so hasten the process. He was getting hungry and wanted his dinner. Then an order came from the Commandant that it was to be stopped — and we hoped again, as we had the night before, that this was the end.

We brought the three poor fellows, pale and trembling, to our end of the hut, and gave them as good a meal as our parcels would afford. One of them had a bayonet wound in his neck, which the N.C.O. had given him. He had jabbed him with the point of his bayonet, to quicken his speed. In spite of their exhaustion, they ate ravenously, and fell asleep at once, worn out with the long hours of working as well as by the brutal treatment they had received.

But there was no sleep for the poor victims — until the long, black sleep of unconsciousness rolled over them and in mercy blotted out their misery — for the N.C.O.'s came for them and dragged them away from us, and the sickening spectacle began again.

There were just eleven of us, British and Canadians, in the camp at this time, twelve of the British having been sent away; and it happened that this was the day, July 4th, that we wrote our cards. We remembered that when the men had written cards about the lice it had brought results: we had no other way of communication with the world, and although this was a very poor one, still it was all we had. We knew our cards would never get out of Germany; indeed, we were afraid they would never leave the camp, but we would try.

We went to the place where the cards were kept, which was in charge of a Polish Jew, who also acted as interpreter. He had been in the Russian Army, and had been taken prisoner in the early days of the war. There was a young Russian with him who did clerical work in the camp. They were both in tears. The Jew walked up and down, wringing his hands and calling upon the God of Abraham and of Isaac and of Jacob! Sometimes he put his hands over his ears — for the cries of his countrymen came through the window.

When we got our cards, we wrote about what had happened. Some of the cards were written to John Bull; some to the British War Office; some to the newspapers; some to friends in England, imploring them to appeal to the United States government at Washington, to interfere for humanity's sake. We eased our minds by saying, as far as we could say it on a card, what we thought of the Germans. Every card was full of it, but the subject was hardly touched. I never knew before the full meaning of that phrase, "Words are inadequate."

Words were no relief! — we wanted to kill — kill —kill.

The running of the Russians went on for days. Every one of them who came in from the farm got it — without mercy. Different N.C.O.'s performed the gruesome rites...

We had only one hope of quick results. The Commandant of the camp at Celle — that is the main Cellelager — had an English wife, and had, perhaps for that reason, been deprived of his command as an Admiral of the fleet. We hoped he would hear of our cards — or, better still, that his wife might hear.

The first indication we had that our cards had taken effect was the change in the soup. Since the first day of the trouble, it had been absolutely worthless. Suddenly it went back to normal — or a little better.

Suddenly, too, the running of the Russians stopped, although others of them had come in. A tremendous house-cleaning began — they had us scrubbing everything. The bunks were aired; the blankets hung on the fence; the windows cleaned; the yard was polished by much sweeping. Evidently someone was coming, we hoped it was "the Admiral." At the same time, the N.C.O.'s grew very polite to us, and one of them, who had been particularly vicious with the Russians, actually bade me "good morning" — something entirely without precedent.

Every day, I think, they expected the Admiral, but it was two weeks before he came. His visit was a relief to the Germans, but a distinct disappointment to us. Apparently, the having of an English wife does not change the heart of a German. It takes more than that. He did not forbid the running of the Russians; only the bayonet must not be used. The bayonet was bad form — it leaves marks. Perhaps the Admiral took his stand in order to reinstate himself again in favour with the military authorities and anxious to show that his English wife had not weakened him. He had the real stuff in him still — blood and iron!

The running of the Russians began again — but behind the trees, where we could not see them...but we could hear...

There are some things it were well we could forget!

The running of the Russians ceased only when no more came in from the farms. Those who had been put out came out of the *Revier* in a day or so — some in few hours — pale and spiritless, and were sent back to work again. They had the saddest-looking faces I ever saw — old and wistful, some of them; others, gaping and vacant; some, wild and staring. They would never resist again — they were surely broken! And while these men would not do much for the "Fatherland" in the way of heavy labour, they would do very well for exchanges!

Bernard Freeman Trotter

Ici Repose

A little cross of weather-silvered wood,
Hung with a garish wreath of tinselled wire,
And on it carved a legend—thus it runs:
"*Ici repose—*" Add what name you will,
And multiply by thousands: in the fields,
Along the roads, beneath the trees—one here,
A dozen there, to each its simple tale
Of one more jewel threaded star-like on
The sacrificial rosary of France.

And as I read and read again those words,
Those simple words, they took a mystic sense;
And from the glamour of an alien tongue
They wove insistent music in my brain,
Which, in a twilight hour, when all the guns
Were silent, shaped itself to song.

O happy dead! who sleep embalmed in glory,
*   Safe from corruption, purified by fire—*
Ask you our pity?—ours, mud-grimed and gory,
*   Who still must firmly strive, grimly desire?*

You have outrun the reach of our endeavour,
*   Have flown beyond our most exalted quest—*
Who prate of Faith and Freedom, knowing ever
*   That all we really fight for's just—a rest,*

The rest that only Victory can bring us—
   Or Death, which throws us brother-like by you—
The civil commonplace in which 'twill fling us
   To neutralize our then too martial hue.

But you have rest from every tribulation
   Even in the midst of war; you sleep serene,
Pinnacled on the sorrow of a nation,
   In cerements of sacrificial sheen.

Oblivion cannot claim you: our heroic
   War-lustred moment, as our youth, will pass
To swell the dusty hoard of Time the Stoic,
   That gathers cobwebs in the nether glass.

We shall grow old, and tainted with the rotten
   Effluvia of the peace we fought to win,
The bright deeds of our youth will be forgotten,
   Effaced by later failure, sloth, or sin;

But you have conquered Time, and sleep forever,
   Like gods, with a white halo on your brows—
Your souls our lode-stars, your death-crowned endeavour
   The spur that holds the nations to their vows.

France, *April* 1917

   (His last poem, the manuscript of which reached his parents the day after he
   was killed.)

First Trooper (*coming upon Boche who has been lying for hours on the wrong side of the parapet*) — Wot's he yelling for Charley?

Second Trooper — Search me! Sounds like "Vasser! Vasser!"

First Trooper (*shareholder in Chesebrough*) — M-m! Try him with some Vasser-line.

James Hanley

THE GERMAN PRISONER

Just as dusk was drawing in, the battalion pulled into Boves. It had marched thirty kilometres that day. The men were tired, black with sweat, and ravenous with hunger. They were shepherded into one of those huge French houses, which now seemed more stable than house, alas. After some confusion and delay they were served out with hot tea, stew of a kind, and bread. The food was attacked with a savagery almost unbelievable. The heavier parts of kit had been thrown off, men sprawled everywhere. They filled the rooms with their sweat; their almost pesty breath.

"The Battalion will move off in three hours' time," announced a sergeant, the volcanic tones of whose voice seemed to shake the house itself. He also made the following announcement.

"Those who have not yet made out wills, had better see the orderly sergeant at once."

Then all became silent as before. In the darkest corner of one of the rooms on the ground floor, lay two men. They were facing each other, and even in this recumbent position their physical contrasts were striking. The taller and more hefty of the two, one Peter O'Garra, said:

"I hope this 'do' won't be as big a balls-up as the last lot."

He spat upon the floor, following up the action by drawing the flat of his hand across his mouth.

"I don't think so," said his companion, a man from Manchester, named Elston.

"You never know," said O'Garra; "these funkin' bastards at the back; you never know what game they're up to."

"We'll see," replied the Manchester man.

Peter O'Garra was forty-four years of age. He came from Tara Street, known as the filthiest street in all Dublin. He had lodged there with a Mrs. Doolan, an old hag who had looked more like a monstrous spider than a woman. O'Garra was very well known in Tara Street. In those fifteen years he had been known as, "a strange man — a misanthrope — a Belfast Bastard (his birth-place — a lousy bugger — a rake — a closet — a quiet fellow — a tub of guts — a pimp — a shit-house — a toad — a sucker — a blasted sod — a Holy Roller — a Tara lemon — a Judas — a jumped-up liar — a book-worm — a traitor to Ireland — a pervert — an Irish jew — an Irish Christ — a clod."

It was rumoured that he had never worked, and had at one time been crossed in love. It was known that he used to stand beneath the clock in Middle Abbey Street, stalking the women, all of whom are supposed to have fled in terror. O'Garra could never understand this, until he discovered it was his ugly mouth that used to frighten the women. It was his most outstanding characteristic. It made him something more than a man. A threat. The children in Tara Street used to run after him, calling him, "Owld click", because he made a peculiar clicking sound with his false teeth. But all Tara Street was surprised when he went for a soldier. Not only the men, women, and children, but even the houses and roofs and chimney pots, the very paving stones, joined in song. They became humanized. And the song they sang was that Peter O'Garra's blood was heavy with surrender.

"His blood is heavy with surrender," they sang.

As soon as the blood is heavy with surrender — *Act.* O'Garra had acted. And Tara Street saw him no more. Perhaps what it had already seen of him was enough. Already there were a number of lines upon his forehead; the years had traced their journey-work through his hair; his eyes resembled the dried-up beds of African lakes. But it was his mouth above all that one noticed. If one wished to know O'Garra, one looked at his mouth. Once Elston had asked him what he thought of the war. He had said:

"Well it's just a degree of blood bitterness, and bitter blood is good blood. Personally, it is a change for me from the rather drab life of Tara Street, with its lousiness, its smells, its human animals herded together, its stinkin' mattresses."

Elston had yawned and remarked:

"My views are different. There is nothing I long for so much as to get back to the smoke and fog and grease of Manchester. I like the filth and rottenness because it is warm. Yes, I long to get back to my little corner, my little world."

In Dublin, a fellow like Elston, a kind of human rat, would get short shrift. To O'Garra he was "the Hungry Englishman" *par excellence*. And he had little time for Englishmen, especially the suck-holing type. Still he remembered that he was his bed-mate, his one companion in this huge mass of desperate life. When first he had set eyes on Elston, he had despised him, there was something in this man entirely repugnant to him. He had once written on a piece of paper, the following lines:

"There's an Englishman named Elston
By the living Christ I swear
Necessity has never hewn
One like him anywhere."

"Have you any idea at all?" asked O'Garra — "as to where we're goin'?"

The Manchester man smiled. His small ferrety eyes seemed to blink.

"Gorman thinks we're marchin' up to the jumpin'-off point, tonight. I suppose they'll want us to take back all the bloody ground the Fifth lost, last year. God blast them."

"Division you mean?" queried O'Garra.

"Yes," replied Elston.

"I suppose we'll be met by a guide. Time they were movin' anyhow. See the time," and he showed Elston his watch. "Remember the last time, don't you? Confusion, delay, roads blocked up. Guide drunk and lost himself. Result. Caught in single file at daylight. One of his 'uckin' observation balloons at work. Next thing a salvo of five-nines and seven men lost."

"Hope it won't be like that this time," said Elston in a quiet voice.

A voice bawled out — FALL IN. And the men filed down the stairs and into the yard. O'Garra and Elston filed out too, and took their places in line with the others. Darkness, gloom, and silence. This darkness was so intense that one could almost feel it. It is just that kind of darkness which falls with the most dramatic suddenness. The men could barely see one another. By feeling with their hands they became aware that they were in line. All was in order. Gorman came out, though he was not discernible. But one recognized the voice. Names were called and answered LEFT TURN. QUICK MARCH.

The files moved. In that blackness they resembled the rather dim outlines of huge snakes, as they turned out of the yard and on to the white road. In the road they halted once more. Nobody spoke. The officers came up. Another order, and the men began to nose their way towards the line. One could not say they walked erect, but just that they nosed their way forward. In five minutes order had given way to confusion. This was inevitable. Roads were blocked. All space around seemed to be festered, suffocated by this physical material; by guns, limbers, ambulances, mules, horses, more guns, more wagons and limbers. And men. Suddenly O'Garra slipped into a hole.

"Jesus Christ! Already," growled Elston.

He dragged O'Garra out, following up the action by falling in himself. One saw nothing. Nothing. There was something infinite about the action of feeling. One was just conscious that the night was deluged by phantom-like movements. That was all. Far ahead the sky was lighted up by a series of periodic flashes. Then a vast concourse of sound, then silence. The roads were impassable. The men were separated, relying on an occasional whisper, an occasional feel of a hand or bayonet, to establish contact with one another. Crawling beneath wagons and guns, now held up by mud. A traffic block.

"Elston man," said O'Garra; "how in hell are they goin' to get all this lot up before daylight? It's impossible. They'll never clear the road."

"Think of yourself," replied Elston. "We have to go a mile and a half yet. And let's hope the guide is there. You know it's not the trenches I hate. No. It's this damned business of getting into them, and out of them again too. Every time I think of those sons of bitches at the base, I get mad."

There was no reply to this remark. The men wormed their way ahead. In that terrible moment when all reason seemed to have surrendered to chaos, men became, as it were, welded together. Occasionally one saw a humped back, the outline of a profile, the shadow of legs. A huge eyeless monster that forged its way ahead towards some inevitable destiny. Nothing more. At last the road seemed a little easier. Elston spoke.

"I was over this same ground, last July. I believe we turn here. The trench-system proper commences somewhere about here. To the right I think. Funny though. I once saw an aerial photograph of these same trenches. Took it off a Jerry who crashed. Looked like a huge crucifix in shape."

"You mean a cross," said O'Garra.

"Yes."

"H'm. Cross. The bloody country is littered with them. I once saw one of those crosses, with the figure of Jesus plastered in shite. Down on the Montauban road."

"Had somebody deliberately plastered it?" asked Elston.

"No. A five-nine landed behind it, and the figure pitched into one of those latrines," replied O'Garra.

"Did you ever make a point of studying the different features of these figures?" asked Elston.

"Saw half-a-dozen. Didn't bother after that. Reminded me of the Irish Christ. All blood and tears."

Again silence. Suddenly a voice whispered — PULL UP.

The order was passed down the line. PULL UP.

More confusion, babble of voices, whisperings, curses, threats.

"What's the matter?"

"Lost the way."

O'Garra shivered. Pulled out his watch and noted the time. He said to the man from Manchester:

"Won't be long before it's light. Must have been over four hours pawing about these blasted roads."

Elston gave a kind of growl. O'Garra growled too. One had to do something. After all, it was better than standing still, helpless. He, O'Garra, once said that the war had quickened his critical spirit:

"After all, the end of man is rather ignominious. No. I don't blame even the simplest of men for endeavouring to go down to the grave in a blaze of glory."

Again an order. In almost a whisper.

"Get contact and move on."

Once more the men moved along in single file. The road seemed clearer here, and the officer knew that but a thousand yards ahead a guide would be waiting to take them up to the old trenches of '16.

That officer, whose name was "Snow-Ball" was at present worrying over his men. He must certainly get them under cover before it got light. It might be too late in half an hour or so, and then progress was so slow. There were, of course, two reasons for this state of mind. Firstly, he might lose a few men; secondly, it might disclose (more important still), the movements of troops, going up for what, to the Germans, would be an attack on the grand scale. Far back, at the very tail end of this file of men, the Irishman was explaining to his English friend that:

"It looked as though the guide had failed to turn up, after all. I had a curious feeling something would happen," he muttered.

"Cheer up," said Elston.

"It's turned half-past six, you fool. Cheer up. That bugger in front wants to cheer up. Doesn't know what to do, I'll bet. Same old thing every time. Flummuxed. I think they get a bug on the brain sometimes."

"Yes. It's getting light now alright," remarked Elston, and there was a frightfulness about the tone in which he uttered these words.

"We can't arse about here much longer. Wonder those fellows up in front don't have something to say to him."

Down on the line came an order. FILE MOVE ON.

The men moved on. And now, what had merely been a germ, became a disease, an epidemic. The torment was no longer private, but general. To all these men it became apparent that something had happened. When something went wrong the more sensitive spirits became agitated. One saw it in their eyes. Like a man conscious of Death, who begins to sense the earthiness of the grave about him. Elston remarked that it was about time they reached the trench.

"I know the ground well, at least I should think I ought to. To the direct north of this trench-network, you'll find a trench once begun but left unfinished. We used it for shelter on one occasion during heavy shelling. We were changing positions one night. It's not much in an emergency, but better than nothing. Only about three feet deep. No covey holes either. Jerry has it spotted too."

Suddenly there was a low whine. Someone ahead shouted LOOKOUT, and the line was thrown into confusion once more. The shell exploded about twenty yards ahead of Elston and O'Garra. There was a scream.

"Christ!" exclaimed Elston. "He's feelin'.' Now we're for it."

"I should think so," growled O'Garra. "It's gettin' light already. When is that bastard in front goin' to do something?"

"He can't do anything if the guide is lost, or failed to turn up."

Already it was light. The men now began to murmur threats against the officer in front. Far ahead somebody had espied a balloon. Somebody shouted from the middle of the file:

"Has that soft runt gone mad? He'll get one bloody quick himself. I suppose he'll ask us to form fours and march in ceremonial style."

It was quite light now. One could see the wilderness all around. Here and there a gnarled tree-stump. Far back one visioned the packed roads and became fearful of consequences. O'Garra thumped Elston.

"Let's go to him. The fool's crazy. Stark staring mad."

LOOKOUT.

There came another shell, exploding right in their midst, so it seemed. Out of the smoke and stench there came sounds of moaning.

"That's only the beginning," said Elston. "Someone caught it alright."

It got seven men. An order was passed down from one to the other.

RUN FOR IT.

Both Elston and O'Garra made for a rise in the ground. Elston said:

"In here. Quick."

Both men sprawled into this unfinished trench.

"This way fellows," shouted Elston.

Soon the remaining men had skeltered across the broken ground, and had jumped into the trench.

"We're here for the bloody day," remarked a lance corporal.

Elston and O'Garra agreed.

The Irishman still saw in his mind's eye, the mangled body of Gorman. Elston had helped him get the papers from his pocket. He had vomited too, for Gorman's brains were splattered on his forehead.

"Think I'll go to kip for a while," said O'Garra. Elston agreed too. The other men were endeavouring to make themselves comfortable, when the sergeant, named Grundy, said he was going to post certain men. On hearing this, all and sundry broke into loud cursings and obscene oaths.

"If that son of a bitch — well by Christ — I — I —"

"I feel rotten tired," sighed Elston.

As soon as darkness set in they were going to move out again, and continue their march until they reached the jumping-off point. An officer was expected up before they moved out. But Grundy knew that no officer would arrive. He was quite prepared to take the responsibility of getting the men up to the jumping-off point mapped out for them.

Finally Grundy had men posted every four hours until nightfall. He knew how lucky they had been to escape so lightly. And what a blasted rotten trench they were in. No protection from flying craft. Exposed to everything.

"If that officer gets here safely," thought the Sergeant, "it'll be a miracle."

At ten-fifteen the men broke cover, and continued on in single file across the broken ground, pitted here and there by yawning shell holes filled with stagnant and stinking water. A voice was heard then.

"TAPE LINE HERE."

And each man felt that at last he was near his final destination. O'Garra himself has espied this tape line, well concealed in the grass. Only the bundles of twigs indicated to the men that that long line of white tape was their infallible guide.

"We follow this I suppose until told to pull up."

"Correct," said the Manchester man. "It won't be long now."

They gripped each other's hand and continued in this fashion until they heard the order to halt. No. They wouldn't be long now.

∞∞∞

At two o'clock rations came along. These were handed down the trench from man to man. Bread, jam, tea. For three hours the men had been standing up to their thighs in water. O'Garra had loosed from his angry and tormented being a series of curses. Likewise Elston. All the men murmured. The orders were now known. Objective five thousand yards. On the right, the Aussies, on the left, the French. Centre body would make for the Albert-Roye road. The barrage would open up shortly after five. Something approaching awe seemed to hang over the trenches. All was silent.

But soon the secret rage lurking in the ground beneath their feet would burst forth. The attack opened up on the very stroke of five.

O'Garra was half drunk. He had very rarely taken his ration of rum, but Elston had used persuasion to such effect that O'Garra had drunk another soldier's ration as well as his own. A whistle blew. The earth seemed to shake. They were over the top.

And now every sound and every movement seemed to strike some responsive chord in the Irishman's nature. He hung on desperately to the Manchester man. For some reason or other he dreaded losing contact with him. He could not understand this sudden desire for Elston's company. But the desire overwhelmed him.

It was not the sound, the huge concourse of sound that worried O'Garra. For somehow the earth in convulsion seemed a kind of yawning mouth, swallowing noise. No. It was the gun flashes ahead. They seemed to rip the very sky asunder. Great pendulums of flame swinging across the sky. In that moment they appeared to him like the pendulums of his own life. Swinging from splendour to power, from terror to pity, from Life to Death. More than that. There was a continuous flash away on his right. It was more than a flash. It was an eye that ransacked his very soul.

"Jesus! Jesus!"

The earth was alive — afire. The earth was a mouth, it was a sea, a yawning gulf, a huge maw. Suddenly Elston was drenched in blood. Like a stuck pig he screamed out:

"O funkin' hell. I'm killed. I'm dead. O'Garra. O'Garra. O'Garra."

"Shut up," growled the Irishman. "Can't you see the bugger behind you? You got a belt in the back with his head. See? He hasn't any now. That whizz-bang took head and arse off him at the same time... Phew! Everybody's mad."

"If ever I get out of this," screamed Elston, "I'll — I'll —"

Grundy came up.

"Shit on you. Get forward. What the hell are you fellows standing here for? You bloody cowards," he roared into their ears.

"What the bloody hell's wrong with you?" growled the Irishman. "This fellow here thought his head was off. Everything alright, isn't it? We're going forward. Are you? You lump of shite.

How long have you been in the line anyhow? When you've learned to piss in your cap, you sucker, you'll have room to talk."

And Sergeant Grundy thought to himself:

"I suppose he thinks he was the only one in the first gas-attack. H'm."

"I'll put a bullet in the first man who wavers," he roared out.

The men struggled forward. It was impossible to see, to hear, to feel. All the senses were numbed. O'Garra's face was almost yeasty with sweat. He spat continually, at the same time cursing Grundy, and endeavouring to keep this man from Manchester upon his feet.

"Oh hell!" he yelled. "Are you utterly helpless? Stand up."

With the speed of terror Elston screamed out.

"Yes. Yes. I'm frightened. Oh mother! Mother! Mother!"

"Shut it, you bloody worm," growled O'Garra, and continued on his way, dragging the Englishman after him.

"Where are they drivin' us to, anyhow?" asked a man from Cork.

"Towards the bloody objective of course. Where in hell d'you think."

"We fairly fanned his backside," yelled another man from Donegal.

The screams of the shells, the *plop-plop* of the gas-shells, the staccato drumming of the machine guns, the shouts and squeals and blubberings, almost upset even a man like O'Garra.

"This is not so bad," he murmured. "The thing is — will these blasted sods come back? That's what we have to look out for."

"Come back," yelled a voice. "Christ, you'll want running pumps to catch the swine."

Then suddenly O'Garra stopped. He no longer heard the sounds of voices. True, the man from Manchester was at his side. But where were the others? And a thick fog was descending. For a moment he seemed to lose contact with the whimperer at his side. And O'Garra shouted:

"Elston. Elston. Hey Elston! Where are you? Something's happened. Can you see? Hey! Hey! Can you see? This bloody fog's thickening."

Elston blinked and stood erect. Then his face paled. He said slowly:

"We must have gone too far. Lost contact somehow. We must search about quickly."

"Too far. Too far," shouted O'Garra, and he burst out laughing.

Yes. There was the possibility of that. He had seemed to eat up distance after that scrap with the sergeant. And then he must have dragged this English coward some distance too. Before they were aware of it, the fog had blotted everything out. They were now conscious only of each other's presence. This fog had separated them from all that madness, that surging desperate mass of matter; that eyeless monster; that screaming phalanx. The fog became so thick it was almost impossible for them to see each other.

"We must do something," said Elston. "God knows where we landed."

"Maybe into his bloody line," growled O'Garra.

They both sat down on the edge of the shell hole to consider their position.

They seemed oblivious of the fact that the attack had not abated. That to the right a team of tanks was shooting forward on to the machine-gun positions; that a thousand yards to the rear a mopping-up party was at work. Oblivious of war and life itself. A strange silence seemed to overwhelm them. O'Garra rested his head in his hands. Suddenly he sat up, gripped Elston by the throat, and said:

"I've a mind to choke you. To put you out of your misery. How funny that in the moment I first realized your cowardice, I became unconscious of my own strength. I must have pulled you a mile, you swine."

The blood came and went across Elston's face in a sudden gust of fear and passion.

"What good would that do you? Especially at this moment?"

O'Garra once more buried his face in his hands, and remained silent. Elston was thinking. What was wrong? And had O'Garra really dragged him a mile? And had they really lost contact? Where in Christ's name had they landed? And did this man really mean to murder him? By God, then the sooner they found the others, the better. Perhaps he had suddenly gone mad? By God. That was it. He had gone mad. Mad.

"O'Garra," called Elston to the man now seated on the edge of the hole. "O'Garra! O'Garra!"

There was no reply, for the Irishman had fallen asleep. This discovery petrified Elston. The consciousness that he was absolutely alone; alone, save for this sleeping figure, caused a kind of icy mist to descend upon his heart, almost suffocating him. He too sunk his head between his hands. The action was profound, for it seemed to the man to shut out thought, action, all external contacts with the world. But O'Garra was not asleep for long. He opened his eyes, looked across at the huddled form of the Manchester man, heaved a sigh, then fell back again into a kind of torpor. O'Garra suddenly began to think, and to think deeply. This process he found painful, as it always is for those who have ceased to think over a period of years. His was an atrophied mind. But now the whole of his past shot across the surface of that mind. He asked himself, if he would not have been better off in Tara Street after all. Even those lonely nights, those fruitless endeavours beneath the clock in Middle Abbey Street, surely they took on a richer texture now. Surely all those commonplace things achieved a certain significance. Those times when his mind had remained simple; when he had been wont to enjoy those sweet charities of life itself. After all there was something in it. Why had he come into all this muck and mud and madness? He could not find any answer to the question. Then again, there was that after-the-war question. Would the men be compensated for all the inconveniences? *All* the inconveniences? All the men? Would they? He had a grudge. Only this morning he had had one against a foolish officer, and yet the sight of that officer's headless body had stirred something deep down in the bosom of his soul. He had borne a grudge. But that was forgiven. There were so many. Did not this state of affairs warrant some kind of vengeance?

Perhaps it did. But how would a man get it? Everyone in the war must bear a grudge. But would they all demand retribution? Would they all wreak a terrible vengeance. Ah! — .

ℰℰℰ

"Elston!"

"Yes."

"Oh! you're awake. I say, we must have slept a hell of a time. My watch has stopped too. This blasted fog hasn't risen yet, either. We'd better move."

"What's that you say?"

"What's up now? Got the bloody shakes again?" asked O'Garra.

"Listen," said Elston.

Somewhere ahead they could hear the movement of some form or other.

"Let's find out," said O'Garra, and jumped to his feet.

"No need now," said Elston. "Here it comes. Look!"

They both looked up at once. Right on top of them stood a young German soldier. His hands were stuck high in the air. He was weaponless. His clothes hung in shreds and his face was covered with mud. He looked tired and utterly weary. He said in a plaintive kind of voice.

"Camerade. Camerade."

"Camerade, you bastard," said Elston, "keep your hands up there."

And O'Garra asked: "Who are you? Where do you come from? Can you speak English? Open your soddin' mouth."

"Camerade. Camerade."

"You speak English, Camerade?"

"Yes — a little."

"Your name," demanded Elston. "What regiment are you? Where are we now? No tricks. If you do anything, you'll get your bottom kicked. Now then — where have you come from, and what the hell do you want?"

"My name it is Otto Reiburg. My home it is Muenchen. I am Bavarian. I surrender, Camerade."

"That's all," growled Elston.

"I am lost, is it," replied the German.

He was a youth, about eighteen years of age, tall, with a form as graceful as a young sapling, in spite of the ill-fitting uniform and unkempt appearance. His hair, which stuck out in great tufts from beneath his forage cap, was as fair as ripe corn. He had blue eyes, and finely moulded features.

"So are we," said Elston. "We are lost too. Is it foggy where you came from? It looks to me as if we'll never get out of this hole, only by stirring ourselves together and making a bolt for it."

"That's impossible," said O'Garra. "True, we can move. But what use is that? And perhaps this sod is leading us into a trap. Why not finish the bugger off, anyhow?"

The two men looked at the young German, and smiled. But the youth seemed to have sensed the something sinister in that smile. He began to move off. Elston immediately jumped up. Catching the young German by the shoulder he flung him to the bottom of the hole, saying:

"If you try that on again I'll cut the bollocks out of you. Why should you not suffer as well as us? Do you understand what I am saying? Shit on you," and he spat savagely into the German's face. From the position the youth was lying in, it was impossible for either of the men to see that he was weeping. Indeed, had Elston seen it, he would undoubtedly have killed him. There was something terrible stirring in this weasel's blood. He knew not what it was. But there was a strange and powerful force possessing him, and it was going to use him as its instrument. He felt a power growing on him. There was something repugnant, something revolting in those eyes, in their leer, and in the curled lips. Was it that in that moment itself, all the rottenness that was his life had suddenly shot up as filth from a sewer, leaving him helpless in everything but the act he was going to commit? O'Garra was watching Elston. He too, seemed to have sensed this something terrible.

His gaze wandered from Elston to the young German. No word was spoken. The silence was intense. Horrible. These three men, who but an hour ago, seemed to be charged for action, eager and vital, looked as helpless as children now. Was it that this fog surrounding them had pierced its way into their hearts and souls? Or was it that something in their very nature had suffered collapse?

One could not say that they sat, or merely lay; they just sprawled; each terribly conscious of the other's presence, and in that presence detecting something sinister; something that leered; that goaded and pricked. Each seemed to have lost his faculty of speech. The fog had hemmed them in. Nor could any of them realize their position, where they were, the possibility of establishing contact with other human beings. What was this something that had so hurled them together?

O'Garra looked across to Elston.

"Elston! Elston! What are we going to do? We must get out of this. Besides the place stinks. Perhaps we are on very old ground. Rotten ground; mashy muddy ground. Christ the place must be full of these mangy dead."

Elston did not answer. And suddenly O'Garra fell upon him, beating him in the face, and screaming out at the top of his voice:

"Hey. Hey. You lousy son of a bitch. What's your game? Are you trying to make me as rotten as yourself, as cowardly, as lousy? It's you and not this bloody Jerry who is responsible for this. Do you hear me? Do you hear me? Jesus Christ Almighty, why don't you answer? Answer. Answer."

The young German cowered in the bottom of the hole, trembling like a leaf. Terror had seized him. His face seemed to take on different colour, now white, now red, now grey, as if Death were already in the offing. Saliva trickled down his chin.

These changes of colour in the face seemed to pass across it like gusts of wind. Gusts of fear, terror, despair. Once only he glanced up at the now distorted features of the half-crazy Irishman, and made as if to cry out. Once again O'Garra spoke to Elston. Then it was that the Englishman opened his eyes, looked across at his mate, and shouted:

"O'Garra! O'Garra. Oh where the funkin' hell are you, O'Garra?"

He stared hard at the Irishman, who, though his lips barely moved, yet uttered sounds:

"In a bloody mad-house. In a shit hole. Can't you smell the rotten dead? Can you hear? Can you hear? You louse, you bloody rat. Pretending to be asleep and all the while your blasted owl's eyes have been glaring at me. Ugh! Ugh!"

"Camerade."

A sigh came from the youth lying at the bottom of the hole. It was almost flute-like, having a liquidity of tone.

"Ah! -uck you," growled O'Garra. "You're as much to blame as anybody. Yes. Yes. As much to blame as anybody. Who in the name of Jesus asked you to come here? Haven't I that bastard there to look after? The coward. Didn't I have to drag him across the ground during the advance? Yes. YOU. YOU. YOU," and O'Garra commenced to kick the prisoner in the face until it resembled a piece of raw beef. The prisoner moaned. As soon as O'Garra saw the stream of blood gush forth from the German's mouth, he burst into tears. Elston too, seemed to have been stirred into action by this furious onslaught on the youth. He kicked the German in the midriff, making him scream like a stuck pig. It was this scream that loosed all the springs of action in the Manchester man. It cut him to the heart, this scream. Impotency and futility seemed as ghouls leering at him, goading him, maddening him.

He started to kick the youth in the face too. But now no further sound came from that inert heap. The Englishman dragged himself across to O'Garra. But the Irishman pushed him off.

"Get away. I hate you. Hate you. HIM. Everybody. Hate all. Go away. AWAY."

"By Jesus I will then," shouted Elston. "Think I'm a bloody fool to sit here with two madmen. I'm going. Don't know where I'll land. But anything is better than this. It's worse than hell."

He rose to his feet and commenced to climb out of the hole. He looked ahead. Fog. And behind. Fog. Everywhere Fog. No sound. No stir. He made a step forward when O'Garra leaped up and dragged him back. Some reason seemed to have returned to him, for he said:

"Don't go. Stay here. Listen. This state of affairs cannot go on for ever. The fog will lift. Are you listening, and not telling yourself that I am mad? I am not mad. Do you understand? Do you understand? Tell me!"

"Is it day or night, or has day and night vanished?" asked Elston.

"It might well be that the whole bloody universe has been hurled into space. The bugger of it is, my watch has stopped. Sit down here. I want to talk. Do you see now? I want to talk. It's this terrible bloody silence that kills me. Listen now. Can you hear anything? No. You can't. But you can hear me speak. Hear that -ucker — moaning down there. They are human sounds. And human sounds are everything now. They can save us. So we must talk. All the while. With resting, without ceasing. Understand? Whilst we are conscious that we are alive, all is well. Do you see now? Do you see now?"

"I thought the bloody Jerry was dead," muttered Elston.

"Dead my arse. Come! What'll we talk about? Anything. Everything."

And suddenly Elston laughed, showing his teeth, which were like a horses!

"Remember that crazy house down in Fricourt? Remember that? Just as we started to enter the God-forsaken place, he began to bomb and shell it.

"Remember? We both went out in the evening, souveniring. Went into that little white house at the back of the hotel. Remember that?"

"Well!"

"Remember young Dollan mounting that old woman? Looked like a bloody witch. I still remember her nearly bald head."

"Well!"

"And you chucked young Dollan off, and got into bed with her yourself."

"Was it a long time ago? In this war, d'you mean?"

"Yes. Are you tapped, or what? Course it was in this bloody war. What the funkin' hell are you thinkin' of, you loony?"

For the first time since they had found themselves in this position, they both laughed. And suddenly Elston looked up into his companion's face, laughed again, and said softly:

"Well, by Christ, d'you know that laugh has made me want to do something."

"Do something?" queried O'Garra.

"Yes," replied Elston, and standing over the prisoner in the hole, he pissed all over him. Likewise O'Garra, who began to laugh in a shrill sort of way.

There is a peculiar power about rottenness, in that it feeds on itself, borrows from itself, and its tendency is always downward. That very action had seized the polluted imagination of the Irishman. He was helpless. Rottenness called to him; called to him from the pesty frame of Elston. After the action they both laughed again, but this time louder.

"Hell!" exclaimed O'Garra. "After that I feel relieved. Refreshed. Don't feel tired. Don't feel anything particularly. How do you feel?" he asked.

"The same," replied Elston. "But I wish to Christ this soddin' fog would lift."

This desire, this hope that the fog would lift was something burning in the heart, a ceaseless yearning, the restlessness of waters washing against the floodgates of the soul. It fired their minds. It became something organic in the brain. Below them the figure stirred slightly.

"*Ah! — Ah! —*"

"The -ucker hasn't kicked the bucket yet," said Elston. He leaned over and rested his two hands on O'Garra's knees. "D'you know when I came to examine things; that time I thought you were asleep you know, and you weren't; well I thought hard, and I came to certain conclusions. One of them was this. See that lump of shit in the hole; that Jerry I mean? You do. Well now, he's the cause of everything. Everything. Everything. Don't you think so yourself?"

"Yes I do," said the Irishman. "That's damn funny, you know. Here is what I thought. I said to myself: 'That bastard lying there is the cause of all this'. And piece by piece and thread by thread I gathered up all the inconveniences. All the actions, rebuffs, threats, fatigues, cold nights, lice, toothaches, forced absence from women, nights in trenches up to your knees in mud. Burial parties, mopping-up parties, dead horses, heaps of stale shite, heads, balls, brains, everywhere. All those things. I made the case against him. Now I ask you. Why should he live?"

"Yes," shouted Elston. "You're right. Why should he? He is the cause of it all. Only for this bloody German we might not have been here. I know where I should have been anyhow. Only for him the fog might have lifted. We might have got back to our own crowd. Yes. Yes. Only for him. Well there would not have been any barrage, any attack, and bloody war in fact.

"Can't you see it for yourself now? Consider. Here we are, an Englishman, and an Irishman, both sitting here like soft fools. See. And we're not the only ones perhaps. One has to consider everything. Even the wife at home. All the other fellows. All the madness, confusion. Through Germans. And here's one of them."

"*Ah! —*"

Elston glared down into the gargoyle of a face now visible to them both, the terrible eyes flaring up at the almost invisible sky.

"Water — *Ah! —*"

A veritable torrent of words fell from Elston's lips.

"Make the funkin' fog rise and we'll give you anything. Everything. Make the blasted war stop, now, right away. Make all this mud and shite vanish. Will you? You bastards started it. Will you now? See! We are both going mad. We are going to kill ourselves."

"Kill me —"

"Go and shite. But for the likes of you we wouldn't be here."

"Water —"

In that moment O'Garra was seized by another fit of madness. Wildly, like some terror-stricken and trapped animal, he looked up and around.

"Fog. Yes fog. FOG. FOG. FOG. FOG. FOG. Jesus sufferin' Christ. FOG. FOG. FOG. HA, HA, HA, HA, HA. In your eyes, in your mouth, on your chest, in your heart. FOG. FOG. Oh hell, we're all going crazy. FOG. FOG."

"*There you are!*" screamed Elston into the German's ear, for suddenly seized with panic by the terrific outburst from O'Garra, he had fallen headlong into the hole. The eyes seemed to roll in his head, as he screamed: "There you are. Can you hear it? You. Can you hear it? You -ucker from Muenchen, with your fair hair, and your lovely face that we bashed in for you. Can you hear it? We're trapped here. Through you. Through you and your bloody lot. If only you hadn't come. You baby. You soft stupid little runt. Hey! Hey! Can you hear me?"

The two men now fell upon the prisoner, and with peculiar movements of the hands began to mangle the body. They worried it like mad dogs. The fog had brought about a nearness, that was now driving them to distraction. Elston, on making contact with the youth's soft skin, became almost demented. The velvety touch of the flesh infuriated him. Perhaps it was because Nature had hewn him differently. Had denied him the young German's grace of body, the fair hair, the fine clear eyes that seemed to reflect all the beauty and music and rhythm of the Rhine. Maddened him. O'Garra shouted out:

"PULL his bloody trousers down."

With a wild movement Elston tore down the prisoner's trousers.

In complete silence O'Garra pulled out his bayonet and stuck it up the youth's anus. The German screamed.

Elston laughed and said: "I'd like to back-scuttle the bugger."

"Go ahead," shouted O'Garra.

"I tell you what," said Elston. "Let's stick this horse-hair up his penis."

So they stuck the horse-hair up his penis. Both laughed shrilly.

A strange silence followed.

"Kill the bugger!" screamed O'Garra.

Suddenly, as if instinctively, both men fell away from the prisoner, who rolled over, emitting a single sigh — *Ah...* His face was buried in the soft mud.

"Elston."

"Well," was the reply.

"Oh Jesus! Listen. Has the fog risen yet? I have my eyes tight closed. I am afraid."

"What are you afraid of? Tell me that. There's buggerall here now. This fellow is dead. Feel his bum. Any part you like. Dead. Dead."

"I am afraid of myself. Listen. I have something to ask you. Will you agree with me now to walk out of it? We can't land any worse place."

"My *arse* on you," growled Elston. "Where can we walk? You can't see a finger ahead of you. I tell you what. Let's worry each other to death. Isn't that better than this moaning, this sitting here like soft shits. That time I fell asleep I did it in my pants. It made me get mad with that bugger down there."

"A thing like that," O'Garra laughed once again.

"Listen," roared Elston. "I tell you we can't move. D'you hear? Do you? Shall I tell you why?

"It's not because there is no ground on which to walk. No. Not that. It's just that we can't move. We're stuck. Stuck fast. Though we have legs, we can't walk. We have both been seized by something, I can't even cry out. I am losing strength. I don't want to do anything. Nothing at all. Everything is useless. Nothing more to do. Let's end it. Let's worry each other like mad dogs. I had the tooth-ache an hour ago. I wish it would come back. I want something to worry me. Worry me."

"Listen! Did you hear that?"

"Well, it's a shell. What did you think it was? A bloody butterfly?"

"It means," said O'Garra, "that something is happening, and where something is happening we are safe. Let's go. Now. Now."

"Are you sure it was a shell?"

"Sure. There's another," said O'Garra.

"It's your imagination," said Elston laughing. "Imagination."

"Imagination. Well, by Christ. I never thought of that. Imagination. By God, that's it."

They sat facing each other. Elston leaned forward until his eyes were on a level with those of the Irishman. Then, speaking slowly, he said:

"Just now you said something. D'you know what it was?"

"Yes. Yes. Let's get out of it before we are destroyed."

"But we're destroyed already," said Elston, smiling. "Listen."

"Don't you remember what you said a moment ago?" continued Elston. "You don't. Then there's no mistake about it, you are crazy. Why, you soft shite didn't you say we had better talk, talk, talk? About anything. Everything. Nothing. Let us then. What'll we talk about?"

"Nothing. But I know what we must do. Yes, by Jesus I know. D'you remember you said these Germans were the cause of the war? And you kicked that fellow's arse? Well, let's destroy him. Let's bury him."

"He's dead, you mad bugger. Didn't we kill him before? Didn't I say I felt like back-scuttling him? I knew all along you were crazy. Ugh."

"Not buried. He's not buried," shouted O'Garra, "Are you deaf? Mad yourself, are you?"

The fog was slowly rising, but they were wholly unconscious of it's doing so. They were blind. The universe was blotted out. They were conscious only of each other's presence, of that dead heap at the bottom of the hole. Conscious of each other's nearness. Each seemed to have become something gigantic. The one saw the other as a barrier, a wall blotting out everything. They could feel and smell each other. There was something infinite in those moments that held them back from each other's throats.

"Not deaf, but mad like yourself, you big shithouse. Can't you see that something has happened? I don't mean outside, but inside this funkin' fog, Savvy?"

"Let's bury this thing. UGH. Everything I look at becomes him. Everything him. If we don't destroy him, he'll destroy us, even though he's dead."

"Let's dance on the bugger and bury him forever."

"Yes, that's it," shouted O'Garra. "I knew an owld woman named Donaghue whose dog took poison. She danced on the body."

And both men began to jump up and down upon the corpse. And with each movement, their rage, their hatred seemed to increase. Out of sight, out of mind. Already this mangled body was beginning to disappear beneath the mud. Within their very beings there seemed to burst into flame, all the conglomerated hates, fears, despairs, hopes, horrors. It leaped to the brain for O'Garra screamed out:

"I hate this thing so much now I want to shit on it!"

"O'Garra."

"Look. It's going down, down. Disappearing. Look," shouted Elston.

"Elston."

"Let's kill each other. Oh sufferin' Jesus —"

"You went mad long ago but I did not know that —"

"Elston," called O'Garra.

"There's no way out is there?"

"'Uck you. NO."

"Now."

"The fog is still thick."

"Now."

The bodies hurled against each other, and in that moment it seemed as if this madness had set their minds afire.

Suddenly there was a low whine, whilst they struggled in the hole, all unconscious of the fact that the fog had risen. There was a terrific explosion, a cloud of mud, smoke, and earthy fragments, and when it cleared the tortured features of O'Garra were to be seen. His eyes had been gouged out, whilst beneath his powerful frame lay the remains of Elston. For a moment only they were visible, then slowly they disappeared beneath the sea of mud which oozed over them like the restless tide of an everlasting night.

Frank Prewett

VOICES OF WOMEN

Met ye my love?
Ye might in France have met him;
He has a wooing smile,
Who sees cannot forget him!
Met ye my Love?—
—We shared full many a mile.

Saw ye my love?
In lands far-off he has been,
With his yellow-tinted hair,
—In Egypt such ye have seen,
Ye knew my love?—
—I was his brother there.

Heard ye my love?
My love ye must have heard,
For his voice when he will
Tinkles like cry of a bird;
Heard ye my love?—
—We sang on a Grecian hill.

Behold your love,
And now shall I forget him,
His smile, his hair, his song;
Alas, no maid shall get him
For all her love,
Where he sleeps a million strong.

L. Moore Cosgrave

1917 – THE LOATHING CHANGES TO A SILENT CONTEMPT, ALWAYS IMPERSONAL, BUT TINGED WITH PITY FOR A HOPELESSLY MISGUIDED PEOPLE, AND AN ACQUIRED DEGENERACY

The year 1917 dawned with the Western Front a stalemate. We had become accustomed to our unnatural existence, supremely confident of ultimate victory for right and humanity, enduring the hardships and dangers, if not cheerfully, then with a stoic indifference — veiling our depression and sadness in the loss and drain of the world's best manhood, in an outer covering of war levity — to the uninitiated and unthinking, verging on callousness. But what a sham this was to us in the midst of it all, whose very souls were like a raw and continually reopened wound — dimly realizing the terrible futility and uselessness of this never-ending destruction and suffering; but ignorant, in our idolatry of precedence, of a better method. And so we fought on, systematically and automatically, destroying and being destroyed, feeling instinctively that we must exterminate those mentally diseased beings who represented Germany and had made foul a beautiful world, in order that a better and more humane world should survive; in which, in the decades to come, even the offspring of those degenerate enemies might be admitted to the council of nations — cleansed and purified of their bar sinister!

And thus our thoughts ebbed and flowed — the unspoken thoughts of a thousand soldier-men, expressing in myriad ways, but always groping toward the same and the right solution; our outer selves sometimes joyously elated and sometimes unutterably depressed as the struggle swayed backward and forward — as we scaled the bastion of Vimy Ridge, swept out on to the plains of Douai, laboriously encircled Lens, battled desperately over the sternly defended ramparts of Hill 70, and finally marched north to that hell on earth — the morass of Passchendaele — a bloodier, fiercer, and still more futile effort than the Somme, where for seemingly endless days and nights we fought to achieve the militarily impossible — and did! By sheer, indomitable Divine Power of each and every man; e'en though not one in a hundred would ascribe aught other agency than man's inherent courage in the face of insuperable difficulties.

And so we emerged from 1917, still struggling, slowly fighting forward toward some vaguely distant goal; our only tangible knowledge of victory, an inherent intuition that, despite all, we would conquer because of that age-old prophecy — "Right shall conquer over Might." As for our thoughts, truly they had passed through an aeon of emotions — for now they had metamorphosed from the cocoon of hate, of loathing, of contempt; and had become as it were, an almost disinterested spectator of some huge, revolting, but necessary sanitation of the world — where we were the sanitary engineers, world's health-inspectors, scavengers — call us what you will — and the German nation was the offal, the waste, the decayed vegetation in the sewers of the world which must be eradicated, ere the world could again move forward on its sweet clean way. Whereas, for the German peoples, their coming generation, their young children, even their *mutiles* who, in their mutilation, had partially expiated their personal guilt in the nation's crime — there came a great pity, tinging our contempt with tolerance and silencing our spoken revilings. The inner contempt remained — but always for that undermined, weak soul of Germany which had permitted the dominance of hell's agents in their native land. But the pity, the pity of a suffering world for all manner of pain and disillusion was there — to remain unaltered. No longer were we possessed of that soul-crushing hate which had so inspired our pioneer efforts, driven the boyish smile from our features and drowned the gladness of our hearts; no longer the after-personal loathing, no longer disgust, no longer, even, that contempt for all things Teutonic, whose every facet we knew so well, remained! For in truth our beings had verily been subjected to, and drained of, every negative human emotion — as though we had passed through some cataclysmic reaction and were about to pass the last and final test — the test of victory — of complete domination — of that long-dreamed-of heaven on earth, the end of this Armageddon. And so we came to 1918.

Frederick George Scott

A Tragedy of War
from *The Great War As I Saw It*

There is nothing which brings home to the heart with such force the iron discipline of war as the execution of men who desert from the front line. It was my painful duty on one occasion to have to witness the carrying out of the death sentence. One evening I was informed by the A.P.M. that a man in one of our brigades was to be shot the next morning, and I was asked to go and see him and prepare him for death. The sentence had already been read to him at six o'clock, and the brigade chaplain was present, but the A.P.M., wished me to take the case in hand. We motored over to the village where the prisoner was and stopped at a brick building which was entered through a courtyard. There were men on guard in the outer room and also in a second room from which a door led into a large brick chamber used as the condemned cell. Here I found the man who was to pay the penalty of his cowardice. He had a table before him and on it a glass of brandy and water and writing materials. He was sitting back in his chair and his face wore a dazed expression. The guards kindly left us alone. He rose and shook hands with me, and we began to talk about his sentence. He was evidently steeling himself and trying to fortify his mind by the sense of great injustice done to him. I allowed him to talk freely and say just what he pleased. Gradually, I succeeded in getting at the heart of the true man which I knew was hidden under the hard exterior, and the poor fellow began to tell me about his life. From the age of eleven, when he became an orphan, he had to get his own living and make his way in a world that is often cold and cruel to those who have no friends. Then by degrees he began to talk about religion and his whole manner changed. All the time I kept feeling that every moment the dreaded event was coming nearer and nearer and that no time was to be lost. He had never been baptised, but wished now to try and make up for the past and begin to prepare in a real way to meet his God.

I had brought my bag with the communion vessels in it, and so he and I arranged the table together, taking away the glass of brandy and water and the books and papers, and putting in their place the white linen altar cloth. When everything was prepared, he knelt down and I baptised him and gave him his first communion. The man's mind was completely changed. The hard, steely indifference and the sense of wrong and injustice had passed away, and he was perfectly natural. I was so much impressed by it that while I was talking to him, I kept wondering if I could not even then, at that late hour, do something to avert the carrying out of the sentence. Making some excuse and saying I would be back in a little while, I left him, and the guard went into the room accompanied by one of the officers of the man's company. When I got outside, I told the brigade chaplain that I was going to walk over to Army Headquarters and ask the Army Commander to have the death sentence commuted to imprisonment.

It was then about one a.m. and I started off in the rain down the dark road. The chateau in which the General lived was two miles off, and when I came to it, I found it wrapped in darkness. I went to the sentry on guard, and told him that I wished to see the General on important business. Turning my flashlight upon my face, I showed who I was. He told me that the General's room was in the second storey at the head of a flight of stairs in a tower at the end of the building. I went over there, and finding the door unlocked, I mounted the wooden steps, my flashlight lighting up the place. I knocked at a door on the right and a voice asked me who I was. When I told my name, I was invited to enter, and an electric light was turned on and I found I was in the room of the A.D.C., who was sitting up in bed. Luckily, I had met him before and he was most sympathetic. I apologized for disturbing him but told him my mission and asked if I might see the General. He got up and went into the General's room. In a few moments he returned, and told me that the General would see me. Instead of being angry at my extraordinary intrusion, he discussed the matter with me. Before a death sentence could be passed on any man, his case had to come up first in his Battalion orderly room, and, if he was found guilty there, it would be sent to the Brigade. From the Brigade it was sent to the Division, from the Division to Corps, from Corps to Army, and from Army to General Headquarters. If each of these courts confirmed the sentence, and the British Commander-in-Chief signed the warrant, there was no appeal, unless some new facts came to light. Of all the men found guilty of desertion from the front trenches, only a small percentage were executed. It was considered absolutely necessary for the safety of the Army that the death sentence should not be entirely abolished. The failure of one man to do his duty might spoil the morale of his platoon, and spread the contagion of fear from the platoon to the company and from the company to the battalion, endangering the fate of the whole line. The General told me, however, that if any new facts came to light, suggesting mental weakness or insanity in the prisoner, it might be possible for the execution to be stayed, and a new trial instituted. This seemed to give hope that something might yet be done, so I thanked the General for his kindness and left.

When I got back to the prison, I made my way to the cell, not of course, letting the condemned man know anything that had happened. By degrees, in our conversation, I found that on both sides of his family there were cases of mental weakness. When I had all the information that was possible, I went out and accompanied by the brigade chaplain, made my way once again to Army Headquarters. The chances of averting the doom seemed to be faint, but still a human life was at stake, and we could not rest till every effort had been made. I went to the room of the A.D.C., and was again admitted to the presence of the Army Commander. He told me now that the only person who could stop the execution was the Divisional Commander, if he thought it right to do so. At the same time, he held out very little hope that anything could be done to commute the sentence. Once more I thanked him and went off. The brigade chaplain was waiting for me outside and we talked the matter over, and decided that, although the case seemed very hopeless and it was now half-past three, one last effort should be made. We walked back through the rain to the village, and there awoke the A.P.M. and the Colonel of the battalion. Each of them was most sympathetic and most anxious, if possible, that the man's life should be spared. The A.P.M. warned me that if we had to go to Divisional Headquarters, some seven miles away, and return, we had no time to lose, because the hour fixed for the execution was in the early dawn.

The question now was to find a car. The only person in place who had one was the Town Major. So the Colonel and I started off to find him, which we did with a great deal of difficulty, as no one knew where he lived. He too, was most anxious to help us. Then we had to find the chauffeur. We managed to get him roused up, and told him that he had to go to Divisional Headquarters on a matter of life and death. It was not long before we were in the car and speeding down the dark, muddy roads at a tremendous rate, whirling round corners in a way that seemed likely to end in disaster. We got to the Divisional Commander's Headquarters and then made our way to his room and laid the matter before him. He talked over the question very kindly, but told us that the courts had gone into the case so carefully that he considered it quite impossible to alter the final decision. If the action of the prisoner had given any indication of his desertion being the result of insanity, something might be done, but there was nothing to suggest such was the case. To delay the execution for twenty-four hours and then to have to carry it out would mean subjecting a human being to unspeakable torture. He felt he could not take it upon himself to run the chance of inflicting such misery upon the man. The Colonel and I saw at once that the case was utterly hopeless and that we could do no more. The question then was to get back in time for the carrying out of the sentence. Once more the car dashed along the roads. The night was passing away, and through the drizzling rain the grey dawn was struggling.

By the time we arrived at the prison, we could see objects quite distinctly. I went in to the prisoner, who was walking up and down in his cell. He stopped and turned to me and said, "I know what you have been trying to do for me, Sir, is there any hope?" I said, "No, I am afraid there is not. Everyone is longing just as much as I am to save you, but the matter has been gone into so carefully and has gone so far, and so much depends upon every man doing his duty to the uttermost, that the sentence must be carried out." He took the matter very quietly, and I told him to try to look beyond the present to the great hope which lay before us in another life. I pointed out that he had just one chance left to prove his courage and set himself right before the world. I urged him to go out and meet death bravely with senses unclouded, and advised him not to take any brandy. He shook hands with me and said, "I will do it." Then he called the guard and asked him to bring me a cup of tea. While I was drinking it, he looked at his watch, which was lying on the table and asked me if I knew what time "IT" was to take place. I told him I did not. He said, "I think my watch is a little bit fast." The big hand was pointing to ten minutes to six. A few moments later the guards entered and put a gas helmet over his head with the two eye-pieces behind so that he was completely blindfolded. Then they handcuffed him behind his back, and we started off in an ambulance to a crossroad which went up the side of a hill. There we got out, and the prisoner was led over to a box behind which a post had been driven into the ground. Beyond this a piece of canvas was stretched as a screen. The firing party stood at a little distance in front with their backs towards us. It was just daylight. A drizzling rain was falling and the country looked chilly and drear. The prisoner was seated on the box and his hands were handcuffed behind the post. He asked the A.P.M. if the helmet could be taken off, but this was mercifully refused him. A round piece of white paper was pinned over his heart by the doctor as a guide for the men's aim. I went over and pronounced the Benediction. He added, "And may God have mercy upon my soul." The doctor and I then went into the road on the other side of the hedge and blocked up our ears, but of course we heard the shots fired. It was sickening. We went back to the prisoner who was leaning forward and the doctor felt his pulse and pronounced him dead. The spirit had left the dreary hillside and, I trust, had entered the ranks of his heroic comrades in Paradise.

The effect of the scene was something quite unutterable. The firing party marched off and drew up in the courtyard of the prison. I told them how deeply all ranks felt the occasion, and that nothing but the dire necessity of guarding the lives of the men in the front line from the panic and rout that might result, through the failure of one individual, compelled the taking of such measures of punishment. A young lad in the firing party utterly broke down, but, as one rifle on such occasions is always loaded with a blank cartridge, no man can be absolutely sure that he has had a part in the shooting. The body was then placed in a coffin and taken in the ambulance to the military cemetery, where I held the service. The usual cross was erected with no mention upon it of the manner of the death. That was now forgotten. The man had mastered himself and had died bravely.

I have seen many ghastly sights in the war, and hideous forms of death. I have heard heart-rending tales of what men have suffered, but nothing ever brought home to me so deeply, and with such cutting force the hideous nature of war and the iron hand of discipline, as did that lonely death on the misty hillside in the early morning. Even now, as I write this brief account of it, a dark nightmare seems to rise out of the past and almost makes me shrink from facing once again memories that were so painful. It is well, however, that people should know what our men had to endure. Before them were the German shells, the machine guns and the floods of gas. Behind them, if their courage failed, was the court-martial, always administered with great compassion and strict justice, but still bound by inexorable laws of war to put into execution, when duty compelled, a grim and hideous sentence of death.

If this book should fall into the hands of any man who, from cowardice, shirked his duty in the war, and stayed at home, let him reflect that, but for the frustration of justice, he ought to have been sitting that morning blindfolded and handcuffed, beside the prisoner on the box. HE was one of the originals and a volunteer.

H.C. Mason

ARTILLERY MAN'S FAREWELL

Horses, harness, wagons, guns,
Steelwork, brasswork, bandoleers,
Messtins, saddles, whizbangs, Huns,
Grooming, bombing, bombardiers,

Limbers, lanyards, gas-masks, mokes,
Breech-blocks, spanners, quick-releases,
Halters, helmets, Belgians, blokes,
Polish, polebars, tugs and traces,

Fusing, firing, S.O.S.,
Dugouts, darkness, double duty,
Wind-up, hardtack, muck and mess,
"Five more kilos!"—"Curse that cootie!"

Horselines, hoofpicks, "Water," "Feed,"
Nosebags, haynets, sack and bale,
Sights, Mark VII, Dial, keyed,
Trigger, traverse, rangedrum, trail,

"Shrapnel, cordite, fuse Eight-O!"
"Lyddite, ballistite, charge three!"
"Three-two fifty!"—"Let 'er go!"
"Right repeat!"—"Sweep one degree!"

Never again, so help me Joe,
Never again no more for me!

Stanley A. Rutledge

HARLAXTON

October 7, 1917

A pilot's efficiency must necessarily depend on his ability to man-oeuvre his aeroplane in such a way as to ward off the opposing plane, and place his opponent in a hazardous position. Thus, he must know how to stunt. If one flies straight a Hun can simply sit on his tail, as the expression goes, and pump lead into one's machine. But suppos-ing the pilot has mastered the plane, then one becomes as slippery as the proverbial eel. One loops, spins, dives, etc., and thus his oppo-nent is thwarted. That is what our programme consisted of. We stunt — one goes aloft and throws the machine about, careless of equilibrium and negligent of the laws of gravity. Thus does man and aeroplane become as one. Thus does a pilot get a great measure of confidence in his ability to meet any contingency in the air.

I do not know of any sensation to equal that of stunting. Suppose one goes up for a loop. The nose of the aeroplane is thrust down until a speed of a hundred miles is registered. Then one pulls the "joy-stick" (control lever) back, and the plane begins to climb. Then, applying pressure gradually one points the nose heavenwards, and the plane stalls and flops over. It is when one is upside down (at the height of the loop) that one gets a sinking feeling like unto nothing I know, and one wonders if the thing will go over or stay upside down forever. Needless to say, this evolution cannot be recommended for women who jump on chairs when rodents appear, or for tremulous men who whistle their way through a cemetery. But the spin is the greatest spectacular stunt. One comes hurtling down, inside out and outside in, as it were. The uninitiated would swear that the aeroplane was out of control and falling to the earth. But generally, all come right. The pilot puts on a little rudder and waggles the "joy-stick," and the "bus," obedient to his touch, straightens out and floats away. Thus do we carry on in the Flying Corps.

The report has just come in that Sir Wilfrid Laurier has resigned. Feel rather sorry for Sir Wilfrid. No doubt he is sincere, but I cannot understand a mind which opposes conscription now. The issue seems so transparently clear. It proves, certainly, that there is no such thing as a fixed and unalterable opinion. Before the war, conscription seemed to me to be the antithesis of liberty, but now it has become the way to liberty. More and more do we see this war as a struggle in which all those principles worth living for are being assailed. In the beginning there was some reason for a doubtful mind. The "gambling" of sovereigns in olden days made us rather sceptical about the cause. But the footprint of the "Beast" through Belgium, through paths of diplomacy, through his cunning espionage are not to be mistaken. Blood is everywhere and we've got to hunt the blond beast down. And we must have every available hunter, because, as Tommy says, "The Hun will get us if we don't get him."

Robert W. Service

ON THE WIRE

O God, take the sun from the sky!
It's burning me, scorching me up.
God, can't You hear my cry?
Water! A poor, little cup!...
See! It's the size of the sky,
And the sky is a torrent of fire,
foaming on me as I lie
Here on the wire... the wire...

Of the thousands that wheeze and hum
Heedlessly over my head,
Why can't a bullet come,
Pierce to my brain instead,
Blacken forever my brain,
Finish forever my pain?
Here in the hellish glare
Why must I suffer so?
Is it God doesn't care?
Is it God doesn't know?
Oh, to be killed outright,
Clean in the clash of the fight!
That is a golden death,
That is a boon; but this...
Drawing an anguished breath
Under a hot abyss,
Under a stooping sky
Of seething, sulphurous fire,
Scorching me up as I lie
Here on the wire... the wire...

Hasten, O God, Thy night!
Hide from my eyes the sight
Of the body I stare and see
Shattered so hideously...

Close to me, close... Oh, hark!
Someone moans in the dark.
I hear, but I cannot see...
Someone is caught like me,
Caught on the wire... the wire...

Again the shuddering dawn,
Weird and wicked and wan;
Again, I've not yet gone.
The man whom I heard is dead.
Now I can understand:
A bullet hole in his head,
Well, he knew what to do—
Yes, and now I know too...
I've suffered more than my share;
I'm shattered beyond repair;
I've fought like a man the fight,
And now I demand the right
(God! how his fingers cling!)
To do without shame this thing.
Good! there's a bullet still;
Now I'm ready to fire;
Blame me, God, if you will,
Here on the wire... the wire...

George Nasmith

POISON GAS

Springtime had come in truth; the hedges of Northern France were beginning to bloom white, and the wild flowers were quite thick in the forest of Nieppe near Merville. It was the time in Canada when the spring feeling suddenly got into the blood, when one threw work to the winds and took to the woods in search of the first violets.

On the twenty-second day of April the very essence of spring was in the air; I felt as if I had to go out into the open and watch the birds and bees, loll in the sun, and do nothing. We struggled along until noon with our routine work, and having completed it Captain Rankin and I left for Ypres. A soldier had been transferred to us, and as we did not need him we decided to register a formal protest and see if he could not be kept with his present unit. Our road lay through Dickebush and we made good time, again reaching Ypres about two o'clock.

It was quite evident to me as I retraversed the streets of Ypres that it had been heavily shelled since I had been there a few days before. Many more houses had been smashed, and unmended shell holes were seen in the roads. As we crossed the Grande Place there was scarcely a soldier visible. The Cloth Hall, which the Captain had not seen before, showed further evidences of shell fire. After viewing the ruins we drove to the little restaurant kept by the pretty milliners, only to find that the place had completely disappeared — literally blown to atoms. Later on we found that a fifteen-inch shell had landed in the building next door and both houses had simultaneously vanished. A well-known officer, Captain Trumbull Warren of the 48th Highlanders, Toronto, coming out of a store on the opposite side of the square had been killed by a flying fragment of the same shell.

We wondered whether the milliners had escaped, and somewhat depressed, drove along in search of another restaurant. A sign

"Chocolat" on a door in a side street made us inquire, and, curiously enough, we found this also to be a little restaurant kept by two other milliners. They informed us that the first three milliners had escaped when the bombardment began, and before their restaurant had been blown up. One's interest in a place or in a battle is often in direct proportion to the number of one's friends or acquaintances there.

After lunch we drove to Brielen, but found that the A.D.M.S., whom we were in search of, and his deputy were both out. We were shown maps of the salient, and had the area pointed out to us where the French joined up with the second and third brigades of Canadians, and where the British troops joined up with the Canadians. When about to leave, a friend, Major Maclaren of the 10th Infantry Battalion, riding a mettlesome horse, rode up and I got out of the car and held the bridle while we had a long talk about the experiences of the Canadians since we had left Salisbury Plain.

We then drove back to the Ypres water pool, which was the largest supply of drinking water in the area. There were at least thirty-five water carts in line waiting their turn to fill up at this presumably good supply. We were told that it was safe because twice a week a couple of pounds of chloride of lime were chucked into the middle of the pool. We took samples of the water and passed on to Wieltze, intending to walk into the salient to see what "No Man's Land" was like. Men had told us that, unlike the rest of the front near the trenches, there were no growing crops, and no birds sang in that desolate, dreary, shell-shattered area, and we wanted to see it for ourselves.

At the outskirts of the village we noticed a peasant planting seeds in the little garden in front of his house. The earth had all been dug and raked smooth by a boy and a couple of children. To our "Bon jour" he replied, and added "Il fait bon temps, n'est ce pas?" looking up at the sun with evident satisfaction.

No motor transport was allowed to pass Wieltze because the road beyond was exceedingly rough, and it would only have been inviting disaster from breakdowns and German shells to have proceeded farther.

As we tramped along towards St. Julien our attention was attracted to a greenish yellow smoke ascending from the part of the line occupied by the French. We wondered what the smoke was coming from. Half a mile up the road we seated ourselves on a disused trench and lit cigarettes, while I began to read a home letter which I had found at Brielen.

An aeroplane flying low overhead dropped some fire-balls. Immediately a violent artillery cannonade began. Looking towards the French line we saw this yellowish green cloud rising on a front of at least three miles and drifting at a height of perhaps a hundred feet towards us.

"That must be the poison gas that we have heard vague rumours about," I remarked to the Captain. The gas rose in great clouds as if it had been poured from nozzles, expanding as it ascended; here and there brown clouds seemed to be mixed with the general yellowish green ones. "It looks like chlorine," I said, "and I bet it is." The Captain agreed that it probably was.

The cannonade increased in intensity. About five minutes after it began a hoarse whistle, increasing to a roar like that of a railroad train, passed overhead. "For Ypres," we ejaculated, and looking back we saw a cloud as big as a church rise up from that ill-fated city, followed by the sound of the explosion of a fifteen-inch shell. Thereafter, these great shells succeeded one another at regular intervals, each one followed by the great black cloud in Ypres.

The bombardment grew in intensity. Over in a field ,not two hundred yards away, numerous coal boxes exploded, throwing up columns of mud and water like so many geysers. General Alderson and General Burstall of the Canadian Division came hurrying up the road and paused for a moment to shake hands, and to remark that the Germans appeared to be making a heavy attack upon the French. We wondered whether they would get back to their headquarters or not.

Shells of various calibres, whistling and screaming, flew over our heads from German batteries as well as from our own batteries replying to them. The air seemed to be full of shells flying in all directions.

The gas cloud gradually grew less dense, but the bombardment redoubled in violence as battery after battery joined in the angry chorus.

Across the fields we could see guns drawn by galloping horses taking up new positions. One such gun had taken a position not three hundred yards away from us when a German shell lit apparently not twenty feet away from it; that gun was moved with despatch into another position.

Occasionally we imagined that we could hear heavy rifle and machine gun fire, but the din was too great to distinguish much detail. The common expression used on the front, "Hell let loose," was the only term at all descriptive of the scene.

Streaking across the fields towards us came a dog. On closer view he appeared to be a nondescript sort of dog of no particular family or breeding. But he was bent on one purpose, and that seemed to be to put as great a distance as possible between himself and the Germans. He had been gassed, and had evidently been the first to get out of the trenches. Loping along at a gait that he could, if necessary, maintain for hours, he fled by with tail between his legs, tongue hanging out and ears well back. And as he passed he gave us a look which plainly said, "Silly fools to stand there when you could get out; just wait there and you will get yours." And on he went, doubtless galloping into the German lines on the opposite side of the salient.

By this time our eyes had begun to run water, and became bloodshot. The fumes of the gas which had reached us irritated our throats and lungs, and made us cough. We decided that this gas was chiefly chorine, with perhaps an admixture of bromine, but that there was probably something else present responsible for the irritation of our eyes.

A lull in the cannonading made it possible to distinguish the heavy rattle of rifle and machine gun fire, and it seemed to me to be decidedly closer.

The Canadian artillery evidently received a message to support, and down to our right the crash of our field guns, and their rhythmical red flashes squirting from the hedgerows, focussed our attention and added to the din.

Up the road from St. Julien came a small party of Zouaves with their baggy trousers and red Fez caps. We stepped out to speak to them, and found that they belonged to the French Red Cross. They had been driven out of their dressing station by the poisonous gas, and complained bitterly of the effect of it on their lungs.

Shortly afterwards the first wounded Canadian appeared — a Highlander — sitting on a little cart drawn by a donkey which was led by a peasant. His face and head were swathed in white bandages.

Soon after, another Canadian Highlander came trudging up the road, with rifle on shoulder and face black with powder. He stated that his platoon had been gassed, and that the Germans had got in behind them about a mile away, in such a manner that they had been forced to fight them on front and rear. Finally the order had been passed, "Every man for himself," and he had managed to get out; he was now on his way back to report to headquarters.

Then came a sight that we could scarcely credit. Across the fields coming towards us, we saw men running, dropping flat on their faces, getting up and running again, dodging into disused trenches, and keeping every possible bit of shelter between themselves and the enemy while they ran. As they came closer we could see that they were French Moroccan troops, and evidently badly scared. Near us some of them lay down in a trench and lit cigarettes for a moment or two, only to start up in terror and run on again. Some of them even threw away their equipment after they had passed, and they all looked at us with the same expression that the dog had, evidently considering us to be madmen to stay where we were. It was quite apparent that the Moroccan troops had given way under the gas attack, and that a break, doubtless a large one, had been made in the French front line.

Then our hearts swelled with a pride that comes but seldom in a man's life. Up the road from Ypres came a platoon of soldiers marching rapidly; they were Canadians, and we knew that our reserve brigade was even now on the way to make the attempt to block the German road to Calais.

Bullets began to come near. Neither of us said a word for a while as we saw spurt after spurt of dust kicked up a few yards in front of us.

"I think we had better move, Colonel," said Captain Rankin at last. As he spoke, a bullet split a brick in the road about three feet away from me, and slid across the road leaving a trail of dust.

"I think we had," I said as I walked over, picked up the spent bullet and dropped it in my pocket. Another bullet pinged over head and another spat up the road dust in front of us. "Those are aimed bullets," I said. "The Germans cannot be far away; it's time to move." It was then about 6:30 and we walked back to Wieltze, near which we met our anxious chauffeur coming out to meet me.

Canadian soldiers with boxes of cartridges on their shoulders ran up the road towards the trenches; others carrying movable barbwire entanglements followed them. A company of Canadians took to the fields on leaving Wieltze, and began advancing in short rushes in skirmishing order towards the German front, while their officer walked on ahead swinging his bamboo cane in the most approved fashion. Another company was just leaving the village, loading their rifles as they hurried along. I overheard one chap say, as he thrust a cartridge clip into place, "Good Old Ross."

As we approached Wieltze we could see ammunition wagons galloping up the other road which forks at Wieltze and runs to Langemarck. Turning into the fields they would wheel sharply, deposit their loads, and gallop wildly off again for more ammunition, while the crashes and flashes of the guns showed that they were being served with redoubled vigor.

At the edge of the village the peasant, whom we had seen preparing his little garden and sowing seeds earlier in the afternoon, came down to the gate and asked rather apologetically if we thought that the Germans would be there tonight; "in any case, did monsieur not think it would be wise for the women and children to leave?"

Behind him, standing about the doorsteps, were the members of his family, each with a bundle suited to their respective ages. The smallest, a girl about six years of age, had a tiny bundle in a handkerchief; the next, a boy about eight, had a larger one. All were dressed in their best Sunday clothes, and carried umbrellas — a wise precaution in the climate of Flanders. We agreed with him that it was wise to move away, because it would be possible to return, if the Germans were driven back, whereas if they stayed they might be killed.

As we talked to the father, the eldest, a boy of eighteen, came down to the gate with his grandmother, a little old lady perhaps eighty years of age, and weighing about as many pounds. The boy stooped down to pick her up in his arms, but she shook her head in indignant protest. Accordingly he crouched down, she put her arms around his neck, he took her feet under his arms, and set off down the road towards Ypres with the rest of the family trailing behind him. About ten o'clock that night my friend, Captain Eddie Robertson, standing with his regiment on the roadside ten miles nearer Poperinge, waiting for orders to advance, noticed a youth with a little old lady on his back, trudging by in the stream of fleeing refugees.

Wieltze was a picture; the kind of moving picture that the movie man would pay thousands for, but never can obtain. The old adage held that you always see the best shots when you have no gun. Small detachments of Canadian troops moved rapidly through the streets. Around the Canadian Advanced Dressing Station was a crowd of wounded Turcos and Canadians waiting their turn to have their wounds dressed. All the civilians were loading their donkey or dog carts with household goods and setting out towards Ypres, sometimes driving their cows before them.

As we climbed into the car, which had been placed for shelter behind the strongest looking wall in the town, and slowly started for Ypres, a section of the 10th Canadian Battalion came along with our friend, Major Maclaren, whom I had talked to at Brielen earlier in the afternoon, at its head. I waved my hand to him and called "Good luck." He waved his hand in answer with a cheery smile. A couple of hours later he was wounded and was sent back in the little battalion Ford car, with another officer, to the ambulance in Vlamertinge. While passing through Ypres a shell blew both officers' heads off.

We picked up a load of wounded Turcos and took them into the ambulance at Ypres. Fresh shell holes pitted the road and dead horses lay at the side of it. One corner in particular near Ypres had been shelled very heavily, and broken stone, pavé and bricks lay scattered about everywhere.

All the while the roar of guns and the whistle of flying shells had increased. We reached the ambulance in Ypres between dusk and dark; it was light enough to see that the front of the building, which had been intact earlier in the afternoon, had been already scarred with pieces of flying shells. The shutters which had been closed were torn and splintered, and the brickwork was pitted with shrapnel. We forced our Turcos to descend and enter the ambulance, though from their protests I judged they would have much preferred a continuous passage to the country beyond Ypres.

As we entered the door Major Hardy (now Colonel Hardy, D.S.O.) was found operating on one of his own men; the man had been blown off a water cart down the street and his leg and side filled with shrapnel. It was rather weird to see this surgeon coolly operating as if he was in a hospital in Canada, and to hear the shells screaming overhead and exploding not far away, any one of which might at any moment blow building, operator and patient to pieces. That is one of the beauties of the army system; each one in the army "carries on" and does his own particular bit under all circumstances.

A terrific bang in the street outside, followed by the rattling and crash of glass and falling of bricks, caused Rankin to remark, "There goes the good old Lozier car." At the same time the piercing shrieks of a woman rang out down the street, shrieks as from a woman who might have had her child killed. We went to the door and looked out; the Lozier was still intact, though later on we found the rounded corner of the metal body of the car bent as though a piece of pavé or metal of several pounds weight had struck it, and the floor of the car was covered with bits of broken glass and brick.

Major Hardy asked us to take his patient on to Vlamertinge as it was doubtful when a motor ambulance would return, and we were glad to do so. After being given the usual dose of anti-tetanic serum, he was wrapped in blankets and made comfortable in the back seat. We shook hands with the Major and started off for Vlamertinge.

It was too risky to go through the centre of the town on account of falling walls, chimneys, and the swiftly descending fragments of houses blown skyward. So we skirted the town and tried to get down a side road to Vlamertinge. It was choked with refugees and transport, and the military traffic policeman strongly advised us to take the main road from Ypres. As there was no alternative we drove back to the water tower in the city. This road was clear, for nobody was going into Ypres at that time by that particular intersecting road.

We made all possible speed to get through the town and into the main Ypres-Vlamertinge road. There, wagons began to pass us going the opposite way, the horses whipped into a gallop as they made haste to get through the town to the bridge-head on the far side. Motor transport lorries also drove at full speed to get by this danger point as quickly as possible. As we cleared the town again, the traffic became heavier, and we gradually worked into and formed part of a great human stream with various eddies and back currents.

It was now dark, and but for the feeble light of a young moon, which sometimes broke through the clouds and faintly illuminated the road, nothing could be seen. All headlights were out, and not even the light of a hand lantern or flashlight was permitted. Yet one's eyes became accustomed to the dark, and when the pale moonlight came through we could dimly see over on our right a line of French Turcos moving like ghosts along towards Vlamertinge. Next to them were the fleeing refugees with their bundles, wagons and push carts, and their cows being driven before them. If there was a cart, the old man or old lady would invariably be seated on the top of the load, sometimes holding the baby.

In the centre of the road we groped our way along with infinite care. A shadow would sometimes bear down on the car, and suddenly swerve to one side as a horseman trotted by. A motor lorry would approach within a few feet of us before the driver would see, and stop before we crashed into each other. On the left were troops standing by all along the roadside, and we felt very proud as we realized that they were Canadians, and that they were the only troops at hand to plug the gap made by the German poison gases.

At one time the road became jammed, and we had visions of staying all night in the midst of a road block. Gradually, with the aid of mounted gendarmes and our military police, the mass, composed of cows, wagons, horses, dogcarts, refugee men, women and children, with hand wagons and baby carriages; motor lorries, horse transport, lumber wagons, motor cycles, touring cars, and mounted horsemen, was dissolved, and slowly began again to flow in both directions. Looking backward we could see the red glow of fires burning in different parts of Ypres and the bright flashes of shells as they burst over that much German-hated city. All around the salient star shells flared into the sky and remained suspended for a few minutes as they threw a white glare over the surrounding country, silhouetting the trees against the skylike ghosts before they died away and fell to earth.

At last we reached Vlamertinge and turned into the yard occupied by No. 3 Field Ambulance. Our car was known, and several officers came forward to see if we had any authentic news. Our patient, whom they recognized as belonging at one time to themselves, was carried into shelter, and we also entered the building. Lying on the floors were scores of soldiers with faces blue or ghastly green in colour choking, vomiting and gasping for air, in their struggles with death, while a faint odour of chlorine hung about the place.

These were some of our own Canadians who had been gassed, and I felt, as I stood and watched them, that the nation, who had planned in cold blood, the use of such a foul method of warfare, should not be allowed to exist as a nation but should be taken and choked until it, too, cried for mercy.

We offered our car to the Colonel of the ambulance for the night, but he had to stay at his work, and the car was not very suitable for evacuating wounded. As we could not be of use, we reluctantly passed on out of the fighting zone toward home, and the refugees being not so numerous we could travel faster.

Near the entrance to Poperinge a British Major came over to our car as we were showing our passes to a military policeman. "Are you Canadian officers?" he said.

"We are," I answered.

"Then would you mind telling your Canadian transport drivers to stop going up and down this road; they insist on doing it, and I can't stop them."

"There is a big battle up in the salient," I said. "Shells and many other things are needed; our men have been sent for them and know what they want; I wouldn't interfere with them if I were you."

He looked at us as though we were hopeless idiots, and we drove on. The motor ambulance convoy, which we had been asked to have sent forward, had already gone, and our last errand was done. Putting on our headlights and opening the throttle, we tore homeward, reaching Merville at eleven o'clock.

When we arrived at the Mess, Captain Ellis, who had been anxiously waiting, said that we looked grey, drawn and ghastly, partly perhaps from the effects of the poisonous gas. We had an intensely interested listener as we recounted our experiences and drew plans of the line as we thought it probably existed at the moment. Whether the Germans could get through or not was the dominant question. Nothing lay between them and Calais but the Canadian Division, and whether the Canadians could hang on long enough in face of this new terror of poison gas until new troops arrived, no one could even venture to guess. We felt that they would do all that men could do under the circumstances, but without means of combating the poison it was doubtful what any troops could do. Supposing the Germans just kept on discharging gas? Nothing under heaven apparently could stop them from walking over the dead bodies of our soldiers, choked to death like drowned men. We could not decide the question that time alone could answer, and we went to bed to spend a long sleepless night longing for the day when we would get news of the battle.

The day after the gas attack I reported to headquarters that, in my opinion, the gas used was chlorine with possibly an admixture of bromine, and that a mask with a solution of "Hypo" to cover the nose and mouth would probably absorb the gas and destroy its effectiveness. I also suggested that the battle area be searched for masks which the Germans were sure to have had prepared as a protection for their own men. (Most of the morning I had spent in bed with an attack of bronchitis suffering from the effects of the gas.)

Later I learned that German prisoners had given the information that the gas was contained in cylinders but would not admit that they knew what kind of gas it was. They also said that the men who operated the tanks wore protective masks and gloves.

All that day the Indians of the Lahore division from our area were passing through our town on the way to Ypres.

At Poperinge we saw a cart on the road beside a house which had been recently blown down by a shell. As we drove slowly by, a wounded old woman was carried out and laid beside the bodies of two other white-haired women who had just been dug out of the ruins. Though fatally injured they were still living, and I shall never forget the pitiful looks on those ashy grey faces as they looked up into my face with eyes like those of sheep about to be slaughtered.

When the French people of the little villages through which we passed saw the name "Canadian" on our car, they nudged each other and repeated the word "Canadien." It was the name in everybody's mouth those days, for it was now general knowledge that the Canadian division had thrown itself into the gap and stemmed the German rush to Calais. The whole world was ringing with the story of how the colonial troops had barred the road to the channel to a force many times its size in men and guns, and armed with poison gas, the most terrible device of warfare that had yet been invented.

Frederick George Scott

The Capture of Vimy Ridge, April 9th, 1917

My alarm clock went off at four a.m. on the great day of April 9th, which will always shine brightly in the annals of the war. I got up and ate the breakfast which I had prepared the night before, and taking with me my tin of bully beef, I started off to see the opening barrage. It was quite dark when I emerged from the door of the château and passed the sentry at the gate. I went through the village of Ecoivres, past the crucifix by the cemetery, and then turning to the right went on to a path which led up to Bray Hill on the St. Eloi road. I found some men of one of our battalions bent on the same enterprise. We got into the field and climbed the hill, and there on the top of it waited for the attack to begin. The sky was overcast, but towards the east the grey light of approaching dawn was beginning to appear. It was a thrilling moment. Human lives were at stake. The honour of our country was at stake. The fate of civilization was at stake.

Far over the dark fields, I looked towards the German lines, and, now and then, in the distance I saw a flarelight appear for a moment and then die away. Now and again, along our nine-mile front, I saw the flash of a gun and heard the distant report of a shell. It looked as if the war had gone to sleep,, but we knew that all along the line our trenches were bristling with energy and filled with men animated with one resolve, with one fierce determination. It is no wonder that to those who have been in the war and passed through such moments, ordinary life and literature seem very tame. The thrill of such a moment is worth years of peace-time existence. To the watcher of a spectacle so awful and sublime, even human companionship struck a jarring note. I went over to a place by myself where I could not hear the other men talking, and there I waited. I watched the luminous hands of my watch get nearer and nearer to the fateful moment, for the barrage was to open at five-thirty. At five-fifteen the sky was getting lighter and already one could make out objects distinctly in the fields below. The long hand of my watch was at five-twenty-five. The fields, the roads, and the hedges were beginning to show the difference of colour in the early light. Five-twenty-seven! In three minutes the rain of death was to begin. In the awful silence around, it seemed as if Nature were holding her breath in expectation of the staggering moment. Five-twenty-nine! God help our men! Five-thirty! With crisp sharp reports the iron throats of a battery nearby crashing forth their message of death to the Germans, and from three thousand guns at that moment the tempest of death swept through the air. It was a wonderful sound. The flashes of guns in all directions made lightnings in the dawn. The swish of shells through the air was continuous, and far over on the German trenches I saw the bursts of flame and smoke in a long continuous line, and, above the smoke, the white, red and green lights, which were the S.O.S. signals from the terrified enemy. In an instant his artillery replied, and against the morning clouds the bursting shrapnel flashed. Now and then our shells would hit a German ammunition dump, and, for a moment, a dull red light behind the clouds of smoke added to the grandeur of the scene. I knelt on the ground and prayed to the God of Battles to guard our noble men in that awful line of death and destruction, and to give them victory, and I am not ashamed to confess that it was with the greatest difficulty I kept back my tears. There was so much human suffering and sorrow, there were such tremendous issues involved in that fierce attack, there was such splendour of human character being manifested now in that "far flung line," where smoke and flame mocked the calm of the morning sky, that the watcher felt he was gazing upon eternal things.

When it got thoroughly light I determined to go on up the road to the 3rd Artillery Brigade which was to press on after the infantry. I found both officers and men very keen and preparing to advance. For weeks at night, they had been making bridges over the trenches, so that the guns could be moved forward rapidly on the day of the attack. I had breakfast with the O.C. of one of the batteries, a young fellow only twenty-three years of age who had left McGill to enter the war. He was afterwards killed in front of Arras. After breakfast I went on up the line till I came to the 3rd Artillery Brigade Headquarters, and there asked for the latest reports of progress. They were feeling anxious because the advancing battalions had given no signal for some time, and it was thought that they might have been held up. Someone, however, looked at his watch and then at the schedule time of attack, and found that at that particular moment the men were to rest for ten minutes before pressing on. The instant the time for advance came, rockets were sent up to show that our men were still going ahead. I went up the road to Neuville St. Vaast, where there was an aid post, and there I saw the wounded coming in, some walking, with bandaged arms and heads, and some being brought in on stretchers. They were all in high spirits and said that the attack had been a great success. Of course, the walking wounded were the first to appear, the more serious cases came afterwards, but still there was the note of triumph in all the accounts of the fighting which I heard. I moved on to a track near Maison Blanche, and then followed up the men. The ridge by this time was secured and our front line was still pressing forward on the heels of the retreating Germans. It was a glorious moment. The attack which we had looked forward to and prepared for so long had been successful. The Germans had been taken by surprise and the important strategic point which guarded the rich coal fields of Northern France was in our possession.

The sight of the German trenches was something never to be forgotten. They had been strongly held and had been fortified with an immense maze of wire. But now they were ploughed and shattered by enormous shell holes. The wire was twisted and torn and the whole of that region looked as if a volcanic upheaval had broken the crust of the earth. Hundreds of men were now walking over the open in all directions. German prisoners were being hurried back in scores. Wounded men, stretcher-bearers and men following up the advance were seen on all sides, and on the ground lay the bodies of friends and foes who had passed to the Great Beyond. I met a British staff officer coming back from the front, who told me he belonged to Army Headquarters. He asked me if I was a Canadian, and when I replied that I was, he said, "I congratulate you upon it." I reminded him that British artillery were also engaged in the attack and should share in the glory. "That may be," he said, "but, never since the world began have men made a charge with finer spirit. It was a magnificent achievement."

Our burial parties were hard at work collecting the bodies of those who had fallen, and the chaplains were with them. I met some of the battalions, who, having done their part in the fighting, were coming back. Many of them had suffered heavily and the mingled feelings of loss and gain chastened their exaltation and tempered their sorrow. I made my way over to the ruins of the village of Thélus on our left, and there I had my lunch in a shell hole with some men, who were laughing over an incident of the attack. So sudden had been our advance that a German artillery officer, who had a comfortable dugout in Thélus, had to run away before he was dressed. Two of our men had gone down into the dugout and there they found the water in the wash-basin still warm and many things scattered about in confusion. They took possession of everything that might be of use including some German war maps, and were just trying to get a very fine telephone when two other of our men hearing voices in the dugout and thinking the enemy might still be there, threw down a smoke bomb which set fire to the place. The invaders had to relinquish their pursuit of the telephone and beat a hasty retreat. Smoke was still rising from the dugout when I saw it and continued to do so for a day or two.

Our signallers were following up the infantry and laying wires over the open. Everyone was in high spirits. By this time the retreating Germans had got well beyond the crest of the ridge and across the valley. It was about six o'clock in the evening when I reached our final objective, which was just below the edge of the hill. There our men were digging themselves in. It was no pleasant task, because the wind was cold and it was beginning to snow. The prospect of spending a night there was not an attractive one, and every man was anxious to make the best home for himself he could in the ground. It was wonderful to look over the valley. I saw the villages of Willerval, Arleux and Bailleul-sur-Berthouit. They looked so peaceful in the green plain which had not been disturbed as yet by shells. The church spires stood up undamaged like those of some quiet hamlet in England. I thought, "If we could only follow up our advance and keep the Germans on the move," but the day was at an end and the snow was getting heavier. I saw far off in the valley, numbers of little grey figures who seemed to be gradually gathering together, and I heard an officer say he thought the Germans were preparing for a counter-attack. Our men, however, paid little attention to them. The pressing question of the moment was how to get a comfortable and advantageous position for the night. Canadians never showed up better than at such times. They were so quiet and determined and bore their hardships with a spirit of good nature which rested on something sounder and more fundamental than even pleasure in achieving victory. About half-past six, when I started back, I met our Intelligence Officer, V.C., D.S.O., coming up to look over the line. He was a man who did much but said little and generally looked very solemn. I went up to him and said, "Major, far be it from me, as a man of peace and a man of God, to say anything suggestive of slaughter, but, if I were a combatant officer, I would drop some shrapnel in that valley in front of our lines." Just the faint flicker of a smile passed over his countenance and he replied, "We are shelling the valley." "No," I said, "our shells are going over the valley into the villages beyond, and the Germans in the plain are getting ready for a counter-attack. I could see them with my naked eyes." "Well," he replied, "I will go and look."

Later on, when I was down in a German dugout which had been turned into the headquarters of our advanced artillery brigade, and was eating the half tin of cold baked beans which my friend, the C.O. had failed to consume, I had the satisfaction of hearing the message come through on the wires, that our artillery had to concentrate its fire on the valley, as the Germans were preparing for a counter-attack.

When I left the warm comfortable dugout, I found that it was quite dark and still snowing. My flashlight was of little use for it only lit up the snowflakes immediately in front of me and threw no light upon my path. I did not know how I should be able to get back in the darkness through the maze of shell holes and broken wire. Luckily a signaller came up to me, and seeing my plight led me over to a light railway track which had just been laid, and told me that if I kept on it I should ultimately get back to the Arras-Bethune road. It was a hard scramble, for the track was narrow and very slippery, and had to be felt with the feet rather than seen with the eyes. I was terribly tired, for I had had a long walk and the excitement of the day and talking to such numbers of men had been very fatiguing. To add to my difficulties, our batteries lay between me and the road and were now in full action. My old dread of being killed by our own guns seemed to be justified on the present occasion. Gun flashes came every few seconds with a blinding effect, and I thought I should never get behind those confounded batteries. I had several tumbles in the snow-covered mud, but there was nothing to be done except to struggle on and trust to good luck to get through. When at last I reached the road I was devoutly thankful to be there and I made my way to the dugout of the signallers, where I was most kindly received and hospitably entertained, in spite of the fact that I kept dropping asleep in the midst of the conversation. One of our signal officers, in the morning, had gone over with some men in the first wave of the attack. He made directly for the German signallers' dugout and went down with his followers, and, finding about forty men there, told them they were his prisoners. They were astonished at his appearance, but he took possession of the switchboard and told them that the Canadians had captured the ridge. One of the Germans was sent up to find out, and returned with the report that the Canadians held the ground. Our men at once took possession of all the telegraph instruments and prevented information being sent back to the enemy in the rear lines. Having done this, our gallant Canadians ordered the prisoners out of the dugout and then sat down and ate the breakfast which they had just prepared.

This was only one of many deeds of cool daring done that day. On one occasion the Germans were running so fast in front of one of our battalions that our men could not resist following them. They were actually rushing into the zone of our own fire in order to get at them. A gallant young lieutenant, who afterwards won the V.C., seeing the danger, with great pluck, ran in front of the men and halted them with the words, "Stop, Boys, give the barrage a chance."

In spite of the numbers of wounded and dying men which I had seen, the victory was such a complete and splendid one that April 9th, 1917, was one of the happiest days in my life, and when I started out from the signallers' dugout on my way back to Ecoivres, and passed the hill where I had seen the opening of the great drama in the early morning, my heart was full of thankfulness to Almighty God for his blessing on our arms. I arrived at my room in the château at about half past two a.m., very tired and very happy. I made myself a large cup of strong coffee, on my primus stove, ate a whole tin of cold baked beans, and then turned in to a sound slumber, filled with dreams of victory and glory, and awoke well and fit in the morning, more than ever proud of the grand old First Division which, as General Horne told us later, had made a new record in British war annals by taking every objective on the scheduled dot of the clock.

Agar Adamson

LETTERS FROM VIMY RIDGE

Top of Vimy Ridge, April 10th, 1917.

My dear Mabel,

We took all our objectives yesterday pushing off at 5:30 A.M. in a rainstorm. The 4th Division on our left, not yet in line with us, having failed in two attempts to gain their objective. We have our flank in the air and are suffering from enfilade fire in newly dug trenches.

A snow storm in progress. Sladen killed. 10 officer casualties, including 3 killed. Pearson shot through lung and spine. Have had him taken out. Other casualties so far equal double Beverly Street number (*150*).

I think we can hang on. Our Brigade did splendidly. Pipes played this Battn. over and are doing great work carrying stretchers, I hope I may get this out by one of them.

Ever Thine,

Agar.

P.S. Our observation over Vimy Ridge is magnificent and if we can hold them till the Artillery push up, we have a commanding position. This Battn. took 400 prisoners, Agar.

Top of Vimy Ridge, 12th April 1917.

Still hanging on wonderfully, well dug in. 4th Division now up in line with us. Their losses heavy. We are suffering a lot from machine gun fire and snipers well hidden and difficult to spot. Also artillery fire, though very general and not concentrated on any one spot.

Estimate of our losses impossible to collect accurate returns. Should not be more than Beverley St. by 3 less 50.

No determined German counter-attack yet launched though R.F.C. report enemy massing in great numbers in front of us. I feel we can stop them in my particular front if their Artillery does not find us too continually.

Agar.

Vimy Ridge, April 1917.

We have done very well, though suffered a lot. The town named after the Ridge will be well in our rear. So far, the fighting has been of an open character. The Germans falling back, fighting hard rearguard action; every place is mined and the whole country, including dugouts and cellars, a mass of booby traps. An innocent-looking canteen standing on the floor being picked up, being connected with a wire, sends off a small mine or bomb. All the wells are poisoned. Every prisoner had a photo of one or more most repulsive naked women. One of our Divinity student sergeants made an officer eat three most filthy postcards. A German Major refused to be sent with prisoners to the rear, except in charge of a Major. He will trouble us no more. Our roads in the new area are very bad, having been smashed by our shell fire. We are having great difficulty in getting guns, etc., up.

I hope you will have a pleasant time in England and give poor little Anthony all the fun of youth and... Agar.

Vimy Ridge, 12th April 1917.

My dear Mabel,

We have pushed them back and are on the outskirts of the town named the same as the ridge. Awful weather. Men absolutely done, awaiting news of a relief which must come. Things have gone splendidly and men awfully cheered. In consequence, if we only had summer instead of winter weather, we could endure more. Thine.

    Agar.

P.S. Eaton of Ottawa killed.

Hartley Munro Thomas

LIEUT. _____, R.F.C., MISSING, BELIEVED KILLED

A RAINDROP on the leaf
Of a rose is here;
The purest form of grief
Is a sunbeam's tear.

The airman who is slain
Has a petal shroud;
And he feels the gentle rain
From the mourning cloud—

Where comrade sunbeams leap
In the open space;
Where the hero fell asleep
With a smiling face.

Hartley Munro Thomas

TWO OF OUR MACHINES ARE MISSING

British official report

Stars of the night, who have travelled the spaces
Farther than ever our feebleness dare,
Say, can you see from your place in the air
The sweeping machines, and the gay boyish faces
Of those whom we knew, and who left us up there?

Often I see in your ocean of shadow
Stars rushing free through the heavens apart;
Say, are they those who with jests at the start
Just rose to the air from our home in the meadow,
Where now are void places—in mess and in heart?

Stars of the night, when you vanish to-morrow
Deep in the shadow that rolls to the west,
Say, will you pass in your voyage o'er the crest
Of horizon, the planes that we search in our sorrow—
The men who were fighting, nor came back to rest?

Brothers are they of the meteor, darting
Fiercely from heaven with flame on its breath;
Say, is it true what the ancient one saith,
"Whom gods would destroy, they make mad?" On departing
Our comrades were scornful of danger and death.

Stars of the morning will fade in the glory
Of daybreak, and gaily we'll bid them adieu.
Say, will they come with a message from you,
Telling, in signals of sunbeams, the story
Of men who will ever sail free in the blue?

Hartley Munro Thomas

A HYMN FOR AVIATORS

O GOD of heaven! wrapt in power,
Grant airmen faith to prove their own;
Be with them in the aching hour,
When searching for Thy highest throne;
Save all who sail the dizzy sky;
Grant airmen courage ere they die.

O God of thunder! grant them might,
That they, despising death and pain,
May purge, as bursts upon their sight,
Each blot upon Thy free domain;
Save all who sail the dizzy sky;
Grant airmen victory ere they die.

O God of sunlight! crowned with pride,
May airmen find their task so dear,
That when grim death tears life aside,
Their pride may stay regret and fear;
Save all who sail the dizzy sky;
Grant airmen peace before they die.

Stephen Leacock

THE BOY WHO CAME BACK

The war is over. The soldiers are coming home. On all sides we are assured that the problem of the returned soldier is the gravest of our national concerns.

So I may say it without fear of contradiction — since everybody else has seen it — that, up to the present time, the returned soldier is a disappointment. He is not turning out as he ought. According to all the professors of psychology he was to come back bloodthirsty and brutalised, soaked in militarism and talking only of slaughter. In fact, a widespread movement had sprung up, warmly supported by the businessmen of the cities to put him on the land. It was thought that central Nevada or Northern Idaho would do nicely for him. At the same time an agitation had been started among the farmers, with the slogan "Back to the city," the idea being that farm life was so rough that it was not fair to ask the returned soldier to share it.

All these anticipations turn out to be quite groundless.

The first returned soldier of whom I had direct knowledge was my nephew Tom. When he came back, after two years in the trenches, we asked him to dine with us. "Now, remember," I said to my wife, "Tom will be a very different being from what he was when he went away. He left us as little more than a schoolboy, only in his first year at college; in fact, a mere child. You remember how he used to bore us with baseball talk and that sort of thing. And how shy he was! You recall his awful fear of Professor Razzler, who used to teach him mathematics. All that, of course, will be changed now. Tom will have come back a man. We must ask the old Professor to meet him. It will amuse Tom to see him again. Just think of the things he must have seen! But we must be a little careful at dinner not to let him horrify the other people with brutal details of the war."

Tom came. I had expected him to arrive in uniform with his pocket full of bombs. Instead of this he wore ordinary evening dress with a dinner jacket. I realized as I helped him to take off his overcoat in the hall that he was very proud of his dinner jacket. He had never had one before. He said he wished the "boys" could see him in it. I asked him why he had put off his lieutenant's uniform so quickly. He explained that he was entitled not to wear it as soon as he had his discharge papers signed; some of the fellows, he said, kicked them off as soon as they left the ship, but the rule was, he told me, that you had to wear the things till your papers were signed.

Then his eye caught a glimpse sideways of Professor Razzler standing on the hearth-rug in the drawing-room. "Say," he said, "is that the professor?" I could see that Tom was scared. All the signs of physical fear were written on his face. When I tried to lead him into the drawing-room I realized that he was as shy as ever. Three of the women began talking to him all at once. Tom answered, yes or no — with his eyes down. I liked the way he stood, though, so unconsciously erect and steady. The other men who came in afterwards, with easy greetings and noisy talk, somehow seemed loud-voiced and self-assertive.

Tom, to my surprise, refused a cocktail. It seems, as he explained, that he "got into the way of taking nothing over there." I noticed that my friend Quiller, who is a war editorial writer, took three cocktails and talked all the more brilliantly for it through the opening courses of the dinner, about the story of the smashing of the Hindenburg Line. He decided after his second Burgundy that it had been simply a case of sticking it out. I say "Burgundy" because we had substituted Burgundy, the sparkling kind, for champagne at our dinners as one of our little war economies.

Tom had nothing to say about the Hindenburg Line. In fact, for the first half of the dinner he hardly spoke. I think he was worried about his left hand. There is a deep furrow across the back of it where a piece of shrapnel went through and there are two fingers that will hardly move at all. I could see that he was ashamed of its clumsiness and afraid that someone might notice it. So he kept silent. Professor Razzler did indeed ask him straight across the table what he thought about the final breaking of the Hindenburg Line. But he asked it with that same fierce look from under his bushy eyebrows with which he used to ask Tom to define the path of a tangent, and Tom was rattled at once. He answered something about being afraid that he was not well posted, owing to there being so little chance over there to read the papers.

After that Professor Razzler and Mr. Quiller discussed for us, most energetically, the strategy of the Lorraine sector (Tom served there six months, but he never said so) and high explosives and the possibilities of aerial bombs. (Tom was "buried" by an aerial bomb but, of course, he didn't break in and mention it.)

But we did get him talking of the war at last, towards the end of the dinner; or rather, the girl sitting next to him did, and presently the rest of us found ourselves listening. The strange thing was that the girl was a mere slip of a thing, hardly as old as Tom himself. In fact, my wife was almost afraid she might be too young to ask to dinner: girls of that age, my wife tells me, have hardly sense enough to talk to men, and fail to interest them. This is a proposition which I think it better not to dispute.

But at any rate we presently realized that Tom was talking about his war experiences and the other talk about the table was gradually hushed into listening.

This, as nearly as I can set down, is what he told us: That the French fellows picked up baseball in a way that is absolutely amazing; they were not much good it seems at the bat, at any rate not at first, but at running bases they were perfect marvels; some of the French made good pitchers, too; Tom knew a *poilu* who had lost his right arm who could pitch as good a ball with his left as any man on the American side; at the port where Tom first landed and where they trained for a month they had a dandy ball ground, a regular peach, a former parade ground of the French barracks. On being asked which port it was, Tom said he couldn't remember; he thought it was either Boulogne, or Bordeaux or Brest — at any rate, it was one of those places on the English Channel. The ball ground they had behind the trenches was not so good; it was too much cut up by long range shells. But the ball ground at the base hospital — where Tom was sent for his second wound — was an A1 ground. The French doctors, it appears, were perfectly rotten at baseball, not a bit like the soldiers. Tom wonders that they kept them. Tom says that baseball had been tried among the German prisoners, but they are perfect duds. He doubts whether the Germans will ever be able to play ball. They lack the national spirit. On the other hand, Tom thinks that the English will play a great game, when they really get into it. He had two weeks' leave in London and went to see the game that King George was at, and says that the King, if they will let him, will make the greatest rooter of the whole bunch.

Such was Tom's war talk.

It grieved me to note that as the men sat smoking their cigars and drinking liqueur whiskey — we have cut out port at our house till the final peace is signed — Tom seemed to have subsided into being only a boy again, a first-year college boy among his seniors. They spoke to him in quite a patronizing way, and even asked him two or three direct questions about fighting in the trenches, and wounds and the dead men in No Man's Land and the other horrors that the civilian mind hankers to hear about. Perhaps they thought, from the boy's talk, that he had seen nothing. If so, they were mistaken. For about three minutes, not more, Tom gave them what was coming to them. He told then, for example, why he trained his "fellows" to drive the bayonet through the stomach and not through the head, that the bayonet driven through the face or skull sticks, and — but there is no need to recite it here. Any of the boys like Tom can tell it all to you, only they don't want to and don't care to.

They've got past it.

But I noticed that as the boy talked — quietly and reluctantly enough — the older men fell silent and looked into his face with the realization that behind his simple talk and quiet manner lay an inward vision of grim and awful realities that no words could picture.

I think that they were glad when we joined the ladies again and when Tom talked of the amateur vaudeville show that his company had got up behind the trenches.

Later on, when the other guests were telephoning for their motors and calling up taxis, Tom said he'd walk to his hotel; it was only a mile and the light rain that was falling would do him, he said, no harm at all. So he trudged off, refusing a lift.

Oh, no, I don't think we need to worry about the returned soldier. Only let him return, that's all. When he does, he's a better man than we are, Gunga Din.

Fanny Kemble Johnson

THE STRANGE-LOOKING MAN

A tiny village lay among the mountains of a country from which for four years the men had gone forth to fight. First the best men had gone, then the older men, then the youths, and lastly the school boys. It will be seen that no men could have been left in the village except the very aged, and the bodily incapacitated, who soon died, owing to the war policy of the Government which was to let the useless perish that there might be more food for the useful.

Now it chanced that while all the men went away, save those left to die of slow starvation, only a few returned, and these few were crippled and disfigured in various ways. One young man had only part of a face, and had to wear a painted tin mask, like a holiday-maker. Another had two legs but no arms, and another two arms but no legs. One man could scarcely be looked at by his own mother, having had his eyes burned out of his head until he stared like Death. One had neither arms nor legs, and was mad of his misery besides, and lay all day in a cradle like a baby. And there was a quite old man who strangled night and day from having sucked in poison-gas; and another, a mere boy, who shook, like a leaf in a high wind, from shell-shock, and screamed at a sound. And he too had lost a hand, and part of his face, though not enough to warrant the expense of a mask for him.

All these men, except he who had been crazed by horror of himself, had been furnished with ingenious appliances to enable them to be partly self-supporting, and to earn enough to pay their share of the taxes which burdened their defeated nation.

To go through that village after the war was something like going through a life-sized toy-village with all the mechanical figures wound up and clicking. Only instead of the figures being new, and gay, and pretty, they were battered and grotesque and inhuman.

He came forward across the foot-bridge with a most ingratiating smile, for this was the first time that day he had seen a child and he had been thinking it remarkable that there should be so few children in a valley, where, when he had travelled that way five years before, there had been so many he had scarcely been able to find pennies for them. So he cried "Hullo," quite joyously, and searched in his pockets.

But, to his amazement, the bullet-headed little blond boy screamed out in terror, and fled for protection into the arms of a hurriedly approaching young woman. She embraced him with evident relief, and was lavishing on him terms of scolding and endearment in the same breath, when the traveller came up, looking as if his feelings were hurt.

"I assure you, Madam," said he, "that I only meant to give your little boy these pennies." He examined himself with an air of wonder. "What on earth is there about me to frighten a child?" he queried plaintively.

The young peasant-woman smiled indulgently on them both, on the child now sobbing, his face buried in her skirt, and on the boyish, perplexed, and beautiful young man.

"It is because he finds the Herr Traveller so strange-looking," she said, curtsying. "He is quite small," she showed his smallness with a gesture, "and it is the first time he has even seen a whole man."

AFTERWORD

by
Margaret Atwood

Two fifteen-year-old Canadian recruits, gassed later at Ypres

In Flanders Fields

In Flanders fields the poppies blow
Between the crosses, row on row,
That mark our place: and in the sky
The larks still bravely singing, fly
Scarce heard amid the guns below.

We are the Dead. Short days ago
We lived, felt dawn, saw sunset glow,
Loved, and were loved, and now we lie
In Flanders fields.

Take up our quarrel with the foe:
To you from failing hands we throw
The Torch: be yours to hold it high!
If ye break faith with us who die
We shall not sleep, though poppies blow
In Flanders fields.

John McCrae

There has been considerable debate as to whether the first line should end in the word "blow" or "grow." McCrae himself could not decide which word was suitable and almost discarded the poem after writing it because he could not come to a conclusion as to which word he should use. The version of the poem published in *Punch* on December 8, 1915, ended the line with "blow." The version on the $10 bill is "grow." Most contemporary anthologists and scholars favour the "blow" version. Ed.

POPPIES: THREE VARIATIONS

In Flanders fields the poppies blow
Between the crosses, row on row,
That mark our place; and in the sky
The larks still bravely singing, fly
Scarce heard amid the guns below.
— JOHN MCCRAE

1.

I had an uncle once who served *in Flanders*. Flanders, or was it France? I'm old enough to have had the uncle but not old enough to remember. Wherever, those *fields* are green again, and ploughed and harvested, though they keep throwing up rusty shells, broken skulls. *The* uncle wore a beret and marched in parades, though slowly. We always bought those felt *poppies*, which aren't even felt any more, but plastic: small red explosions pinned to your chest, like a *blow* to the heart. *Between the* other thoughts, that one *crosses* my mind. And the tiny lead soldiers in the shop windows, *row on row* of them, not lead any more, too poisonous, but every detail perfect, and from every part of the world: India, Africa, China, America. *That* goes to show, about war — in retrospect it becomes glamour, or else a game we think we could have played better. From time to time the stores *mark* them down, you can get bargains. There are some for us, too, with *our* new leafy flag, not the red rusted-blood one the men fought under. That uncle had *place*-mats with the old flag, and cups *and* saucers. The planes *in the sky* were tiny then, almost comical, like kites with wind-up motors; I've seen them in movies. The uncle said he never saw *the larks*. Too much smoke, or fog. Too much roaring, though on some mornings it was very *still*. Those were the most dangerous. You hoped you would act *bravely* when the moment came, you kept up your courage by *singing*. There was a kind of *fly* that bred in the corpses, there were thousands of them, he said; and during the

bombardments you could *scarce* hear yourself think. Though some-
times you *heard* things anyway: the man beside him whispered,
"Look," and when he looked there was no more torso: just a red hole,
a wet splotch in *mid*-air. That uncle's gone now too, the number of vets
in the parade is smaller each year, they limp more. But in the windows
the soldiers multiply, so clean and colourfully painted, with their little
intricate *guns*, their shining boots, their faces, brown or pink or yellow,
neither smiling nor frowning. It's strange to think how many soldiers
like that have been owned over the years, loved over the years, lost
over the years, in backyards or through gaps in porch floors. They're
lying down there, under our feet in the garden and *below* the floor-
boards, armless or legless, faces worn half away, listening to every-
thing we say, waiting to be dug up.

2.

Cup of coffee, the usual morning drug. He's off jogging, told her
she shouldn't be so sluggish, but she can't get organized, it involves
too many things: the right shoes, the right outfit, and then worrying
about how your bum looks, wobbling along the street. She couldn't
do it alone anyway, she might get mugged. So instead she's sitting
remembering how much she can no longer remember, of who she
used to be, who she thought she would turn into when she grew
up. We are the dead: that's about the only line left from *In Flanders
Fields,* which she had to write out twenty times on *the* blackboard,
for talking. When she was ten and thin, and now see. He says she
should go vegetarian, like him, healthy as lettuce. She'd rather eat
poppies, get the opiates straight from the source. Eat daffodils, the
poisonous bulb like an onion. Or better, slice it into his soup. He'll
blow his nose on her once too often, and then. *Between the* rock and
the hard cheese, that's where she sits, inert as a prisoner, making lit-
tle *crosses* on the wall, like knitting, counting the stitches *row on row,
that* old trick to *mark* off the days. *Our place,* he calls this dump. He
should speak for himself, she's just the mattress around here, she's

just the cleaning lady, *and* when he ever lifts a finger there'll be sweet pie *in the sky*. She should burn *the* whole thing down, just for *larks; still,* however *bravely* she may talk, to herself, where would she go after that, what would she do? She thinks of the bunch of young men they saw, downtown at night, where they'd gone to dinner, his birthday. High on something, *singing* out of tune, one guy's *fly* half-open. Freedom. Catch a woman doing that, panty alert, she'd be jumped by every creep within a mile. Too late to make yourself *scarce,* once they get the skirt up. She's *heard* of a case like that, in a poolhall or somewhere. That's what keeps her in here, in this house, that's what keeps her tethered. It's not *a mid*-life crisis, which is what he says. It's fear, pure and simple. Hard to rise above it. Rise above, like a balloon or *the* cream on milk, as if all it takes is hot air or fat. Or will-power. But the reason for that fear exists, it can't be wished away. What she'd need in real life is a few *guns*. That and the technique, how to use them. And the guts, of course. She pours herself another cup of coffee. That's her big fault: she might have the gun but she wouldn't pull the trigger. She'd never be able to hit a man *below* the belt.

3.

In school, when I first heard the word *Flanders* I thought it was what nightgowns were made of. And pyjamas. But then I found it was a war, more important to us than others perhaps because our grandfathers were in it, maybe, or at least some sort of ancestor. The trenches, the *fields* of mud, the barbed wire, became our memories as well. But only for a time. Photographs fade, the rain eats away at statues, *the* neurons in our brains blink out one by one, and goodbye to vocabulary. We have other things to think about, we have lives to get on with. Today I planted five *poppies* in the front yard, orangey-pink, a new hybrid. They'll go well with the marguerites. Terrorists *blow* up airports, lovers slide blindly in *between the* sheets, in the soft green drizzle my cat *crosses* the street; in the spring regatta the young men *row on, row* on, as if nothing has happened since 1913, and the crowds wave and enjoy their tall drinks with cucumber and gin. What's wrong with *that*? We can scrape by, more or less, getting from year to year with hardly a *mark* on us, as long as we know *our place*, don't mouth off too much or cause uproars. A little sex, a little gardening, flush toilets and similar discreet pleasures; *and in the sky* the satellites go over, keeping a bright eye on us. The ospreys, *the* horned *larks*, the shrikes and the woodland warblers are having a thinner time of it, though *still bravely* trying to nest in the lacunae left by pesticides, the sharp blades of the reapers. If it's *singing* you want, there's lots of that, you can tune in any time; coming out of your airplane seat-mate's earphones it sounds like a *fly* buzzing, it can drive you crazy. So can the news. Disaster sells beer, and this month hurricanes are the fashion, and famines: *scarce* this, scarce that, too little water, too much sun. With every meal you take huge bites of guilt. The excitement in the disembodied voices says: you *heard* it here first. Such *a* commotion in the *mid*-brain! Try meditation instead, be thankful for the annuals, for the smaller mercies. You listen, you listen to the moonlight, to the earthworms revelling in the lawn, you celebrate your own quick heartbeat. But below all that there's another sound, a ground swell, a drone, you can't get rid of it. It's the guns, which have never stopped, just moved around. It's the guns, still firing monotonously, bored with themselves but deadly, deadlier, deadliest, it's *the guns*, an undertone beneath each ordinary tender conversation. Say pass the sugar and you hear the guns. Say I love you. Put your ear against skin: *below* thought, below memory, below everything, the guns.

Biographies

Acland, Peregrine (1891-1963). Acland served in a Montreal Highland Regiment and survived the war and lived during the 1930s in Toronto. His novel, *All Else is Folly*, was published in 1929. In his introduction, novelist Ford Madox Ford called it "the first really authentic work of imaginative writing dealing with the War to come out of one of the great British Dominions." Prior to the war he had written a poem, *The Reveille of Romance*.

Adamson, Agar (1865-1929) enlisted at the age of forty-eight and got a commission as an officer in the Princess Patricia's Light Infantry and served for three years in the trenches. His letters to his wife, Mabel, remain one of the most detailed and quoted references of Canada's experience of the First World War. He won the Distinguished Service Order for bravery in 1916.

Audette, A(dalard) (dates unknown). After serving as a Corporal in the 22nd Battalion at Zillebeke and Courcelette, Audette survived the war and wrote two small pamphlets about his experiences, *Verses Written in the Trenches* (1917) and the French volume *Histoire et poèsies de la grande guerre: écrites dans les tranchées même composées par A. Audette* (1919).

Brophy, John Barnard (1893; killed in action 1916). John "Don" Brophy was born in Ottawa to a "lace curtain" Irish family, and educated at McGill University and Ottawa University before leaving to take a job in the civil service prior to the war. He was recruited for the Royal Flying Corps in 1915, and served until his death. These excerpts from his airman's diary, one of two in *A Rattle of Pebbles: The First World War Diaries of Two Canadian Airmen*, edited by Brereton Greenhous, was published in 1987 by the Ministry of Supply and Services.

Carveth, Berta (1891 – 1984) was born in Toronto and raised in Scarborough. Eager to serve in some way during the war, she went off to Rochester, New York, in 1914 where she studied nursing at the Rochester Homeopathic Hospital, graduating in 1915 and arriving at the Queen's Military Hospital, Beachborough Park, a few weeks later. As part of the Canadian War Contingent Association under the direction of Lt. Colonel Sir William Osler, she served until the war's end in 1918. Following the war she never nursed again.

Cosgrave, L. Moore (dates unknown). Cosgrave was a Lieutenant Colonel in the Canadian Field Artillery of the Canadian Expeditionary Force. He appears to have been a member of the First Contingent, and survived the war to write *Afterthoughts of Armageddon: The Gamut of Emotions Produced by the War, Pointing a Moral That Is Not Too Obvious* (1919). He was awarded the DSO for his services overseas.

Dent, W. Redvers (1900 – ?). Served in the Canadian Army and survived the war. His novel *Show Me Death* is — among collectors — one of the rarest books in Canadian literature. It was re-written by a ghost writer, the poet and short story author Raymond Knister. Little is known about Dent other than that he worked periodically as a newspaperman after the war.

Dixon, Frank P. (1898; died of wounds 1918). Signaller Frank P. Dixon was born in Elkhorn, Manitoba, and served in the 10th Brigade of the Canadian Field Artillery. His mother, Ellen M. Dixon, published a slim, posthumous volume of his poems written in the trenches, *War-Time Memories in Verse* (1937).

Hanley, James (1901 – 1985). Hanley, best-known for his numerous detective novels written during the 1930s and 1940s, was born in Dublin and spent his early years as a seaman's boy on merchant ships. At the age of 15, he jumped ship in Saint John, New Brunswick, and enlisted in the Canadian Army, and saw action in the C.E.F. until he was wounded in 1918. *The German Prisoner*, perhaps the least-known of Hanley's works, was privately printed in a limited edition by the author in 1930, and featured an introduction by British author and war poet, Richard Aldington.

Harrison, Charles Yale (1898 – 1954). Born in Philadelphia, worked as a journalist in Montreal before enlisting in the Royal Montreal Regiment. He was wounded at Amiens in 1918. His novel, *Generals Die in Bed*, appeared in 1928, the same year as Hemingway's *A Farewell to Arms*, Remarque's *All Quiet on the Western Front*, and Robert Graves' *Goodbye to All That*, and was named by the *New York Evening Post* "the best of the war books."

Imrie, Walter McLaren (dates unknown) was a Canadian short story writer whose story "Remembrance" appeared in Raymond Knister's *Canadian Short Stories* (1928). Imrie published a collection of short fiction, *Legends* (1920). It is unclear whether Imrie served in the Canadian Army during the war, but details in the story suggest that he had a solid grasp of the realities of life and death near the front.

Johnson, Fanny Kemble (1868 – ?). Although an American, born and educated in Virginia, her story "The Strange-Looking Man" appears in this anthology because it is set in Nova Scotia and deals directly with the consequences of the war suffered by Canadians. The story appeared in E.J. O'Brien's *Best Short Stories of 1917*.

Langstaff, J(ames) M(iles) was born near Toronto in 1883 and died at Vimy Ridge on March 1, 1917. A promising scholar and a medal-winning law student at Osgoode Hall in 1912, he rose in the ranks to Major and was recommended for the Military Cross shortly before his death.

Leacock, Stephen (1869 – 1944), humorist, educator, economist, was born in Swanmoor, England, and educated at Upper Canada College and the University of Toronto. He taught at McGill University from 1903 to 1936. His volume of war observations, *The Hohenzollerns in America* (1919), contains his uncommonly serious and sensitive "The Boy Who Came Back."

Logan, John Daniel (1869-1922) was born in Antigonish, Nova Scotia, and served in France as an over-age volunteer until 1918. He was educated at Dalhousie and Harvard University, taught at the University of South Dakota, and, at Acadia University, was the first professor in Canada to teach a course on Canadian Literature.

Mason, H.C. (dates unknown). Served in and survived the War to become a farmer in western Ontario. He was elected several times as president of the Middlesex and Western Ontario Jersey Breeders Association. Sometime in the late 1940s, Mason published a small volume of his verse, *Three Things Only*, which contained poems based on his war experience.

McClung, Nellie (1873 – 1951). Born in Chatsworth, Ontario, she was raised in Manitoba. McClung became a national figure because of her groundbreaking work in women's rights. She was the first woman to sit in the Canadian Senate. She was acclaimed in her lifetime for her novels and stories, and her selections in this volume are from *Three Times Out* (1918), co-authored with a Private Simmons.

McCrae, John (1872 – 1918). McCrae was born in Guelph, Ontario, and graduated in medicine from the University of Toronto. He served in the South African War from 1899 – 1900 and then worked at McGill University. He died of pneumonia in France in 1918, having seen his poem, "In Flanders Fields," published in *Punch* in 1915. It became universally known among the Allied troops of the Western Front. His volume, *In Flanders Fields*, containing his poems, letters and a memoir, was published in 1919.

Nasmith, George (1878-1965) was born in Toronto and educated at the University of Toronto. He was deputy officer of health for the city and served in France where he was in charge of water purification for the Canadian Corps. It was Nasmith who discovered that poisoned gas, first used on Canadians at the First Battle of Ypres, was comprised of chlorine. To remedy this, Nasmith invented the gas mask that became standard issue for the Allies. After the war he wrote several books, including a biography of Timothy Eaton. His experiences in World War One were recorded in his memoir, *On the Fringe of the Great War* (1918).

P. (dates unknown) was a contributor to Lady Byng's volume of stories, verse and pictures contributed by members of the Canadian Expeditionary Force, *Oh Canada!* It was published in 1916.

Peat, Harold (dates unknown). Peat, author of *Private Peat* (1917), a book of war memoirs, advice to soldiers and civilians, and anecdotes about the front, served in the 3rd Battalion of the First Canadian Contingent until he was severely wounded in 1916. The volume, *Private Peat*, contains the story of the "Canadian Golgotha," and is one of the first non-press accounts of the atrocity.

Prewett, Frank (1893 – 1962) was born in Kenilworth, Ontario, and educated at the University of Toronto before enlisting in the Eaton Machine Gun Battery. He was promoted to the Royal Artillery and wounded in January 1918. During his recuperation, he was befriended by Siegfried Sassoon who introduced him to W.B. Yeats, T.S. Eliot, Thomas Hardy, D.H. Lawrence, and Virginia Woolf, who hand-set and published his first book, *Poems* (1922), with the Hogarth Press. Following the war, Prewett lived in England where he broadcast on the BBC, established England's milk distribution system, taught at the Agricultural Economics Institute at Oxford, and edited *The Farmer's Weekly* for Lord Beaverbrook and *The Countryman* magazine before serving as Mountbatten's administrator for food distribution in Ceylon during World War Two. He died in Scotland. A posthumous volume, edited by Robert Graves, appeared in 1964. *The Selected Poems of Frank Prewett*, edited by Bruce Meyer and Barry Callaghan, was published in 1987 and was reissued in the Picas Series from Exile Editions.

R.L. was a member of the First Contingent of the Canadian Expeditionary Force, and a contributor to *Oh Canada!* (1916), published in London and edited by Lady Byng.

Roberts, Theodore Goodridge (1877 – 1953), the brother of poet Charles G.D. Roberts, was educated at the University of New Brunswick. He became a war correspondent during the Spanish-American War. The author of over thirty novels and historical romances, his collected poems, *The Leather Bottle* (1934), contains much of his war poetry, including "A Billet in Flanders." He died in Digby, Nova Scotia.

Rutledge, Stanley A. (dates unkbown). Born in Fort William, Ontario, Rutledge was training to be a lawyer when he enlisted in the Canadian Army in 1915. After serving in the trenches where he wrote most of his only volume, *Pen Pictures from the Trenches* (1918), he transferred to the Royal Flying Corps and was killed in action in 1917.

S.F.L. (dates unknown), author of the vignette, "The Battalion Bard," was a member of the First Contingent of the Canadian Expeditionary Force. His prose piece was published in *Oh Canada!* (1916), edited by Lady Byng.

Sarson, H(enry) Smalley (dates unknown). Sarson, who published two slim volumes of poetry, *From Field and Hospital* (1916) and *A Reliquary of War* (date unknown), was a Private in the First Canadian Contingent of the C.E.F. and was wounded at Ypres in 1916. His poems, as he notes in the cryptic introduction to *A Reliquary of War*, were written during his convalescence.

Scott, F(rederick) G(eorge) (1861 – 1944). Scott, the father of poet and constitutionalist, F.R. Scott, was born in Montreal and educated at Bishop's College. Ordained as an Anglican clergyman, rising to the rank of canon, he was chaplain for the Royal Regiment of Canada during the War. He was wounded and awarded the DSO. Known for his poetry before and after the war, the selections in this volume are from his memoir, *The Great War As I Saw It* (1922).

Service, Robert W. (1874 – 1958). Service was born in Preston, England, and raised in Scotland before adventuring to North America where he made his way to the Klondike in 1902 and worked for the Canadian Bank of Commerce. His volumes *Songs of a Sourdough* (1907) and *The Spell of the Yukon* (1907) made him an international success. He moved to Paris where he lived during the early years of the war. Following the death of his brother Albert at the front in 1915, Service enlisted in the Ambulance Service, making daily ventures into No Man's Land to rescue wounded. His verse about the war, *Songs of a Red Cross Man* (1916), from which the poems in this volume are excerpted, also became successful, but hid much of the reality of the war he witnessed. Following the war, he penned a lengthy memoir of his experiences in the Ambulance Service, but burned the manuscript. He continued to write poetry and novels until his death in the south of France.

Simmons (dates unknown). Private Simmons was the source and subject of Nellie McClung's third book, *Three Times and Out* (1918).

He appears to have been from Edmonton, and was captured during the battle of Ypres, interned in German camps for the duration of the war, and made three failed attempts at escape.

Thomas, Hartley Munro (1896 – 1974). Thomas was a student in History and Political Science at Queen's University when he enlisted in the Canadian Army. He eventually transferred to the Royal Flying Corps where he wrote many of the poems in his volume *Songs of an Airman and Other Poems* (1918). He survived the war and became a noted historian and Professor of History at the University of Western Ontario.

Trotter, Bernard Freeman (b.1890; killed in action 1917). Trotter, born into a literary family in Toronto, was raised in Wolfville, Nova Scotia, and California. He was educated at Woodstock College and McMaster University (then in Toronto) and began his graduate work at the University of Toronto and Oxford before receiving a commission in the 11th Leicesters. He was killed in the spring of 1917. His posthumous collection, *Canadian Twilight and Other Poems of War and Peace,* appeared later that year.

Willson, Beckles (1869 – 1942). An author and historian prior to the war, Willson published *Early Days at York Factory* (1899), the novel *Drift* (1895), and an important history of the Hudson's Bay Company, *The Great Company* (1900). During the war he served as a Major in the Canadian Expeditionary Force, and survived the conflict to write historical studies of North American and European diplomatic relations. His memoir, "A Visit to France's Colonials," which appears in this volume, was first published in *Oh Canada!*, a collection of writing by members of the C.E.F., edited by Lady Byng and published in London, 1916.

GLOSSARY

A.D.M.S.: Assistant Director of Medical Service.

Amiens: The Battle of Amiens was fought from early August to early September, 1918 and involved divisions from Britain, France, Canada, Australia and America. During the nine mile advance, the Allies took 30,000 German prisoners. The Germans suffered 75,000 casualties, the Allies approximately 46,000 casualties.

Ammonal: A high explosive used by British and Allied troops.

A.O.C.: Army Ordinance Corps or the department of the army that supplies the troops with uniforms, boots, helmets, etc.

Archies: Nickname given by the Allied troops for the Germans. See also Bosche, Fritzies, Huns.

Armentieres: A town near Lille in France that was held first by the Allies and then by the Germans before being retaken in September 1918 by the Allies. Memorialized in the song, "Mademoiselle from Armentieres," it came to symbolize the Western Front of the First World War.

Arras: The Battle of Arras was fought from early April to early May, 1917, with Canadian troops seeing much of the action. The total number of Allied casualties there numbered 84,000 while the Germans lost 70,000.

ballistite: An explosive material used to propel heavy shells in large pieces of field artillery.

Bantams: A name given to battalions composed of men who were shorter than that regulation of height of five-foot-three.

Bapaume: Was within the German lines until 1917 when the Kaisers' troops withdrew. A battle followed there during late August and early September of 1918, fought mainly by Australian troops.

Barrage: Concentrated shell-fire on a sector of the enemy lines.

Billet: A house belonging to members of the public where soldiers are housed when away from the front lines.

Biscuit: An army food consisting of a hardened bread that can keep indefinitely and softened when dipped in tea or beef stock.

Bivouac: A tent-like structure made out of waterproof sheets that can be set up in open fields or under harsh conditions.

Boche (es) or **Bosch**: A nickname given by the Allied troops for the Germans.

Bois de Ploegsteert: The wooded area of the Ypres Salient battleground contested several times during the war, including the First Battle of Ypres in 1915.

Cannister: A German trench mortar shell filled with scraps of iron and nails.

CEF: Abbreviation for the Canadian Expeditionary Force. Created in 1914 with the Canadian government's offer to supply Britain with a division, it originally consisted of 31,000 men. It was in action in France from early 1915 on, and eventually grew to 619,636 men and nursing sisters. 59,544 were killed and 172,785 were wounded or injured.

Communication Trench: A trench leading from the rear lines to the forward lines for the purpose of allowing men and supplies to move below the line of fire.

Courcelette: Was the site of a major Canadian attack in September of 1916 as part of the Battle of the Somme. The battle, which lasted for only a week, cost the Canadians 7230 casualties.

C.S.M.: Company Sergeant Major.

C.S.S.: Casualty Clearing Station. A field hospital set up at or near the front line for triage of the wounded.

DCM: The British empire medal known as the Distinguished Conduct Medal, was created in 1854, and was given for "gallantry in action."

DSO: Abbreviation for the Distinguished Service Order. The medal was established in 1866 for meritorious and distinguished service in war. The medal was given during World War One only to commissioned officers who had been mentioned "in despatches" for bravery under fire.

Dugout: An area in the trenches that is deeper than the actual trench and reinforced with roof and beams and often metal doors for the purpose of giving shelter from fire.

Festubert: Several battles were fought at Festubert, the chief ones being in 1914 and the spring of 1916. In May of 1915, the Canadians followed an attack by Indian troops, but failed to make any significant gains. The battle of May 1915 cost the Canadians 2468 casualties.

Field Post Card: A postcard with a series of boxes to be checked off indicating their status. These were usually sent to family member from the front.

Firing Step: A ledge in the front trench which enabled soldiers to shoot over the top of the trench.

Firing Squad: A group of soldiers gathered together (usually by lots) to execute a fellow soldier for a crime or misdemeanour.

Five-Nines: A German artillery shell approximately 5.9 inches in diameter.

Fokkers: A manufacturer's brand of German aircraft used in the First World War, beginning with the Fokker E or "Eindekker" monoplane, the Fokker DII biplane, and the famous Fokker DIII or triplane flown by Manfred von Richtofen, the Red Baron. By the latter part of the war, the

Fokker DVII, such as the one flown by Hermann Goering, was the principal fighter aircraft of the German Jagdgeschwader or squadrons.

Fritzies: A nickname coined by the Allies for the Germans.

Givenchy: An area north of Arras which was the scene of constant fighting throughout the war.

G.S. Wagon: Another name for a four-wheeled supply wagon.

G.S.W.: Gun shot wound.

Gum boots: Another name for rubber boots issued for soldiers in wet, front-line trenches.

Haversack: A small canvas bag originally intended for emergency rations but used by the troops for carrying personal items such as pipes, tobacco, bread, letters, and souvenirs.

howitzer: A short-muzzled, low-velocity artillery piece with a steep angle of fire. These pieces were usually used in short-range barrages.

Hunland: A nickname given by the Allied troops for Germany.

Huns: Nickname given by the Allied troops for the Germans. See also Bosch, Fritzies, Archies.

Labour Battalion: A battalion assigned for digging. Considered by some of their fellow soldiers to have an easy job, the labour battalions, especially the Cape Breton Miners battalions, were instrumental to the Canadian success at Vimy Ridge. A number of "Black" or African Canadian battalions were assigned labour duties until they were permitted to see action in the front ranks.

lazaret: A small locker or storeroom for personal belongings not taken to the front.

Lee Enfield: Standard issue rifle used by the British army. At the Second Battle of Ypres, Canadian troops were issued with the "Ross Rifle," a longer weapon that overheated, jammed on ammunition and had to be used as a butt-end club against the enemy. The bad reputation of the Ross Rifle has been exaggerated as part of the mythology of Canadian bravery at Second Ypres.

listening post: A post, usually located in No-Man's Land and extremely close the enemy lines where two to three soldiers would be stationed to detect the enemy's movements.

LVG: A two-seater German observation aircraft in service from 1915 through to 1918. The observer who sat in the rear seat of the aircraft did double duty as a machine gunner.

lyddite: An explosive, used particularly in mines and timed explosions composed of fused picric acid.

Maconachie: A canned stew eaten by the Canadian troops.

M.G.C.: Machine Gun Corps. Frank Prewett originally joined the Eaton Machine Gun Corps in Toronto, an M.G.C. unit sponsored by the T. Eaton Company, a famous department store in the city. His unit went into battle wearing the delivery man flashes of the company on their shoulders. Prewett's unit was eventually dispersed to the Royal Artillery.

Military Medal: The medal was created in 1916 for "Bravery in the field." Roughly 43,000 were awarded during the First World War to British empire troops of any rank.

Minenwerfer: A German trench mortar.

NCO: Abbreviation for Non-Commissioned Officers.

Nine Point Two: A German howitzer shell. A Howitzer was a large gun that could deliver shells from miles away.

Night Ops: A slang term for operations and attacks at night, usually raids as in *Generals Die in Bed*.

Observation Balloon: A balloon, tethered to the ground, sent into the air for the purpose of observing enemy troop movements. These balloons, on both sides of the war, were heavily defended by anti-aircraft fire and took a huge toll on the Royal Flying Corps. The average "balloon buster" squadron pilot lasted only three missions, on average.

OC: Abbreviation for "Officer-in-Charge."

ops: Abbreviation for the word "operation," pertaining either to a military action or to medical surgery.

Over the Top: The order given for soldiers to leave the relative safety of their trenches and attack the enemy over open ground.

parados: A bank (usually consisting of sandbags) piled around a trench to give protection from enemy fire. Also the term parados was often the name given to the rear wall of the trench. These rear walls were sandbagged to prevent bullets from ricocheting into the backs of soldiers on the firing steps.

Passchendaele: Also known as the Third Battle of Ypres was fought by Canadians in June of 1917 and cost Canada over 15,000 dead or wounded. Remembered for its horrifically muddy conditions, it was a major victory for the C.E.F.

Pats: The popular nickname for the Princess Patricia's Canadian Light Infantry organized in 1914. The regiment served under the British Army command before joining the Canadian 3rd Division. It participated in all the major Canadian battles of the First World War. The regiment is based in Calgary.

QCMH: Abbreviation for the Queen's Canadian Military Hospital, located outside Folkestone in England.

RFC: Abbreviation for the Royal Flying Corps.

Respirator: One of the original names given to the gas mask by the soldiers.

St. Eloi: The Battle of St. Eloi took place in April 1916 when Canadian troops battled the Germans for control of large craters in No-Man's Land that had been created by the detonation of underground mines. Canadians lost 1373 killed, wounded or missing in the action, and eventually, after several days of fighting took all but one of the occupied craters from the Germans.

Somme: The Battle of the Somme lasted from late June 1916 to early November of that year with the height of the battle beginning on July 1 when the British and empire forces lost 21,000 men on a single day. The Canadian corps entered the Somme fighting in September of 1916 under the command of General Julian Byng whose wife edited *Oh Canada!* The Allies, in gaining only 125 square miles of territory, lost over 600,000 men. Canadian casualties numbered 24,029 killed, wounded or missing.

Stand-to: Order to mount the firing step.

Stand-down: Order given to soldiers at dawn to let them know that their night watch duties are over. Also a general command stating that soldiers can take a rest from hyper-vigilence.

Star shells: A shell that bursts at a pre-set altitude and creates a large, bright flare in order for soldiers to see where they are going during a night attack or to illumine the enemy's movements during their attacks at night. A large, flare-type shell.

strafebarcke: The sound of constant shelling.

Taking Over: Getting into a trench and relieving the previous company.

Terriers or Territorials: Units that were composed of peacetime regular army forces.

Tommies: Nickname given to British soldiers. The full name given to a British soldier was "Tommy Atkins," regardless of his real full name.

Trench foot: A rot in the toes and soles of the feet caused from standing too long in water, especially the water of flooded trenches.

Very Lights: A star shell or flare or shorter duration intended to illumine a specific area at night. These could be fired from mortars or from flare guns and were often used to signal commands during night attacks or night raids.

Vickers gun: A machine gun that was belt-fed. A machine gun that was canister fed with ammunition was a **Lewis gun**. These were the principle machine guns used by Canadians in the trenches of the First World War. Vickers guns were heavier and were placed in machine-gun bays or in aircraft on the top cowling of the engine. Lewis guns, lighter and more portable, could be carried easily from location to location, mounted in the observer's seat of a two-seater aircraft, or on the top wing of a bi-plane.

Vimy: A heavily fortified high ground north of Arras that had been contested by the French and Australians from 1915 through to 1917 when it was captured by Canadian troops on April 9, 1917 in what was, perhaps, Canada's greatest victory of the war. Canada lost 3598 killed and 7004 wounded in the action.

Washout: An attack or manoeuvre that was considered to have accomplished nothing.

whizzbangs: A high speed shell that made a high-pitched noise as it approached, followed by a loud explosion.

Woodbine: A cigarette made of paper and old hay. During the war, a British author (invented by the propaganda machine) who was supposedly a trench padre was named "Woodbine Willy."

Ypres: Three major battles were fought at Ypres, the first in October-November of 1914 involving British Expeditionary Forces; the second from late April to late May 1915 involving Canadian units who suffered 6,000 casualties out of a force of approximately 10,000 – most suffering the horrendous effects of chlorine gas warfare; and the third battle involving the struggle for Passchendaele in June of 1917 where the mud and horrendous conditions not only claimed the majority of the Royal Newfoundland Regiment, but 15,654 Canadians dead or wounded.

Zillebeke: A minor action, in the scope of the entire Western Front, that took place in 1915 when Canadian Forces were trapped with their backs to a small lake in Flanders. Canadian losses in the action were significantly large for the importance of the battle.

Related Reading

Original Works

Acland, Peregrine. *All Else is Folly*. Toronto: McClelland and Stewart, 1929.

Adamson, Agar. *Letters of Agar Adamson*. (ed. N.M. Christie). Nepean: CEF Books, 1997.

Audette, A. *Verses Written in the Trenches*. No publisher. 1917.

Brown. E.K. *On Canadian Poetry*. Toronto: Ryerson Press, 1943.

Cosgrave, L. Moore. *Afterthoughts of Armageddon: The Gamut of Emotions Produced by the War, Pointing a Moral that is Not Too Obvious*. Toronto: S.B. Gundy, 1919.

Dixon, Frank P. *War-Time Memories in Verse: Written While Overseas*. Self-published, 1918.

Empey, Arthur Guy. *Over the Top*. New York: G.P. Putnam's and Sons, 1917.

Garvin, John. *Canadian Poems of the Great War*. Toronto: McClelland and Stewart,1918.

Hanley, James. *The German Prisoner*. Toronto: Exile Editions, 2006.

Harrison, Charles Yale. *Generals Die In Bed*. New York: A.L.Burt Publishers, 1928.

Leacock, Stephen. *The Hohenzollerns in America and Other Impossibilities*. London: John Lane, The Bodley Head, 1919.

Mason, H.C. *Bits O'Bronze*. Toronto: Thomas Allen, 1918.

Mason, H.C. *Three Things Only...* Toronto: Thomas Nelson and Sons Limited, n.d.

McClung, Nellie L. *Three Times Out: Told by Private Simmons*. Boston: Houghton Mifflin Company, 1918.

McCrae, John. *In Flanders Fields and Other Poems*. Toronto: William Briggs, 1919.

Nasmith, George. *On the Fringe of the Great Fight*. Toronto: McClelland, Goodchild, and Stewart, 1917.

Peat, Harold R. *Private Peat*. Indianapolis: Bobbs Merrill Company, 1917.

Prewett, Frank. *Selected Poems of Frank Prewett*. (ed. Bruce Meyer and Barry Callaghan). Toronto: Exile Editions, 1987.

Rutledge, Stanley. *Pen Pictures from the Trenches*. Toronto: William Briggs, 1918.

Scott, Frederick George. *Collected Poems*. Vancouver: The Clarke and Stuart Company, 1934.

Scott, Frederick George. *In the Battle Silences: Poems Written at the Front*. London: Constable and Company Limited, 1917.

Scott, Frederick George. *The Great War As I Saw It*. Toronto: F.D. Goodchild and Company, 1917.

Service, Robert. *Rhymes of a Red Cross Man*. New York: Barse and Hopkins, 1916.

Thomas, Hartley Munro. *Songs of an Airman and other poems*. Toronto: McClelland, Goodchild and Stewart, 1918.

Trotter, Bernard Freeman. *Canadian Twilights and other Poems of War and Peace*. McClelland, Goodchild and Stewart, 1917.

Young, Fred. *Poems by the Late Sgt. Fred Young 53180*. 18th Battalion. 1954.

Baetz, Joel. *Canadian Poetry from World War One: An Anthology*. Toronto: Oxford University Press, 2009.

Buitenhuis, Peter. *The Great War of Words: British, American and Canadian Propaganda and Fiction, 1914-1933*. Vancouver, University of British Columbia Press, 1987.

Gwyn, Sandra. *Tapestry of War: A Private View of Canadians and the Great War*. Toronto: Harper Perennial, 1992.

Questions for Discussion

1. Discuss how you perceived the First World War before you encountered any of the works in this anthology. Was it something you were familiar with? Did it seem real to you or just a story someone was telling? How have your thoughts and reactions changed after reading some of the works in this anthology?

2. What roles do love and affection play in the war? Is war purely about aggression or does it leave room for experiences such as friendship, comradeship, and even love?

3. There are moments in war when the absurd takes over – when things simply do not make sense or seem out of place. How do these moments impact on the authors who experience them and what role do they play in either making the experience of the war hideous or more human?

4. Examine the four pieces by L. Moore Cosgrave. How do his perceptions of the war change over the years of his service? What do these changes in outlook and belief say about the nature of the war from the perspective of those who served in it?

5. In the diaries of Berta Carveth, she relates the experience of being a nurse at a hospital for the severely wounded in the south of England. What do her experiences tell us about the role of women in the war? What does she bring to the experience of the war that the male writers to not?

6. What do you perceive are the differences between the realities of the war and the home-front perceptions of it? How do the soldiers view the way the home-front sees the war? If you were a soldier in the trenches and returned home, what would you say about the actualities of combat? Could you say anything? Examine Leacock's "The Boy Who Came Back" for ideas.

7. How do the soldiers in the book communicate the horror of the war? Refer to Frank Prewett's poem "The Card Game" for material for this discussion.

8. Why is the language of Harrison's prose so spare in his poems? What impact does this have, and what does Harrison achieve by being so brief?

9. What is the impact of the capture of Vimy Ridge as perceived by Scott and Adamson? What makes this event significant for them out of all the events in the war?

10. What does Charles Yale Harrison gain by writing "Generals Die in Bed" in the present tense? Does his language qualify as literary language or is it simply the language of reporting, and what impact does the sense of actuality have on the reader?

11. Did the soldiers who participated in World War One share a premonition that their sacrifice might be forgotten in their lifetime by the Canadian public? Discuss this idea in terms of Bernard Trotter's "Ici Repose" and Frank Prewett's "Voices of Women."

12. In F.G. Scott's "The Tragedy of War," he writes of the execution of a soldier who has breached a rule of military conduct. What alternative does a soldier have to facing death in combat? How unjust does this seem and what kind of response can one offer to such an event?

13. Describe the role that neurasthenia or shell shock plays in the reality that the soldiers faced after the war, especially as it is described in Frank Prewett's "I Stared at the Dead." Discuss how you would consider dealing with the memory of horrific events and traumas if you had to endure them. Would you be able to cope?

14. War is punctuated by moments of strange peace, as described by Charles Yale Harrison in "London," Frank Prewett in "A Strange War Story," or Beckles Wilson in "A Visit to France's Colonials." In light of other realities recorded by the soldier writers in this collection, do these moments seem absurd? If so, why?

15. What role do women have in the selections in the collection? Are they merely observers who watch the follies of war or are they active participants? See, especially, Harrison's "London."

16. Describe how the "enemy" is portrayed throughout the book. Does direct contact with the German soldiers change the attitude to them or humanize them in any way? Consider this in light of Charles Yale

Harrison's "Bombardment" or Stanley A. Rutledge's "Willie Gierke" or Robert Service's "My Mate."

17. What role does love play in the war? Discuss the role of love in H. Smalley Sarson's "Love Song," Prewett's "Voices of Women," and the Anonymous "Cupid in Flanders." Can one have still have feelings in the face of such horror?

18. What role does diary-keeping play in recording the realities of war? Discuss this in terms of Berta Carveth's diary or John McCrae's entries in his diary, or the reflections of John Barnard Brophy. What role does a consciousness of time or lack of consciousness of time play in keeping track of the experience of the war?

19. Small mercies, small gifts, small treats, are often welcomed by the soldiers in this collection. Discuss the ways in which these offerings are perceived by the soldiers in A. Audette's "Complimentary Dinner" and Frank Dixon's "Cigarettes." What do these pieces tell us about the deprivations of war?

20. Hartley Munro Thomas and John Barnard Brophy were both airmen in the First World War who recorded their thoughts and reactions to their experience. How does the war in the air, from their perspective, compare to the war on the ground?

21. Why does John McCrae use the symbolism of poppies in his poem "In Flanders Fields?" A number of critics have disliked this poem because of McCrae's use of the flowers. What are the flowers a metaphor or symbol for, and why poppies?

22. What do the Canadian soldiers feel they share in common with the German soldiers? Apply this question to numerous pieces in the book.

23. What role does humour play in a number of the pieces? Is there anything laughable or funny about war? Do the soldier writers purposely try to find humour in their situation and what, if anything, does laughter allay?

24. The soldier authors use the vocabulary of the war – the specific names for things they use to fight and for the peculiarities of their lives at the front. How difficult is it for a non-military person to perceive

the details of what they are saying in this very specific vocabulary and what impact do you think this vocabulary had on readers at home and after the war?

25. From your own reading of this book, discuss why you think Canada's literature of the First World War was neglected and dismissed for many years. What do you think made Canadian readers resistant to the realities of war presented by these writers?

Acknowledgements

Every effort has been made to contact the estates of those whose works have been included in this anthology. In many cases, however, the estates of the authors have not been traceable owing to the length of the time since their deaths. Excerpts from *Generals Die in Bed* are published by permission of Potlatch Publications. Works by Hartley Munro Thomas are published by permission of his estate. James Hanley's *The German Prisoner* (© 1930 Liam Hanley) comes from *The Last Voyage and Other Stories* (The Harvill Press) and appears by permission David Higham Associates. Agar Adamson's letters appear by permission of CEF Books. The editors would like to thank Norman Christie, Chris Adamson, Gil Adamson, and the estate of Agar Adamson. The Afterword, "Poppies: Three Variations", is reprinted from *Good Bones* and published by permission of Margaret Atwood. The editors of this book would like to thank the following individuals for their generosity and assistance: John D. Snider, Jane Youngs, Bernard Freeman Trotter, Marcia McClung, Madelaine Thomas, Greg Gatenby, Antonio D'Alfonso, Bruce Whiteman, Carl Spadoni, Steven Temple, Sebastian Hergott, Edna Aitken, Antoinette Fernandez, Gabrielle Somer, Kerryn Johnston, Claire Weissman Wilks, Christopher Doda, Nina Callaghan and Tim Hanna.

THE EXILE CLASSICS SERIES ~ BOOKS 1 TO 27

THAT SUMMER IN PARIS (No. 1) ~ MORLEY CALLAGHAN
Memoir and Essays 6x9 280 pages 978-1-55096-688-6 (tpb) . $19.95
It was the fabulous summer of 1929 when the literary capital of North America had moved to the Left Bank of Paris. Ernest Hemingway, F. Scott Fitzgerald, James Joyce, Ford Madox Ford, Robert McAlmon and Morley Callaghan... amid these tangled relationships, friendships were forged, and lost... A tragic and sad and unforgettable story told in Callaghan's lucid, compassionate prose. Also included in this new edition are selections from Callaghan's comments on Hemingway, Joyce and Fitzgerald, beginning in that time early in his life, and ending with his reflection on returning to Paris at the end of his life.

NIGHTS IN THE UNDERGROUND (No. 2) ~ MARIE-CLAIRE BLAIS
Novel 6x9 190 pages 978-1-55096-015-0 (tpb) $19.95
With this novel, Marie-Claire Blais came to the forefront of feminism in Canada. This is a classic of lesbian literature that weaves a profound matrix of human isolation, with transcendence found in the healing power of love.

DEAF TO THE CITY (No. 3) ~ MARIE-CLAIRE BLAIS
Novel 6x9 218 pages 978-1-55096-013-6 (tpb) $19.95
City life, where innocence, death, sexuality, and despair fight for survival. It is a book of passion and anguish, characteristic of our times, written in a prose of controlled self-assurance. A true urban classic.

THE GERMAN PRISONER (No. 4) ~ JAMES HANLEY
Novella 6x9 64 pages 978-1-55096-075-4 (tpb) $13.95
In the weariness and exhaustion of WWI trench warfare, men are driven to extremes of behaviour. (see advertisement at the end of this book)

THERE ARE NO ELDERS (No. 5) ~ AUSTIN CLARKE
Stories 6x9 159 pages 978-1-55096-092-1 (tpb) $17.95
Austin Clarke is one of the significant writers of our times. These are compelling stories of life as it is lived among the displaced in big cities, marked by a singular richness of language true to the streets.

100 LOVE SONNETS (No. 6) ~ PABLO NERUDA
Poetry   6x9   225 pages   978-1-55096-108-9 (tpb) $24.95
As Gabriel García Márquez stated: "Pablo Neruda is the greatest poet of the twentieth century – in any language." And, this is the finest translation available, anywhere!

THE SELECTED GWENDOLYN MACEWEN (No. 7)
GWENDOLYN MACEWEN
Poetry/Fiction/Drama/Art/Archival   6x9   352 pages
978-1-55096-111-9 (tpb) $32.95
"This book represents a signal event in Canadian culture." —*Globe and Mail*
The only edition to chronologically follow the astonishing trajectory of MacEwen's career as a poet, storyteller, translator and dramatist, in a substantial selection from each genre.

THE WOLF (No. 8) ~ MARIE-CLAIRE BLAIS
Novel   6x9   158 pages   978-1-55096-105-8 (tpb) $19.95
A human wolf moves outside the bounds of love and conventional morality as he stalks willing prey in this spellbinding masterpiece and classic of gay literature.

A SEASON IN THE LIFE OF EMMANUEL (No. 9) ~ MARIE-CLAIRE BLAIS
Novel   6x9   175 pages   978-1-55096-118-8 (tpb) $19.95
Widely considered by critics and readers alike to be her masterpiece, this is truly a work of genius comparable to Faulkner, Kafka, or Dostoyevsky. Includes 16 ink drawings by Mary Meigs.

IN THIS CITY (No. 10) ~ AUSTIN CLARKE
Stories   6x9   221 pages   978-1-55096-106-5 (tpb) $21.95
Clarke has caught the sorrowful and sometimes sweet longing for a home in the heart that torments the dislocated in any city. Eight masterful stories showcase the elegance of Clarke's prose and the innate sympathy of his eye.

THE NEW YORKER STORIES (No. 11) ~ MORLEY CALLAGHAN
Stories   6x9   158 pages   978-1-55096-110-2 (tpb) $19.95
Callaghan's great achievement as a young writer is marked by his breaking out with stories such as these in this collection... "If there is a better storyteller in the world, we don't know where he is." —*New York Times*

REFUS GLOBAL (No. 12) ~ THE MONTRÉAL AUTOMATISTS
Manifesto 6x9 142 pages 978-1-55096-107-2 (tpb) $21.95
The single most important social document in Quebec history, and the most important
aesthetic statement a group of Canadian artists has ever made. This is basic reading for
anyone interested in Canadian history or the arts in Canada.

TROJAN WOMEN (No. 13) ~ GWENDOLYN MACEWEN
Drama 6x9 142 pages 978-1-55096-123-2 (tpb) $19.95
A trio of timeless works featuring the great ancient theatre piece by Euripedes in a
new version by MacEwen, and the translations of two long poems by the contempo-
rary Greek poet Yannis Ritsos.

ANNA'S WORLD (No. 14) ~ MARIE-CLAIRE BLAIS
Novel 5.5x8.5 166 pages ISBN: 978-1-55096-130-0 $19.95
An exploration of contemporary life, and the penetrating energy of youth, as Blais looks
at teenagers by creating Anna, an introspective, alienated teenager without hope. Anna
has experienced what life today has to offer and rejected its premise. There is no point
in going on. We are all going to die, if we are not already dead, is Anna's philosophy.

THE MANUSCRIPTS OF PAULINE ARCHANGE (No. 15)
MARIE-CLAIRE BLAIS
Novel 5.5x8.5 324 pages ISBN: 978-1-55096-131-7 $23.95
For the first time, the three novelettes that constitute the complete text are brought
together: the story of Pauline and her world, a world in which people turn to violence
or sink into quiet despair, a world as damned as that of Baudelaire or Jean Genet.

A DREAM LIKE MINE (No. 16) ~ M.T. KELLY
Novel 5.5x8.5 174 pages ISBN: 978-1-55096-132-4 $19.95
A Dream Like Mine is a journey into the contemporary issue of radical and violent solu-
tions to stop the destruction of the environment. It is also a journey into the uncon-
scious, and into the nightmare of history, beauty and terror that are the awesome land-
scape of the Native American spirit world.

THE LOVED AND THE LOST (No. 17) ~ MORLEY CALLAGHAN
Novel 5.5x8.5 302 pages ISBN: 978-1-55096-151-5 (tpb) $21.95
With the story set in Montreal, young Peggy Sanderson has become socially unaccept-
able because of her association with black musicians in nightclubs. The black men

think she must be involved sexually, the black women fear or loathe her, yet her direct, almost spiritual manner is at variance with her reputation.

NOT FOR EVERY EYE (No. 18) ~ GÉRARD BESSETTE
Novel 5.5x8.5 126 pages ISBN: 978-1-55096-149-2 (tpb) $17.95
A novel of great tact and sly humour that deals with ennui in Quebec and the intellectual alienation of a disenchanted hero, and one of the absolute classics of modern revolutionary and comic Quebec literature. Chosen by the Grand Jury des Lettres of Montreal as one of the ten best novels of post-war contemporary Quebec.

STRANGE FUGITIVE (No. 19) ~ MORLEY CALLAGHAN
Novel 5.5x8.5 242 pages ISBN: 978-1-55096-155-3 (tpb) $19.95
Callaghan's first novel – originally published in New York in 1928 – announced the coming of the urban novel in Canada, and we can now see it as a prototype for the "gangster" novel in America. The story is set in Toronto in the era of the speakeasy and underworld vendettas.

IT'S NEVER OVER (No. 20) ~ MORLEY CALLAGHAN
Novel 5.5x8.5 190 pages ISBN: 978-1-55096-157-7 (tpb) $19.95
1930 was an electrifying time for writing. Callaghan's second novel, completed while he was living in Paris – imbibing and boxing with Joyce and Hemingway (see his memoir, Classics No. 1, *That Summer in Paris*) – has violence at its core; but first and foremost it is a story of love, a love haunted by a hanging. Dostoyevskian in its depiction of the morbid progress of possession moving like a virus, the novel is sustained insight of a very high order.

AFTER EXILE (No. 21) ~ RAYMOND KNISTER
Poetry 5.5x8.5 240 pages ISBN: 978-1-55096-159-1 (tpb) $19.95
This book collects for the first time Knister's poetry. The title *After Exile* is plucked from Knister's long poem written after he returned from Chicago and decided to become the unthinkable: a modernist Canadian writer. Knister, writing in the 20s and 30s, could barely get his poems published in Canada, but magazines like *This Quarter* (Paris), *Poetry* (Chicago), *Voices* (Boston), and *The Dial* (New York City), eagerly printed what he sent, and always asked for more – and all of it is in this book.

THE COMPLETE STORIES OF MORLEY CALLAGHAN (No. 22-25)
Four Volumes ~ Stories 5.5 x 8.5 (tpb) (tpb) $19.95
v1 ISBN: 978-1-55096-304-5 352 Pages / v2 978-1-55096-305-2 344 Pages
v3 : 978-1-55096-306-9 360 Pages / v4 : 978-1-55096-307-6 360 Pages

The complete short fiction of Morley Callaghan is brought together as he comes into full recognition as one of the singular storytellers of our time. "Attractively produced in four volumes, each introduced by [Alistair Macleod, André Alexis, Anne Michaels and Margaret Atwood], and each containing 'Editor's Endnotes.' The project is nothing if not ambitious... [and provides for] the definitive edition." —*Books in Canada*

So that the reader may appreciate this writer's development and the shape of his career – and for those with a scholarly approach to the reading of these collections – each book contains an on-end section providing the year of publication for each story, a Q&A section related to each volume's stories, and comprehensive editorial notes. Also included are historical photographs, manuscript pages, and more.

CONTRASTS: IN THE WARD ~ A BOOK OF POETRY AND PAINTINGS (No. 26) ~ LAWREN HARRIS
Poetry/16 Colour Paintings 7x7 168 pages ISBN: 978-1-55096-308-3
(special edition pb) $24.95
Group of Seven painter Lawren Harris' poetry and paintings take the reader on a unique historical journey that offers a glimpse of our country's past as it was during early urbanization. "This small album of poetry, paintings, and biographical walking tour ought to be on every 'Welcome to Toronto' (and 'Canada') book list. Gregory Betts's smart, illustrative writing, which convinces by style as well as content, and Exile Editions' winning presentation, combine to make *Lawren Harris: In the Ward* a fresh look at the early work of one of Canada's most iconic modernists." —*Open Book Toronto*

WE WASN'T PALS ~ CANADIAN POETRY AND PROSE OF THE FIRST WORLD WAR (No. 27) ~ ED. BRUCE MEYER AND BARRY CALLAGHAN
Poetry/Prose 5.5x8.5 320 pages ISBN: 978-1-55096-315-1 (tpb) $18.95

2014 marks the 100th anniversary of the start of the war...

The Exile Classics, and Exile Related Reading titles, are available for purchase at:
www.ExileEditions.com

genuine at work on the printed page, Brown declared in his study *On Canadian Poetry* (1941) that "nothing of significance was written in Canada" about the First World War.

What resulted from Brown's dismissal was that an entire era of Canadian literature vanished into oblivion. The publication in 2000 of *We Wasn't Pals: Canadian Poetry and Prose of the First World War*, edited by Barry Callaghan and me, made some strides in correcting that element of silence, though the anthology came so many years after the war itself as to have offered no recompense to those who survived the years of horror. To cut Brown some slack, it would be fair to say that the realities of war outstripped the capabilities of literature. What Brown viewed as "literary content" was far from the horrors experienced by writers such as Frank Prewett, Charles Yale Harrison and Peregrine Acland. Denying the trench writers their place in the catalogue of Canadian literature was Brown's admission, in some respects, that he could not accept nor understand the aesthetics of war; that he was, when it came right down to it, an incapable critic. In the mud, the madness and the despair of Canada's experience on the Western Front, a new vocabulary was taking shape. This new language, a tongue without containment, was brutal, honest, uncivilized, savage and explicit; yet it was real. Literature, as the twentieth century taught readers through many hard and painful lessons, was not about what we can bear, but about what we need to say even though it may be unbearable.

THE GERMAN PRISONER ~ JAMES HANLEY
(EXILE CLASSICS No. 4)
Fiction/Novella 6x9 64 pages 978-1-55096-075-4 (tpb) $13.95

In the weariness and exhaustion of WWI trench warfare, men are driven to extremes of behaviour... James Hanley, best-known for his numerous detective novels written during the 1930s and 1940s, was born in Dublin, but at the age of 15 he jumped ship in Saint John, New Brunswick, and enlisted in the Canadian Army. He saw action as a Canadian fighting man until he was wounded in 1918. *The German Prisoner*, brilliant in its stark depiction of trench warfare, was privately printed in a limited edition, in 1930. Until now, this battle classic has remained little known in obscurity.